BREAKING FREE

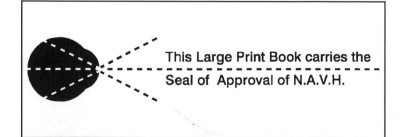

This Large Print Book carries the
Seal of Approval of N.A.V.H.

BREAKING FREE

LAURAINE SNELLING

THORNDIKE PRESS

A part of Gale, Cengage Learning

GALE
CENGAGE Learning™

Detroit • New York • San Francisco • New Haven, Conn • Waterville, Maine • London

GALE
CENGAGE Learning™

Copyright © 2007 Lauraine Snelling.
Thorndike Press, a part of Gale, Cengage Learning.

LIBRARY OF CONGRESS CATALOGING-IN-PUBLICATION DATA

Snelling, Lauraine.
    Breaking free / by Lauraine Snelling.
      p. cm. — (Thorndike Press large print Christian romance)
    ISBN-13: 978-1-4104-0861-7 (hardcover : alk. paper)
    ISBN-10: 1-4104-0861-2 (hardcover : alk. paper)
    1. Women prisoners — Fiction. 2. Horses — Training —
Fiction. 3. Divorced men — Fiction. 4. Children with disabilities
— Fiction. 5. Large type books. I. Title.
PS3569.N39B74 2008
813'.54—dc22   2008014263

Published in 2008 by arrangement with Grand Central Publishing, a
division of Hachette Book Group USA, Inc.

To animal rescuers, the people who give of their time and money to help care for lost, wounded, or abandoned animals, many of them former pets or, as in this book, retired Thoroughbreds. In return, the animals give unconditional love that helps heal humans, a winning circle for all.

ACKNOWLEDGMENTS

Research is always an adventure and this time I traveled to Wallkill, New York, and visited Wallkill Correctional Facility, the first prison to take in retired Thoroughbreds for rehabilitation. I cannot thank Jim Tremper, the vocational instructor, enough for sharing information and making it easy to talk with the inmates involved in the Thoroughbred Retirement Foundation. My two days there were eye opening to say the least. Also thank you to the superintendent who gave us permission to tour the main facility, besides the horse program. Everyone there was most helpful, including the inmates who talked so openly. I patterned Los Lomas, the prison I made up, on all I saw and learned at Wallkill.

Diana Pikulski, Executive Director of the Thoroughbred Retirement Foundation, helped set all this up and then added to our information, including a visit with her own rescued horses. Thanks to her, I visited the TRF facility at the Horse Park in Lexington, Kentucky, and talked with Linda Dyer, the vocational instructor who runs the program at Blackburn Correctional Facility. I learned more about the open houses from Nikki Smith of TRF at the Horse Park, she introduced me to Chris Irwin who was there training riders and horses. His book, *Dancing with Your Dark Horse,* and videos were great information on horse training.

Therapeutic riding trainers make such a difference in people's lives, but not only children like I thought before I started the research on this book. I visited various programs and talked with people involved, again volunteers who are rescuers at heart.

We have rescued two Basset hounds so far in our lives, Chewy from Daphneyland Rescue Ranch in Acton, California, owns us now, so I offered a contest to Basset lovers to have their hound star in this book, the proceeds going to Daphneyland. Our contest winner, Bonnie, belongs to Don and Pam Bullock and is a hound with a story all her own.

Having a good editor is critical, and I can't thank Christina Boys enough, along with all the staff at FaithWords, an imprint of Hachettc Book Group USA. I had to catch my breath when I first saw the incredible cover for this book. Thank you all.

I have an amazing team, Kathleen and Chelley, who read and critique for me, Cecile, my invaluable assistant, my Round Robin friends who both encourage and pray, and my A plus agent and friend, Deidre Knight. Thank you, my friends.

What an adventure this book has been and I'm always grateful for my husband and best friend Wayne who loves adventuring as much as I do. Thanks also to all my faithful readers who make it possible for me to continue to write more books. Come along for more adventures. Above all, to God be the glory. You can learn more about the background of this book, along with TRF information and pictures of Bonnie, at my Web site www.laurainesnelling.com.

Blessings,
Lauraine

ONE

Maggie recognized menace as it slid over DC's face right before the female tank, shielded by her groupies, slammed her against the chain-link fence. "Too late to run, Miss Prissy White Girl. I been waitin' for you."

Trying to swallow with the woman's forearm pressing against her throat, Maggie clutched at the woman's arm. *Someone, guard, please.* Already spots floated before her eyes. *Air, I need air.*

"That's enough." Maggie heard the words from a distance, and air, blessed air returned to her lungs as DC lurched backward, propelled by a black hand sunk into her shoulder.

"Beat it." Kool Kat hissed as she slid in front of Maggie. Both women smiled and kept their voices low so as not to attract the attention of the correctional officers, who were safe in their bulletproof shelter by the fence. She turned to Maggie. "Keep walkin' like nothin' wrong."

Maggie kept from staggering and resumed her walk, fear flailing her shoulders like a crazed jockey.

After the big black woman sauntered back to the exercise yard population, Maggie rubbed her throat. Four months until her review by the parole board and she'd almost not lived to see it. She tried to breathe evenly to calm the deep trembles. Seven years of keeping her head down, three of them here at Los Lomas and she'd only this once had any trouble. She'd been afraid at her sentencing, afraid of being alone with her memories, afraid with the terror of a normal woman — as she used to see herself — in an abnormal environment. But now, with DC having marked her, she knew real fear.

"Roberts, I've got something for you." Ms. Donelli, head of the occupational programs, beckoned from The Bubble where the correctional officers stayed, watching the prisoners in the concrete exercise yard. DC had made sure none of the COs had seen her little activity. There was always a way not to be seen. Until a few moments ago, Maggie thought she knew most of them.

She trotted over to the gate, managing a

wave at the correctional officer who checked her name off the roster as she passed through the gate.

"What's up?" Maggie asked, voice still raspy from the attack. At five-five she felt like a dachshund next to a Great Dane. Elegant was the word for Ms. Donelli, a word and concept Maggie had left behind with her entry into the penal system. They entered the three-story, cut-stone building that housed A wing and climbed two flights of concrete stairs. Even with freshly painted green walls, the bars on the windows screamed prison.

"A new program. You're a fit. Parole in four months instead of release in a year and a half." Ms. Donelli smiled down at Maggie and nodded at another inmate they met.

Smiles were a precious commodity in Maggie's life so she horded this one, just like she had done since the accident that sent her here.

"Your record's good," Ms. Donelli continued. The officer of the day sat at the front desk and greeted them both as they turned down the hall to the offices.

Which meant she'd stayed out of trouble with both inmates and staff. Until today. How fast would the grapevine travel and this carrot be removed?

"And I heard you like horses."

"I did . . . as a kid."

Donelli ushered Maggie into her private office and motioned to sit beside her on a love seat that, like the other furnishings in the room, had seen better days. Donelli lived by the rule she touted. The budget was better spent on helping inmates than decorating offices. "An organization called The Thoroughbred Retirement Foundation has contracted with us to rehabilitate horses that can no longer race for one reason or another. The program pioneered in New York, but we will be the first one in a women's prison. If you agree to do this, you will care for the horses along with taking classes in stable management."

"So are you saying this will be a paid job, like working on the beef ranch?"

"Yes, they'll actually be appropriating the unused barns at the beef ranch. Are you interested?"

Pictures of the horses she'd cared for at the riding stable in her teens flashed through her mind. Dusty with the loose lower lip who loved lemon drops; Jefferson who nosed her pockets for carrots; old Silver who acted like he was going to kick the daylights out of you but once you laid a hand on his rump, nickered a soft hello. Did she want to work with horses again — did dogs bark? A tiny sliver of — what? excitement? — shivered down her spine.

"Yes, please." She brushed a straw-like hank of hair from her eyes. It needed trimming with her nail scissors again. She'd realized that anyone who had known her as the wife of a rising executive and stay-at-home mom wouldn't recognize her now. Back then, she'd known she was attractive with sun streaked brown hair and laughing blue eyes. Her husband Dennis often told her how beautiful she was. Now the mirror said mousy, nondescript — a perfect cover for safety's sake.

"Good. We'll be starting with ten inmates and ten horses. Our occupational trainer is a man named Trenton James. He's managed horse farms for years. Comes highly recommended as both a teacher and a trainer."

"When do we start?"

"Tomorrow."

Tomorrow she would be safer — far away at the barns — safe from DC. Even though she knew no one was ever really safe on the inside of prison fences. "Thank you."

"You're welcome. Do you have any suggestions for others who might be interested?"

The immense bulk of Kool Kat plucking

DC's arm off Maggie's throat skittered across her mind. She owed a debt. "Kool Kat."

Donelli seemed surprised by the suggestion. Everyone knew Kool Kat was regarded as one of the tougher prisoners and had been called many uncomplimentary names by more than a few. Starting in her teens, she'd been incarcerated enough times to know her way around prison rules and make some of her own.

"She's inner-city LA, probably never seen a horse in real life," Donelli said dismissively.

"I know, but she told me once when we were working in the kitchen that she likes animals. She's a hard worker." *And strong as a sumo wrestler, fortunately for me.*

"I'll consider it."

Maggie knew that possibly doing someone a favor was stepping out of character and might cost her. She'd lived her life in prison by the words an old woman told her when she first came in: "Just get through." Staying to herself all these years had gotten her through. But Kool Kat had saved her *life.* It wasn't the same as conferring favors with contraband perfume. This was different. Besides, she had read that change started in

16

the mind. No matter if she was in prison or not.

The next morning Maggie joined the small group waiting for the van to take them to the beef ranch, part of which would soon be a horse farm.

Kool Kat, her black hair braided and looped in intricate swirls, stopped beside Maggie. She lowered her voice. "What you be wantin'?"

Keeping her eyes directed toward the floor, Maggie whispered back. "We're even." The snort from the woman who dominated the prison yard made her wonder if she'd done the right thing. She'd seen firsthand what happened when someone crossed Kool Kat; that woman's face bore a scar for life.

A broad shouldered man with the standard issue clipboard strode through the door. Square jawed with a golden tan that matched his short-cropped hair and eyes that crinkled, he wore assurance and contentment like a longtime favorite shirt. He stopped by the desk and waited for the conversations to cease. "I'm Mr. James and I'm the occupational trainer with this new program. Please answer when I call your name, and we'll get on the road." He was dressed in jeans and a blue plaid western shirt instead of the usual tan uniform, and the tone and timber of his voice set Maggie at ease.

Maggie's name was fifth. "Here." She raised her right hand. At his nod, she followed the others out the door to the waiting bus. While she'd been so careful not to get involved, Maggie knew all the women who'd agreed to the program. Blonde Sim was in for bank robbery; she'd driven the getaway car and missed her two kids so badly she'd do anything to keep out of trouble. Like Maggie, parole was a possibility in the near future. Petite JJ with the charming smile and dubious methods of anger management; Brandy, the youngest of them all, in for possession and dealing, wore cockiness like armor and had gotten on the bad side of the COs more than once.

Weren't there supposed to be ten women? Maggie'd only counted nine. As she turned around to sit down in the middle seat next to the window, she heard Mr. James talking to someone and a moment later, a woman boarded the bus. Maggie's stomach leaped to her mouth, and it was all she could do not to hurl the cold cereal she'd eaten at breakfast.

DC swaggered in, her gaze riveted on Maggie. For the veriest of seconds, she slowed by the bench seat where JJ sat next to Maggie. DC was up for possession and armed robbery, along with other violent crimes, but like many others she said she'd been framed. Her record in prison according to the COs sounded like she sang in the church choir, but the inmates knew better. Her infrequent smile sported two gold front teeth.

The door shut and another man took the driver's seat while Mr. James stood in the well by the door.

"First of all, our driver is my assistant, Mr. Creston. Besides driving, he'll be in charge if for any reason I have to be absent. Next I have some announcements to make. We'll be going by the prisoner's handbook, which I am sure you all have memorized, but I have a few additions. Number one: there is no second chance. If you mistreat either animals or humans, you are out of here and back to the yard. I'll teach you all that I can, but like the saying goes: you can lead a horse to water, but you can't make him drink. You can lead a man — or a woman in this case — to knowledge, but you can't make her think." He paused and looked them each in the eye. "I hope you . . . well, learn all you can. It's the first time this program has been offered to women.

Women have a reputation for good intuition with horses as well as compassion. Horses are honest, what you see is what you get, not like humans who play games. If you have trouble with a horse, you might want to look inside yourself and see if you can figure what he sees and is reacting to."

Maggie let his words sink into her mind. Could she do that? Learning from the horses would be easy, but look inside herself? She shuddered. She'd spent the last seven years avoiding herself, along with all the groups' and counselors' probing — just getting through.

The bus stopped in front of a long, low shed. "You'll be helping some men who have volunteered to build stalls and fencing. Horses have a knack for tangling up in wire so we're installing all wooden fences here. We have ten days to get ready. I'll be checking out the tools, and at the end of our session, you need to check them back in. Can I see a show of hands if you've ever used a hammer?" He counted and nodded. "And a saw?" Noting something on his clipboard he led the way down the stairs. As they filed down the three steps he said their name and pointed either to the left or the right.

"Ms. Jackson."

"Kool Kat," she replied, meeting his eyes.

"You'd rather be called that?"

"Yeah, man."

"Mr. James."

"Yeah, Mr. James, that's what I said."

At his smile, a spate of chuckles blew through the group. He nodded toward the left.

"Ms. Roberts."

"Maggie."

"Maggie it is." He nodded for her to follow Kool Kat.

The driver of the vehicle handed them each a hammer. "You'll find nails at the building site. Follow the instructions of Mr. Hansen, he's the foreman."

Maggie nodded and sucked in a deep breath of real air. Air not tainted by chainlink fences topped with concertina wire and the hot concrete of the yard, nor by the misery and hostility of those inhaling and exhaling. Free air that had passed over pastures and lingered in the trees. She inhaled again and raised her face to the sun. Soon she would be breathing free air 24/7 — if they granted her parole and DC didn't kill her first.

She'd always loved being outdoors, her garden and yard had born testimony to that. Camping and hiking, they'd loved the mountains, especially the Sierras.

She blinked in the dimness of the building before her eyes adjusted from the sun. A stack of rough-sawn lumber filled the aisle in front of timbers that were already concreted into the dirt floor. Sawhorses topped with sheets of thick plywood held a chop saw where two men were cutting the boards to the proper lengths.

"If you'll come on over here," another man called, beckoning them to one of the stalls. "We're nailing the walls up; the nails are in the bucket. Put three nails in each end, like the one you see here. The sooner you learn to hit the nails square, the faster they'll go in. I take it you've all used hammers before?"

Maggie nodded as she looked at the stack of boards. From the size of it, she'd be nailing until she got paroled. Tapping nails to hang pictures with her husband didn't look to have anything in common with building walls for horse stalls.

An hour later, with repeated help from the foreman, Kool Kat and Maggie began to make progress, although their fingers and thumbs bore witness to their inexperience.

By the time they had to return to the correctional facility for head count and lunch, her back ached, her thumb throbbed, and they had nailed one wall up to six feet.

"We ahead of the others." Kool Kat returned from looking at the other stalls.

Maggie stared at her partner. "We're not in a race here."

Kool Kat leaned into Maggie's face, her voice taking on a hiss. "I play, I win."

The threat made Maggie take a step backward. And they were supposed to be partners? She headed for the bus, keeping a watch out for both Kool Kat and DC.

"Good work, ladies," Mr. James said as they filed off the bus. "See you in a few."

"Not if I see you first," Kool Kat grumbled.

"You aren't going back?" Maggie asked, hope flaring.

"Course I'm goin' back." A fierce look accompanied her reply. "But I never worked so hard in my entire life. Feels like my arm's about to fall off."

"I wish mine would." Maggie flexed her right arm and stretched her neck from side to side. When she looked at her palm, the blisters were no surprise. Kool Kat raised hers, and even though she had dark skin, the seeping showed.

"I'll get us bandages and leather gloves," Kool Kat said matter-of-factly.

Maggie knew Kool Kat had ways of getting things. "Us? Why would you do that?"

"Simple. I don't quit." She paused, her eyes narrowed. "And these partners are gonna win." She tapped Maggie on the shoulder.

Maggie heard the unspoken words, "at any cost." Nine more days until the horses, four months until probation. She would pound all the nails they wanted for that.

Ten days later the remaining nine women — one had backed out — were lined up as a horse van pulled into the driveway. Ten stalls, all with doors that swung on hinges, with sliding latches waited for the guests. Maggie and Kool Kat had put up more boards than all the others put together, and they both had the muscles and calluses to prove it. Maggie often felt like she was being towed along by a freight train.

DC brushed by Maggie, bumping her with her hip. Maggie went sprawling. Mr. James turned.

"Sorry, clumsy," Maggie lied, getting to her feet, not looking at DC.

As the first Thoroughbred limped down the ramp, Kool Kat backed up. "What they bring us, giants?"

Maggie rolled her eyes and shook her head. What was that feeling in her face? Her lips even twitched.

"This is Dancer's Delight, eight years old and won $750,000 in his years on the track. If you look at his left hind leg, you'll see the bow in his tendon. Maggie, since you've worked with horses before, you take him to stall ten."

Blinking back something in her eyes, Maggie walked forward and stopped in front of the horse, allowing him to sniff her hand and up her arm. She reached slowly for the lead shank.

"Easy fella, you're safe now." Shank in hand, she led him around the van to the stalls, half listening to Mr. James' voice as he used her as an example on how to handle the horses.

Maggie moved slow-and-easy-like around her cross-tied horse, keeping watch on his ears. Dancer, as she had decided to call him, not only had leg and foot problems, but someone or many someones had treated him with less than gentle hands. His upper lip wore a scar from the use of a twitch, an age-old and cruel control mechanism that pinched a horse's upper lip. The tremors that shook him possibly came from abuse too — or neglect.

"Easy fella, no one's going to hurt you here." She kept up her soothing singsong as she took up a soft brush and worked on his neck again. Gentle strokes, gentle hands. Like petting a dog. "Pet him gently, son, like this," she'd told her toddler when they met a dog at the park.

She closed her eyes, clamping off the memory. Why so many memories today? Usually they didn't attack her until just before she slipped into sleep, jerking her awake.

She could feel the horse begin to relax, the quivers dying until he finally released one sigh and then another.

As did she. All the forced labor had indeed been worth it.

Before it was time to leave, all six of the horses were in their stalls with fresh hay and water, examined by Mr. James and assigned to an inmate, who was being instructed on the type of care her charge needed.

"You did well with Dancer's Delight, keep it up," Mr. James commented as she passed by him to board the bus.

A compliment. How long had it been since she had received a compliment, and from a man no less? Maggie stored it away in her heart to be taken out and polished when she needed a lift.

"Thank you. I will." *I will. I can do this.*

Maggie returned to her room before lunch, grateful that she didn't have to share a cell, like she had at the other places where she'd been incarcerated. Here at Los Lomas, she had a room three feet longer than her bed and three feet wider, with a door that closed to which she owned the key.

Sitting down on her bed, she looked at her hands, held them to her nose, and smelled them. Her mother used to tell her to go wash as soon as she came back from the stable because she stunk of horse. *But I don't stink,* she told herself. *I smell of horse, and this afternoon I will smell of horse again.*

Not of prison.

A knock on her door brought her back to the moment. "Yes?"

"Maggie, it's Kool Kat."

Maggie stood and crossed to unlock the door. "Come in."

"No." Kool Kat leaned against the door frame, eyes narrowed as if searching for a fight. She stared hard at Maggie. "Will you help me?"

Maggie started, knowing what the words cost her. "With what?"

"My horse."

Maggie stared at the woman still glaring at her. "What's the problem?"

"He don't like me."

"How do you know?"

"He bit me." She showed the bruise on

her arm. It was a nasty one and would soon turn black-purple.

"He's afraid. It has nothing to do with liking or disliking you."

"Well he ain't nearly afraid of me much as I be afraid of him. He one big . . ."

"Horse," Maggie said softly before Kool Kat could revert to her usual language.

One eyebrow rose as the woman leaning against the doorjamb smiled real slow like. "Yeah, horse. That's another thing. Mr. James say we got to learn — all the parts of the horse."

Maggie knew the other inmates thought her stuck-up because she didn't mix well, but early on she'd learned that staying to herself was safer. Just get through this, as the old woman had told her. And that's just what she had done before drawing the attention of DC. She'd kept from making friends all these years, if she gave in now she knew something bad was going to happen. But she still found herself saying, "I'll help you this afternoon." Maggie paused, still staring at Kool Kat. "Why are you staying with the program? You don't have to."

The narrowed eyes made Maggie wish she'd not said anything.

"I tole you, I ain't no quitter. . . . Let's go eat."

The next day three more horses arrived. Mr. James introduced each one, again listing earnings, age, injuries, treatment, and who he assigned to care for the horse. Maggie now had two of the Thoroughbreds to care for, making her look at him with questions in her eyes.

"I can tell you know what you're doing. And when you have them settled in, I want you to show the others how to lead a horse out to graze." Mr. James then began the day's lecture on hand-feeding, adjusting halters, tying knots, and leading a horse. He gave them ropes to practice tying the knots and made them take turns putting halters on one of the easier-to-handle horses. "Tomorrow we'll do grooming and bathing," he announced at the end of the lesson.

"Ain't no tub big enough." The soulful look on Kool Kat's face made everyone laugh. Except for Maggie whose lips did no more than twitch again.

By the end of two weeks, they'd lost Sim, who'd been paroled and tearfully gone back to her kids, and gained two more women: Jules who was serving life without parole and was known as a scholar and Willy who asked for a transfer to the horse program from the laundry. James assigned Brandy and JJ, who were now considered experienced, to one of the newer horses, who needed far more care than the others. His feet and legs had to be soaked every day, using canvass boots that reached past his knees. After the vet came and floated the horse's teeth so he could chew decently again, the women mixed up a mash with ground grain, molasses, vitamins, an antibiotic, and warm water to try to build their charge back up.

"How could anyone starve him like this?" JJ, short for Janice and known for her fiery Latino temper, asked. "Why not just sell him?"

"I think he was left in a stall, and maybe they forgot him," Maggie answered, stroking the horse's nose.

"They oughta be shot." JJ used a cloth to stroke the horse's neck. "He has hives so bad he can't even be brushed." This from a woman so high on crack she'd once shot her boyfriend when he brought home the wrong-sized serving of fries from McDonald's.

Two weeks later the stronger and more easily handled horses were let loose in the paddocks, some alone while others had progressed to tolerating other horses nearby, forming a small herd. The inmates gathered at the fence for their daily lecture at the usual spot when it wasn't held in the large area at the far end of the barn.

"Okay, ladies, here's your quiz for today." Mr. James handed a paper with the outline of a horse to each of them as they sat on the grass. "Take out your pencils and fill it in, no cheating. Soon as you are finished, hand it to me and go about your chores."

While there were the normal groans, no one said much until Brandy asked, "Does spelling count? How do you spell 'withers'?"

Mr. James ignored the giggles. Brandy asked the same question every quiz.

"How come we can't have multiple choice?" Kool Kat got another chuckle. The girls were all in good form this day. The cool breeze helped.

Finished long before the others, Maggie lifted her face to feel both the sun and the breeze. Watching the grazing horses was about as close to freedom as she could get now, but soon she'd be living without bars. She turned her head at the sound of a truck shifting down and watched it haul a trailer along the drive to the horse barn.

"Were we expecting a new horse today?" she asked as she stood and handed in her paper.

The trailer shook from the hooves pounding inside. "Not that I know of." Mr. James studied the vehicle. "Collect the rest of the papers, would you?" He handed hers back to her and headed toward the driveway.

"What's happening?" JJ asked.

Maggie shrugged as she accepted several of the papers, and the women leaned against the fence, watching the show.

"He be a mean one." Kool Kat handed in her paper.

"Hey, Mr. Creston, make sure the number one stall has clean bedding," Mr. James called from the side of the truck. "Water and hay too."

A scream from the trailer made the hair on the back of Maggie's neck stand on end. She figured her eyes were as round as the others'.

"That from the horse?" Brandy asked, moving closer to Maggie as if seeking safety.

Maggie nodded, the scream still echoing in her mind. She'd never heard a horse make a noise like that.

"Who gets that horse? Not me," Brandy whispered.

The tailgate sent up dust puffs as it hit the dirt, and the trailer rocked from the force within.

"Bring him out easy," Mr. James ordered.

32

"This horse don't do easy." One of the haulers backed out of the trailer. "Ya better get two ropes on him." More scuffle as the other man tried to do as he was told. A string of profanity announced his feelings about the horse.

"Okay, I've got him."

The blood bay horse backed out of the trailer in a rush, dragging the two handlers with him. When his front feet hit the dirt, he reared, slashing the air with both front hooves. One of the men ducked and shouted at the other. "Tighten up on your rope before he kills me."

"Bring him over to that open door." Mr. James pointed to the open barn door.

"Right, like we can lead him anywhere." The horse reared again and came down teeth bared, lunging at one of the men. "Tighten up, I said."

"I am."

"I ain't takin' that horse, no way." Kool Kat hugged the fence. "I'll go back to the yard afore that."

Once near the barn, the horse headed for the open stall door, dragging the men behind him. When he stormed in, Mr. James slammed both the top and bottom halves shut. A frenzy of hooves pounding the walls rewarded his quick action.

"I'll get your ropes back to you after he calms down."

"Good luck. Only one solution for that one . . . a fast bullet." The two men climbed back in the truck and drove off. The horse screamed again, his hooves thundering on the stall walls. The crack of wood told of the power of his kicks.

Mr. James settled his straw wide-brimmed hat tighter on his head and glanced down at the paper one of the men had given him. "Sounds like Breaking Free is trying to do just that. If we can't get him under control, he'll have to be put down. He could put the whole Thoroughbred program in jeopardy." He looked at each of the dumbstruck women. "Stall one is off limits, you understand?"

Two

"Dad, it's time."

Gil Winters looked up from the contracts he was trying to catch up on to see his son waiting in the doorway to his home office. Not already. He glanced at his watch. "Give me five minutes, okay?"

"But Dad, we'll be late."

With a sigh, Gil slicked back the lock of hair that no matter how much gel he applied always fell forward. His son's hair did the same. Their matching hazel eyes with long lashes, the envy of most women, were further proof of their relationship. Maria would take Eddie, all he had to do was ask. Maria had been their housekeeper since he'd married and taken over the care of the baby boy when Sandra, his ex-wife, couldn't accept a less than perfect baby. Spina bifida definitely came under the heading of imperfect.

He knew he had promised to take Eddie

to the therapeutic riding school. Had promised himself he'd use this activity to get closer to his son, hoping he wasn't too late. But somebody has to earn the money here, he reminded himself, though grateful as always he was in a position to be able to take time away from business when necessary.

He heard the retreating squeak of his son's wheelchair, one of the wheels needed oiling. He shoved his cordovan leather chair back. "No, Eddie, don't leave. I'm coming." Grabbing his keys and billfold from the tray on the ebony credenza where he always left them, he followed Eddie out the double doors and down the ramp. Rust and orange marigolds lined both sides of the redwood ramp, another example of Maria's devotion to their stucco home. She never believed the hired gardeners took care of the flower beds as well as she could.

While Eddie couldn't walk, in spite of several surgeries that promised miracles and didn't deliver, he propelled his own wheelchair rather than using an electric one. At ten, he certainly had a mind of his own. While his legs failed to function, his facile brain amazed his father at times.

Gil clicked the key ring that raised the back door of the modified van and lowered the lift for Eddie to roll on to. Here he did need his father's help. Gil pushed the wheelchair in, locked the wheels in place, and handed his son the seat belt. "You have your helmet?"

"Of course." Eddie pointed to the box where he kept his riding equipment. Gloves, helmet, and safety belt. Eddie always put his things away.

Knowing he'd earned the silent treatment, Gil got in the front seat, latched his own seat belt, and started the car. Glancing in the rearview mirror, he watched his son. A worried look at being late eclipsed the usual grin. To Eddie, being late was almost as bad as not showing up. They had driven out of the gated housing development before Eddie relented.

"Dad?"

"What?"

"Can we buy a horse?"

"Sorry, bud, but we've no room for a horse."

"We could stable one at the Rescue Ranch."

Gil let out a sigh. He'd been afraid this was coming. "But who'd take care of it? Horses take a lot of care."

"They have people that do that, and I can do some of the things. I could feed and water him."

"I think you need to learn a bit more and then we'll see." He knew he was copping out on the issue but at these riding classes, his son was protected. People who were trained in assisting therapeutic riding worked with Eddie. Have a horse of his own — was Eddie nuts?

But Gil couldn't say that. Not when he was the one who always told Eddie he could do anything he wanted, if he wanted to bad enough. Gil turned on to the highway, thinking he should keep his mouth shut. His words tended to come back to haunt him.

When they drove under the tree trunk posts and carved beamed entry to Rescue Ranch, he glanced back again to watch his son. The smile had returned and Eddie leaned slightly forward, staring out the side window at the horses grazing in a green pasture. Green because they were irrigated. Here in Southern California if the land wasn't irrigated, it was brown — or gold as the pundits tried to convince residents and tourists alike.

If they bought a horse and boarded it out here, either he or Maria would spend half of their life at the ranch because that was what Eddie would want to do. Nearly two years they'd been coming out here. So much for letting Eddie ride with the hopes he'd learn from it and go on to something else. He parked the van in the shade of a huge cottonwood tree and opened the rear door.

Eddie had already leaned down and un-snapped the locks on the wheels, spinning his chair to go down the ramp, riding helmet in place. As he propelled himself toward the incline made for those in wheel-chairs to get up on the mounting block, he shouted greetings to the instructor and laughed when someone called him dynamo.

Gil choked back the "be careful." No wonder Maria had been encouraging him to take his son to his riding lessons. She'd told him there had been big changes, but he'd only half-listened. When she got so upset with him that she switched to Span-ish, he knew he'd better come. She was right.

One of the men lifted Eddie up into the saddle, and they buckled him in. Then with a guard on each side, but no one leading, Eddie clucked the horse forward. While they had placed his feet into the stirrups, there was no muscle tone to guide the horse or help in balance.

Gil knew that. But with the special saddle and a well-trained horse, his son was basically riding alone. He heard someone come up beside him but didn't take his gaze from the action in the arena.

"Good to see you, Mr. Winters."

He glanced to the side where a dark-haired woman wearing sunglasses also watched his son. What was her name? Starting with A, he skimmed through the alphabet, hoping that would trigger his memory, an old trick he'd learned years ago. He'd met her before. Carolyn, no, Carly, that was it. With a small sigh of relief he answered, "Good to see you, Carly."

Her quick smile told him she was impressed he remembered her name. "He is doing well."

"I can see that. If you had told me — what's it been? eighteen months ago? — that he'd ride by himself, I'd not have believed you."

"I did tell you that, and you're right, you didn't believe me. Eddie is one of the most tenacious students we have. When you tell him something, he doesn't quit until he can do it. He often quotes you, you know?"

He wished she'd take off her glasses so he could see her eyes. But then, he'd have to remove his. Dark glasses were a necessity in Southern California, besides being a fashion statement. His noncommittal "hmm" made her snort.

"He said you always tell him he can do whatever he wants if he is willing to give it all he has."

"I never want him to think of himself as a cripple."

"Or handicapped?"

"Or disabled or whatever word is PC at the moment. Somehow you can find a way to do most anything."

"Other than walk?"

"True, but I keep hoping that with all the medical advances, he'll even be able to do that someday. He can manage for a time on crutches, but the wheelchair is more flexible."

"And faster."

"And we all know Eddie likes faster."

"He'd like to enter in a horse show that's coming up."

"Is that possible, I mean, is there a class for . . . for . . . ?"

"Kids with special needs?"

He stared from his dark glasses into hers. "Are you encouraging him to do that? I mean, there he wouldn't have his two guards."

"Aides. I don't think he's quite ready, but I'm not saying no."

She should say no, he might fall and get

hurt. No, he was the father, *he* should say no. Gil swallowed, blew out a puff, and sighed. Should and could were two entirely separate things. "What horse would he ride?"

"The one he is on. To ease your concern, the show is held here as a fund-raiser, and we encourage our students to enter."

"I see." He turned to look at her, noticing for the first time that she was an attractive woman. "If there is any way you can discourage this for now, I'd greatly appreciate it."

She laughed. "We have some of our horses voice trained for riders like Eddie who haven't the leg power. It doesn't take a lot of time to train a horse to voice commands."

"I see." *And you're telling me this why?*

"He wants his own horse too." She slipped the words in under his resolve, like a stiletto between the ribs.

"I know, he told me that. But you don't understand. We live in a gated community that has limited yard space and strict regulations. Even dogs require special dispensation if they will be outside much."

The tilt of her head told him what she thought of his excuse. "We have room for another horse here."

"Right. Then I might as well move in too.

Coming out here twice a week for lessons is one thing, driving out every day or even two times a day to take care of a horse is beyond the time I have available." *And besides, I have a life too. I work and I . . . work.*

"I see." Her tone indicated she didn't.

I'm sure you don't. Being a single parent and running my own corporation. . . . Gil caught himself up short. Whining doesn't become anyone. At least he hadn't said anything out loud. He turned his attention back to his son. The aides had dropped back when Eddie ordered the horse to trot.

Carly turned, a slight smile curving her lips. "If you should ever decide to buy a horse for Eddie, I'd be happy to assist you. In the meantime, good to see you again." She held out her hand, forcing him to shake it.

"Thank you, for the offer." *Right, good manners, but lady it'll be a cold day in that hot spot before I buy a horse.* "And thanks for all you do for Eddie. This is an amazing place."

"Thank you, and thank you too for your generous donations."

"You're welcome." He nodded. Feeling his cell phone vibrate, he patted his pocket. "Excuse me, please. I need to get this."

"Have a good rest of the day." She nod-

43

ded and strode off in the loose-limbed manner of an athlete. He'd seen her ride before. She made it look so easy, he almost wanted to try it. Almost, but not enough to do anything about it. He flipped open his cell. "Winters here." Listening to Amy, his secretary, he kept one eye on Eddie and dug in his pocket for his PDA. "All right. You go ahead." He gave her instructions and flipped his PDA closed again, thinking about the pile of work waiting on his desk. Since he'd started working more from his home office in order to spend time with Eddie, he felt more fractured than ever.

His heart skipped as, in seeming slow motion, his son slipped to one side. Gil grabbed the fence. Eddie hung with one arm clamped around the front of the saddle. He wanted to scream, to shout at the aides who were rushing to Eddie's assistance. He *might break his neck if he hits the ground.* In spite of his inner shouting, he heard Eddie order the aides not to help him. *Don't listen to him, help him back up.* But halfway over the fence, Gil watched the horse stand and wait as Eddie slowly righted himself, thanks to the strong arms he'd developed by propelling his wheelchair. He settled himself back upright in the saddle and patted his horse's neck, nodding at the comments and congratulations from the two aides. When the horse stepped forward again, Gil allowed himself to breathe. Too close, that one was too close.

And Carly thinks I should buy him a horse of his own? What kind of crazy was the woman?

THREE

What was it about Breaking Free that made her care about him so quickly? Like an instant attraction, soul to soul. Maggie knew it sounded silly, but that's what she felt. Was it the rage in his eyes and every line of his body, so like the impotent rage that woke her, sweating and panting, at night? Or was it fear that made him crazy? She understood fear. She breathed it, ate it, and slept with it. It reminded her to stay invisible. Don't go rocking any boats, head down; don't volunteer anything, even a word.

But those years ago, when she was young, she'd not been afraid of anything. She'd called the horse Harry instead of his fancy registered name — the owners had left him at the stable while they were transferred to some place in Europe. She'd been assigned to take care of him, train and exercise the big brute and hopefully get him over a few bad habits. By the time she showed him at a regional horse show, they'd won a stack of ribbons of all colors, finally taking top honors. Her heart nearly broke when the owners returned and moved him to their new home way north. Then her family moved away, and she never wanted to hurt that badly again so she didn't look for a new stable to work at. Maggie lay in her bed in her room staring at the ceiling. Did Breaking Free remind her of Harry, was that the pull?

Breaking Free. What a name! What a horse! She closed her eyes again, the better to see him. Even rough as his coat was, the sun shot fire in the red of him. Flame would have been a great name. His one white sock would flash when clean. Black mane and tail. She'd braided a tail like that back when prepping another horse for the show ring, but he'd not had the fire of this one. Nor murder in his eyes.

The next morning when they all answered roll call and climbed into the bus, she sat in the front so she could ask Mr. James some questions.

Kool Kat stared down at her, one eyebrow cocked.

She'd taken Kool Kat's seat. Maggie memorized her fingers, now knit together to keep them from shaking.

Kool Kat's grin showed a front tooth outlined in gold as she slid into the seat beside her. "Move your skinny butt over."

Maggie shifted, although she was already against the wall, her shoulder pressed to the cool window. Kool Kat sat down, pulling her extended leg in just enough so the others could get by, barely.

"All right, ladies. . . ."

Mr. James' comment always brought a snort or two from the women. At first she'd thought he was being sarcastic, but now she knew that Trenton James did not indulge in sarcasm. He meant what he said and he said what he meant. A jingle from one of the Dr. Seuss books she'd read to . . . She bit down on her lip so hard she tasted blood. A little boy's giggle echoed in her memory. Please, someone, say something. She wanted to clap her hands over her ears, anything to drown out the sounds inside.

She looked up to see Mr. James watching her. Had she been so obvious? What was happening to her? After all these years of never talking about what happened and burying the memories so deep they couldn't surface while she was awake, here she was on a sunny day going to her closest place to freedom and the memories burst in her head like rockets in a barrage.

Just get through. Two months and eighteen days and she would be up for parole.

"Mister James . . ." She had to clear her throat so he could hear her. "Breaking Free. Did you go back and check on him?"

"I did. He'd settled some."

"You think he's on Equipoise?"

"I'm sure of it. Take two months at least for it to leave his system."

"Echo pa . . . ?" Kool Kat tried spitting out the rest of the word. "What's that?"

"A medication they give racehorses to make them perform better. Like a steroid."

"They give horses stuff like that?"

James nodded. "Although some drugs are illegal, this one isn't."

"So they make horses pee in a bottle?" Her bark of a laugh said what she thought of such a thing.

"The winner can't leave the track until he's been drug tested."

"Now that'd be some job, gettin' a horse to pee in a bottle." Kool Kat slapped her knee, laughing and shaking her head. Others behind her joined in.

Trenton James tried to keep a straight face, but his smile broke out in spite of himself.

Maggie turned to look out the window.

She'd take that job. Collecting horse urine would beat time behind bars. Any job would beat time behind bars.

"All right, listen up." Mr. James had his clipboard in hand as the vehicle turned the last corner into the driveway to the horse barns. "We have two new horses coming in today before lunch so we need to move two others to the small pens and those in the small pens to the larger one." He read off the names of the horses. "JJ, you take your filly out to that empty paddock. Lead her around a bit before you turn her loose."

He gave the rest of them instructions, finishing with, "Class will be this afternoon right after lunch, so make sure you bring paper and pencils back with you."

"Not another test?" The universal groan of students everywhere rocked the bus.

"Just come prepared."

Once off the bus, he fell into step with Maggie, causing her to look up at him. "About Breaking Free. I'll hold him while you bring in hay and water."

"What about cleaning his stall?" she asked.

"We'll see how this goes."

Maggie brought a bucket out of the tack room and filled it at the faucet. After setting it by the stall door, she peeled several flakes of hay off the bale and waited for Mr. James to finish giving instructions to Brandy. She could hear Breaking Free moving around in his stall. At least he wasn't kicking the daylights out of it. He snorted and moved off from the stall door again.

"You ready?"

She nodded and picked up the bucket.

When James unlatched the upper part of the door, a hind foot rapped against the far wall. He swung the door open slowly and looked in. Breaking Free stood in the back corner, ears back, nostrils flared.

"Okay, horse, we're just going to make sure you have enough to eat and drink, then we'll leave you alone." As he spoke, James kept his eyes on the horse and unlatched the bottom door. He eased inside and waited.

Breaking Free snorted and shifted but remained at the back of the double stall.

Nodding to Maggie, he said, "All right, move slowly and keep an eye on him. If you're afraid, he'll know it."

Maggie did as she was told, aching with the desire to go to the horse. She dumped the hay in the rack, filled the water bucket, and eased back out of the stall.

As Trenton James slid out of the stall, he latched the lower door and let out a sigh that in Maggie's mind sounded like relief.

"He did well," she said.

"Yes, he did. Better than I feared, not as good as I hoped." Mr. James nodded. "We'll leave the top of the door open, let him look around, get comfortable."

"Good." Maggie picked up her bucket, heaving a quiet sigh of relief of her own. She fed her other two horses, petting necks and talking to them as she used the hose to refill their drinking buckets. "You'll be outside for a while," she told a dark bay gelding named His Too, whose right front foot wore a special boot to help repair the damage to hoof and ankle, or fetlock, as Mr. James had called it when he'd told Maggie what she needed to do. She had to soak it and wrap the other leg as well.

"Take Dancer out to the last small pen," Mr. James said as she walked up. "Let him get a taste of freedom."

"Hey, Dancer, you want to go outside?" Snapping a lead shank on his halter, Maggie led the horse outside and across the dirt lane to the rail enclosed area. She took him inside and walked him around once, then rubbed his neck and ears the way she knew he liked before unsnapping the lead shank and walking away.

"He's followin' you." Several of the women had gathered to watch the release.

Maggie turned around. "Go, you're free." He rubbed his forehead against her shoulder. "Just because someone's nice to you, you get all mushy." She scratched his cheek and stepped away again, this time out of the gate and shut it behind her. "Go on now, see what freedom feels like."

"Ten minutes." The warning call was Mr. Creston's job.

Time flew out here where air moved around Maggie, flirting with her, teasing her hair in the back, instead of canned recirculated air that had been fresh maybe during the Reagan administration. Never enough time with the horses either. But then, she thought as she boarded the bus, watching Dancer rolling on his back and kicking his feet in the air, a little time was better than never.

That afternoon Maggie stopped by Breaking Free's stall and leaned on the top of the lower door. "You're doing better, you know," she told him. "In spite of yourself. Look at you; you're listening to me instead of glaring at me." The horse shifted but kept his ears forward. *He's going to make it,* she told herself. *I just know it.*

"Yes, he's calmed down, but don't you go trusting him." Mr. James checked his watch.

53

"Let's take this next step slowly and get him fed and watered."

Maggie nodded, holding several flakes of baled hay under one arm and the full water bucket in the other. She'd kept a peppermint candy back for Breaking Free, just in case he'd take it from her. "I hope he calms down soon. I didn't get his stall cleaned out, and if we don't pick his hooves pretty soon, he's going to end up with thrush."

"Better thrush than being kicked through the wall." Mr. James slid open the latch and keeping his attention on the horse, slipped into the stall, Maggie right behind him. She'd just tossed the hay into the rack when without warning, Breaking Free charged out of the dimness like a demon from hell. He slammed Mr. James into the wall and with teeth bared went for Maggie.

"Get out, get out," James grunted.

Acting solely on impulse, Maggie heaved the full water bucket at the horse at the same time his teeth grazed her shoulder. Both she and Mr. James fled through the open door, slamming both the upper and lower portions shut behind them and sliding the latches in place.

"Are you all right?" he gasped, forcing his shoulders straight and rubbing one.

"He got you worse than me."

"That's because you threw the bucket at him. Good thinking." He stared at the door that quivered under the tattoo of Breaking Free's back hooves. "I didn't expect this."

Maggie felt tears twisting her eyes and throat. She hadn't either. This wasn't helping the horse's chances to stay alive. She kept from rubbing her shoulder or checking to see if there was blood on her shirt only through hardheaded stubbornness. Breaking Free wasn't afraid to act out his pain, she reflected. She had to give him credit for that. So unlike herself, her pain stuffed back down at the slightest hint of an upheaval.

Mr. James flexed his shoulder. "I missed his halter by an inch."

The two of them stood outside the stall, back far enough to be out of range, but close enough to hear the horse charge the stall door again.

"He got a real mad on." Jules, who rarely spoke, commented. When Maggie turned around, the rest of the group stood behind them, gawking.

"That's why I told all of you to stay back, not to walk near that stall door." He turned to Maggie. "Are you sure you're not hurt?"

Maggie nearly flinched at the gruff tone. She'd not heard him speak like that before.

"Well, there's no blood." She walked over to the fenced pen to check on Dancer. When she leaned her head to the opposite side, her shoulder screamed at her. She glanced around to make sure no one was watching and pulled her cotton knit shirt away from her neck. Looked more like a scrape than a real bite, but either way, she knew she'd have a bad bruise to show for it. At least there was no running blood. Ice pack would be good but that would be admitting Breaking Free had injured her.

Just the thought of the fiery daggers in Breaking Free's eyes kicked up her heart rate. What would it take to gentle him? He must have been abused so badly that anything they did to try to control him would only cause more rage. The only comment she'd heard was that he injured several of his grooms, to the point no one wanted to take daily care of him, let alone see to his injuries. But they had to get feed and water in to him.

When Dancer avoided her attempts to catch him, she turned and soon felt him blowing on the back of her neck. Now why was Dancer so gentle and yet Breaking Free fought back with everything in his power? Dumb question. At some point in his life in spite of the scars from a twitch, someone

56

had lavished a lot of love and attention on this old boy and not on Freebee. "Freebee, where did that come from?" Maggie slowly turned toward Dancer and stroked his nose. "Okay, fella, let's get you to soaking." She took hold of his halter and led him over to the gate to be let out. Snapping the lead shank in place, they walked back to the stalls, staying clear of Breaking Free, who punished the walls of his stall anytime he heard someone come close.

"See, you're missing out on all kinds of good things by being so cranky," she told the closed stall doors as they passed. Since she'd already dumped feed in his box, she cross-tied Dancer in his stall and let him eat while she worked on his foot and leg.

"How's he going?" Mr. James stopped in the stall doorway.

"He still favors it, but I think it's improving. Less swelling."

"He'll make a great riding horse, even a jumper maybe."

"I wish I could adopt him." Maggie knew she was dreaming, but years ago, dreaming had been a delight.

"We're all like that. But every one of them that we keep out of the slaughterhouse is one more victory."

"The thought of eating horse meat makes

me gag."

"The French and the Japanese think it's a delicacy."

Maggie closed her eyes and swallowed hard.

"He's just kiddin' ya." Kool Kat stopped beside Mr. James.

"No, it's true. I read about it." Maggie pulled two brushes out of the bucket and went to work on Dancer. The smell of horse and the rhythm of stroke with one hand, then the other combined to make her relax too. Dancer cocked one back foot, his head hanging further and further.

"Now, there's a picture of contentment." Mr. James nodded as he spoke. He turned to the other women, who had drifted over. "It doesn't take a whole lot to make a horse happy. Food, water, attention, a good brushing."

"She turn him loose, he go roll, you watch." Kool Kat stuck her hands in her back pockets. "Jes like any man, clean 'em up, they go get dirty again."

Mr. James rolled his eyes, but all the women laughed as they drifted back to their own chores.

Maggie kept on brushing and a small tune flitted through her mind, keeping time with the brush strokes. When she finished brushing the horse, she dropped the brushes back in the bucket and unsnapped the tie ropes. "Come on, fella, back out in the fresh air for you." And me. She couldn't get enough of the sunshine, the breeze, and blue sky that went on forever.

"Why don't you take him over to graze that patch by the south paddock?" Mr. James suggested.

Maggie paused with Dancer at her side. "You know, I was thinking. How about we drill a hole in the stall wall so we can stick a hose in there to fill Freebee's bucket?"

"Freebee?"

She shrugged. "Easy to say."

"Good idea. I'll look into it after I write his attack on the report."

"But . . ." She clamped off her protest. Stay invisible. If you react, you can get hurt. She turned back to Dancer. "Come on, fella." All the time she walked away, she wanted to whirl and yell at him. *He didn't really hurt anyone. Well, except you and me.* But Mr. James didn't know about her shoulder. *It could have been a lot worse,* the voice in her head reminded her. *Either you or he could have been seriously injured, not just bruised.* No horse is worth that. What would he do if she begged him not to write that report? Probably nothing, he seemed to think that following protocol was pretty important. But then, not following the rules could put the entire program in jeopardy. Sometimes being able to see both sides of a situation didn't make one feel any better.

The next day when they arrived at the barns, a hole had been drilled into the wall so a hose could be inserted, and the top half of the stall door had been left open.

"Keep way back from Breaking Free's stall. Hopefully his curiosity will help him calm down." Mr. James announced to them all, with a direct look at Maggie.

On her way back to the barn, after taking Dancer to the paddock, she paused, careful to keep a safe distance away from Breaking Free's stall. While he pulled his head back from the stall door, she could see him standing in the shadows, rather than hugging the back wall.

"Hey, fella." His ears stayed forward. She studied him, running one of Mr. James' early lectures through her mind. He had taken them around to all the horses and pointed out their body language.

"You watch the horse to see what he is trying to tell you. Horses never lie. What you see is what you get. See that one throw his head up, we startled him. You want to see relaxation, go watch Ghost snoozing in the corner. His head hanging even with his withers, lower lip drooping. Ears go back for a reason. What is it?"

"The horse is mad," JJ called.

"Kinda like you?" Brandy grinned at her own words.

"Used to be like me." JJ spoke firmly but without the rage and slashing fingernails a comment like that might have caused before.

"Exactly. Watch the ears and the tail, easy indicators of what the horse is feeling. When that tail starts to twitch, back off. Give him some space."

Breaking Free moved to the back of his stall and now seemed to ignore her. When he cocked a back foot, she knew he was relaxed again. She inched closer to the stall door. Her action brought his head back up, and he shifted his front feet.

More of Mr. James' words came back to her. "Watch his eyes. It's easy to mix up fear and anger. But remember, either way, the horse wants to get away from whatever is bothering him. He wants to run."

"These guys always want to run, they's Thoroughbreds," Kool Kat had quipped, making everyone laugh as usual.

Making people laugh, a gift Maggie had

always dreamed of having but never saw happen. *Except for my baby.* The thought struck right to the target of her heart, like an arrow after flight. Her hands clamped against the shaking that came with the arrow.

Breaking Free snorted and shifted again, his eyes rolling white in the dimness. Could he pick up on her feelings that quickly? He'd recognized them almost before she did. She took a deep breath and forced her hands and shoulders to relax. Someday she'd have to let those thoughts out but not today. Not here.

That afternoon she stopped by the door, only moving forward a tiny bit and then waiting until he settled down again before repeating the action. He settled more easily the third move so she left and went about her chores. Make it easy for him to do what you want. She'd read that in a horse training book. Surely the same would work with people.

"You ever worked a lunge line before?" Mr. James asked her as she stepped off the bus at the ranch the next day.

She nodded, all the while wracking her brain, trying to remember everything she'd learned almost twenty years ago.

"Good, take Fashion Sense over to that corral," he pointed to the one at the south end of the long barn, "and work him slow for a bit, then pick up the pace. Most of these horses have cooled out on hot walkers so you should have no trouble with him. The whip is in the tack room."

By the time she had the horse in the corral, Mr. James had gathered the others around. He was good at using everything available to teach about horses, instilling new information in their heads every chance he had.

"Okay, Maggie, you loosen him up while I give a little quiz here."

"A test, that ain't fair, you din't warn us." As usual Kool Kat's voice rose above the rest.

He raised his hands for silence, which happened fairly quickly these days. These last weeks had accomplished as much among the inmates as with the horses. "Now, tell me what was wrong with this horse when he came in?"

Maggie led the dark bay gelding to the center of the corral and, clucking him forward, slowly let out the lunge line. She snapped the whip behind him to get him moving away from her. Keeping one ear on the discussion, she kept both eyes on the horse.

"He was skin and bones. Nobody taked care of him."

"His feet were a mess." Brandy was getting braver about answering.

"Meaning?" James asked.

"Growed out, hooves cracking. Smelled so bad I almost heaved."

"And what is that called?"

Brandy screwed up her face. "I don't remember."

"Anybody help her?"

"Thrush?" JJ asked.

"Good. Anything else?"

"He had a bad cough."

"Good, and what have we done for him?"

"Put him on good food." Kool Kat threw in.

"Trimmed his hooves." JJ picked it up. "And treated the infection."

"Dewormed him." Back to Kool Kat.

They had come a long way in their horse sense. Maggie turned with the horse, flicking the whip along the ground, unconsciously keeping her body in line with his. The sun beat down hot, a breeze danced with the dust stirred by the horse hooves and slowly Fashion Sense picked up his feet. He even snorted once and bobbed his head.

"So, tell me what you see." Mr. James returned to his questions.

After a pause, Kool Kat took up the challenge. "I see a horse that still got a long way to go."

"True. But what do you notice?"

"He not limpin' any more. Coat looks better. Ribs and hip bones don't stick out so much." Kool Kat raised her arms in the air and danced, stepping high in place and making everyone laugh.

"Good. Now watch Maggie. What is she doing?" He kept eye contact with Kool Kat, encouraging her further.

"Showing off." DC's voice.

Showing off could get you hurt. Maggie swallowed and focused on the horse. It wasn't the first time DC had made a comment about Maggie's "uppity" attitude, different duties, and how she got them. How the woman slipped below Mr. James' watchful eye, Maggie did not know, but she did.

Kool Kat squinted her eyes to think. "Makin' him go with the whip."

"How is she using the whip?"

"She keep it low and behind him."

"Watch her body."

"For why?" The others groaned with her.

"Go, Kool Kat," Brandy chanted.

"See how relaxed she is? If she tightened

up, so would the horse. She's easy and keeps moving with him. So, if he is throwing his head and jerking on the lead, what is he telling you?"

"He scarder'n me?" Kool Kat's answer brought snickers from the group.

"He might be head shy. What would cause that?"

"Someone smacked him around."

His nod brought other murmurs and comments.

"No one should be smacked around." JJ spoke with deadly certainty.

"I agree." Mr. James looked them each in the eyes. "Not horses, not people."

For a moment, silence hung.

Then, "Okay, who'd like to trade places with Maggie?"

A hand went up and JJ entered the corral.

"Now, you go stand by Maggie and begin by copying everything she does."

Maggie had to keep her attention on the horse or she knew she'd start to freeze up. Having someone this close always sent her into a retreat within herself.

"Go ahead and hand her the whip."

She passed it to JJ and joined the others around the pen.

Sweat trickled down her back, and she lifted her hat to finger comb her hair back and let the breeze cool her. She might have looked relaxed out there, but the scrutiny made her sweat. Interesting how the rhythm came back to her. Besides, Fashion Sense was an easy horse, grateful for his good treatment.

What about Breaking Free? If she was able to bring him out here and work him like that. . . . Not if, but when, she reminded herself, remembering a comment Marion, their group leader, had drilled into them at Bible study every Tuesday evening. Maggie sometimes found it hard to believe the good things when everything around her screamed hide, get through. Don't let anyone in.

Later that day, she brought Dancer in from the small pen so another horse could be let out. *We really need more small pens,* she thought. More horses would keep coming in, but then they'd not get a group this big all at once again.

She rubbed her shoulder, using the whip had made it ache. But she'd made it without Mr. James noticing anything was wrong. Picking up a bucket with brushes, she headed for another stall. Giving this guy a bath would be a good time. She glanced at her watch — an hour to go, surely she could finish in time.

By the time she dumped the scraper in the bucket, her shoulder felt like it was on fire.

"He sure is pretty now," JJ said, walking over to stroke the horse's shoulder and up his neck. "He liked that."

"Sure, he's used to getting all cleaned up. Pretty soon he'll shine again, just like he should."

"Five minutes," Mr. Creston called.

"Can you put him back in his stall? I'll take this stuff back to the tack room." Maggie dug in her pocket and palmed the last quarter of her apple. "You're a good fella."

"Where's the whip?" Mr. James asked when she set the bucket in its place.

"Ah, JJ had it. I'll go ask her." Maggie trotted back to the stall. No JJ. She turned and scoped the area. Where would it have been left? She ran out to the corral. No whip. Time was running out, if they were late, they'd all get demerits. Back to Dancer's stall. Sure enough, the whip leaned against the wall just inside. She snatched the whip and trotted back to the tack room.

"Remember, you take it out, you bring it back." His censure smarted.

She nodded, in her mind screaming, *but I didn't use it last!* Now she had a mark against her, and it wasn't even her fault.

"We're late, let's hustle."

Mounting the bus steps, she moved down the aisle to her regular seat. DC had taken her place, smirking at her. Fight for it or go on? The thought caught her by surprise. She'd never fought for anything in her entire incarceration. She lowered her gaze and took a seat to the rear.

That evening in her room, she made a list of the questions about Breaking Free she wanted to ask Mr. James, determined she wouldn't lose her nerve again, and planning ways to avoid contact with DC.

In the morning on her way out to the bus, she was mentally reviewing her list when she heard the warden's voice coming from behind the closed door of his office. She kept her gaze forward but slowed slightly.

"Put him down! We cannot keep a vicious animal here!"

Maggie froze.

"But Warden . . ."

"You heard me, Trenton. I'm sorry, but that's the way it has to be."

No, it cannot be. *Please God, it cannot be. We've not had enough time.*

FOUR

He can't mean Breaking Free.

"But . . ."

"I can't have it." The warden interrupted Mr. James. "Someone gets hurt and the lawyers will be all over us like ducks on a June bug. Now you know that."

"We need more time."

"Time is something I can't safely give you. Either put him down or I put him back out on the auction."

Maggie tried to swallow, but her mouth couldn't even work up enough spit to move the muscles. She stared at the door and stepped back when it opened, staring at Mr. James. When the warden walked out behind him, she found herself walking over to them without ever realizing she was going to move.

"Please, Warden Brundage, please can I have a word with you?" She clamped her fists so hard her nails bit into the heels of her hands.

The man stared at her face, then her name on her shirt. "You know you should make an appointment."

"I — there's not time."

"You're working at the horse barn, aren't you?"

"Yes, sir. I — Breaking Free isn't a bad horse, sir. You know people lash out when they're scared. He's no different. You'd give an inmate time, solitary maybe, but time. Please, three weeks. Just give me . . . ," she glanced at Trenton James, "us, three weeks. I know we can bring him around. He's too good a horse to let go like this. Besides, it might be the Equipoise that's contributing to his, his . . . and that has to get out of his system. Same as if an inmate got high and turned mean." She closed her eyes. "Please, sir."

She could feel his gaze drilling into her so she raised her eyes to meet his, putting please into every muscle and cell of her body. She'd never begged for anything like this in her entire life, as if she would disintegrate if he refused.

The warden turned to Trenton James. "Do you agree with her?"

"Yes, sir."

Brundage's gaze swept from James to

Maggie and back. "No one else is to touch him or even go near him. I hear of one more episode, and he's history."

Maggie fought back the tears that made her need to sniff. She blinked and wet her lips. "Yes, sir, thank you, sir. You'll see." She reached out to shake his hand, took a step back but before she dropped her hand, he met her offer and shook her hand.

"I hope to heaven you're right." His dark eyes drilled into hers, as if seeking any morsel of doubt.

"Thank you, sir. I'll keep you posted." Mr. James nodded to Maggie. "They're waiting for us. Let's go."

Maggie fell into step beside him and blinked in surprise when he held the door for her. No man had held a door for her in nearly eight years. It felt mighty good.

Once outside, her knees went weak, and she stumbled going down the steps. He caught her by the elbow. "You all right?"

"I — I can't believe I did that." She laid her hand to her chest, feeling her heart thumping like it wanted to escape.

"Caught me by surprise, too. We sure got our work cut out for us. Come on, let's get cracking."

"What happen to you?" Kool Kat whispered as Maggie collapsed in the seat next to her. She didn't have the strength to walk down the four rows to her usual place. Not past DC.

"Tell you later."

James ran through roll call and then motioned to the driver to get moving. "We just had a discussion with Warden Brundage and the results are that we have three weeks to turn Breaking Free around. In that time, no one is to touch him or get near enough for him to injure you. Basically he is in quarantine, with only Maggie or me working with him. Maggie will have most of the responsibility for his care and rehab. Any questions?"

"Who's going to take care her other horses?" Jules asked from the back of the bus.

"I'll spread them out among the rest of you for now."

DC's low remark probably didn't reach Mr. James' ears, but it smacked Maggie's. "Figures Miss Uppity'd spread around her leftovers."

Mr. James checked his clipboard. "Class is at two thirty today so you need to hustle."

By the time they reached the barn, Maggie had gotten over the shakes. All but those in her mind. What had she been thinking? She hadn't, that was the problem. She let her feelings get in the way. She used to show her feelings, her husband used to tease her when she cried at the movies or while reading a book. She cried when she was happy or sad. But back then when she got angry, if she went silent he knew there was trouble.

She thought back to the last several days. Breaking Free had been settling in but then he tried to hurt them. . . . She paused at that thought. Hurt them. He could have caused serious damage, no mistake about that, but . . . come on, think. What all happened? The horse had charged and slammed Mr. James with his shoulder. He had raked her with his teeth but didn't clamp down. "Freebee, you're a big fake."

She heard Mr. James' boots crunching the dirt and glanced over her shoulder at him. At the same time Breaking Free snorted and slammed one back hoof against the wall. Head high, nostrils wide, ears back, he was now the picture of an angry horse. Maggie stared from the man to the horse. Was the horse only angry because he was so afraid?

"He was calm and fine, at ease, until you came up." She kept her tone low and conversational.

"You were talking to him?" Mr. James stood back from the stall door.

She nodded. "And while he didn't come

to me, he didn't attack either. He even licked his lip." She paused at the next idea, catching it to let it grow. "Maybe it's men." Of course it is. Her voice gained both surety and excitement. "Men abused him. Makes sense, given his prior life."

Mr. James was silent so long Maggie ever so carefully turned her head toward him. "So what do we do?"

"You're going to have to out-horse him," Mr. James said once he'd thought a bit more. "You are the leader here, and he has to understand that. But men have mistreated him so he takes out his fear on all humans. It's our job to show him that he can put away the fear and anger."

"I don't blame him for being angry."

"Me either, but Maggie, it's us or him."

"So what do I do?"

"Well, when a stallion wants his herd to move, he nips the other horses on the rump and drives them forward."

"You want me to bite him on the butt?"

He glanced at her, then a smile broke his face. "Smart aleck."

Maggie stared down at her shoe, digging a dent in the hard-packed dirt. She fought the smile all the way up from her toes and finally trapped it before it reached her face. He then reminded her of her work with

Dancer, how she'd used the whip to move him forward.

"We'll do the same with Breaking Free, only in the beginning I'll keep another rope on him to keep him from charging you. And no audience, other than JJ. We'll need her to slip the gate bar in place."

When Maggie walked back to the stall with the lead shank and lunge line, Breaking Free had his head out of the upper door, watching both her and the other activities. His ears pricked forward. But as soon as Mr. James walked up, the ears went back, and the horse withdrew into his stall.

"You ready?" Mr. James asked, stopping at the stall.

She nodded.

He unlatched the door, and Maggie eased into the stall and stood beside the wall. "Easy, fella, no need to get all heated up. Just take it easy."

Breaking Free snorted from his retreat in the back corner. Swallowing hard, Maggie felt the throbbing of the bruise from the attack and hoped today would be different. For her and Breaking Free. *C'mon, boy, you can do this,* she telegraphed to him with her eyes.

Mr. James entered the stall, taking the other wall, and JJ slid the bar in place.

"We'll just stand here a minute and let him settle."

"Good boy, see you can behave yourself." Maggie kept her gaze on the horse, noting his heavier breathing, shifting front feet, and swishing tail. When he threw his head up and snorted, she wanted nothing more than to reassure him that all was well. "Easy now. Easy."

"Okay, be ready, we walk forward together and take hold of his halter like we do this every day."

"Right." Her heart picked up and her mouth dried. She kept up a singsong murmur as she moved forward and grasped his halter with a firm hand. James did the same and quickly snapped the lead shank to the ring under the horse's chin. "Now you thread yours up and over, then I'll do the same."

Breaking Free tossed his head, stepping backward at the same time. His ears flattened and he shook his head, jerking to shake them off. If this big horse decided to lift them both straight up in the air, he could do it, but Maggie sincerely hoped he wasn't in the mood. When she tightened the lead shank over his nose, he stopped. A small victory.

"Good, now we'll walk him out to the

round pen and see how he does. Pay attention to his every move."

She didn't need to be reminded of that. Reaching up, she stroked his neck. "Hey, fella, do you ever need a good brushing. Would make you feel lots better." Keeping one hand close to his halter, she held the lead firmly with the other.

"Let's go."

No one else showed a face as they led Breaking Free to the round pen. JJ followed to close the gate behind them, just like she had the stall door. Once in the round pen, the horse stood with head up, like a king surveying his kingdom. When he snorted, tiny drops spattered her face. While she wanted to wipe it off, she kept both hands on his lead shank.

"All right, boy, you've had a look around, now let's walk." Mr. James rubbed the horse's cheek and neck with his knuckles as he talked. Breaking Free's ears lay back for a moment and then returned to attention.

They made a circle around the pen, three dancers tied together by tension. When Breaking Free tried to pull away, both humans tightened their leads, keeping a firm pressure from either side. Maggie sang her litany of encouragement as Breaking Free did a high stepping tight walk.

"Time for a bite on the rump," Mr. James said.

Maggie jerked her head toward him, then nodded. "Like yesterday?"

"You don't want to nick him with it, just pop it near him. That whip is the same as a bite on the butt."

When they came back around to the gate, Maggie exchanged the lead shank for the lunge line, and together they walked back out. While she let the line out trailing it through her fingers, Mr. James led Breaking Free out toward the edge of the pen. With ears flat against his head, Breaking Free pulled against the lead rope, all his attention focused on the man walking beside him.

"Let him go," Maggie called.

"What if he charges you?"

"I think it's you he's fighting."

Mr. James considered that for a moment. "If you get hurt, you know it's over for him."

"I know." Maggie inhaled courage and exhaled fear. "Let him loose."

As soon as the lead shank was removed from over his nose, Breaking Free shook his head and jigged around a bit, but when Maggie popped the whip right behind him, he leaped forward and ran around the circle, head high, neck arched, staring over the walls, ignoring Maggie. It struck her she'd spent her years in prison that way — until the morning DC shoved her against the fence — running in circles, staring over the walls of her heart, ignoring everyone. She and this horse definitely had a connection.

After half an hour of back and forth turning and popping, she thought her arms would fall off at her shoulders. But when his head finally went down and he walked forward flat-footed, her chest swelled like she'd just crossed the finish line at a marathon. She stepped back, and he kept on walking.

She caught Mr. James' thumbs-up sign and wished she could throw the line to the outside and go hug on that beautiful horse. She nodded her gratitude. When she took a couple of steps toward him, Breaking Free moved forward, but when he turned to look at her, full face, not just furtive glances, she took a couple of steps back. Any time he responded the way she wanted, she took the pressure off by stepping back. Just like in the book she'd read, he came forward. How often did things happen like they were supposed to? Not much in Maggie's recent life. This was a nice change. *Breaking Free, you are breaking free of your past.* Like partners dancing the cha-cha, they moved two steps forward, two back. She gathered in some of the lunge line, turned around, and walked away. She could hear him following her. *I'm communicating with him, talking the language of horse, and it is working.* A thrill, almost unidentifiable since it had been so long since she felt it, tickled her backbone.

When she stopped, the horse kept on coming. He stopped so close she could feel his heat. She was trembling, her mouth dry as a Santa Ana wind.

"Okay, fella, looks like we did some joining up. Good thing, 'cause I don't know how much longer I could have kept going." She turned slowly. He stood still except for his ears that swiveled to catch every nuance. When she tugged on the lunge line, he came forward. "Good boy. Ah, what a good boy you are." He tightened up when she reached for the snap under his halter and shook his head when she released it. But now, when he could have run away, he chose to stay. When she stepped back, he came forward. He wanted to be near her. He was beginning to trust her. Tears of joy erupted inside her, but she clamped both eyes and hands so they wouldn't escape. Because she and Mr. James chose to try to understand him and his fears, they had given him a chance to live.

Mr. James' voice interrupted her thoughts.

"Send him around again, make sure this imprints on his mind. You all right?"

She nodded and stroked the horse's neck. "About as all right as I'll ever be, long as I'm still an inmate. But that won't be for long." She kept her words low, only for the horse's ears, and he'd never tell. Having witnessed the horse's willingness to overcome . . . Well, that bore thinking about on lots of levels, especially tonight, when sleep ignored her summons.

"Use your lead shank instead of the whip to keep driving him forward."

She did as Mr. James told her, having more trouble schooling her face into blankness than the horse. Breaking Free watched her, and he stopped when she stopped, each time turning slightly so he could see her with both eyes. When she turned and walked the other way, he followed.

Never before the other day with Dancer had a horse followed her without a lead shank. She picked up a jog. So did the horse. She did a figure eight, so did he. Her trembling had ceased and adrenaline surged through her clear to her fingertips. Surely climbing Mount Everest would be no bigger thrill than this.

FIVE

"What's this?" Gil asked.

Maria glanced over from squeezing orange juice. "The newspaper?"

"No, this?" Gil pointed to the page laid on top. The headline read *Horse Country* in twenty-point type. "And what's that?" Now he pointed to the blue nylon harness hooked over the back of a kitchen chair.

"Eddie bought that yesterday, used his own money. He says our new house is in there." She nodded at the page in Gil's hand.

"All right, Maria, what is going on?"

"You ask Eddie." She set his regular plate of scrambled eggs with two strips of bacon, no toast, in front of him. "More coffee?" She paused and gave him one of her looks. "Decaf."

Gil frowned. Ever since she'd read that he should cut back on caffeine, she served him one cup regular, the second and third decaffeinated. Sometimes he wondered who was the boss.

"Hey, Dad." Eddie spun his lightweight all-terrain style wheelchair into the kitchen. "Maria."

"Buenos días, chico."

"Hey yourself. Where's Bonnie?" Gil asked.

"She went back to bed," Eddie answered.

"On your bed?"

"Of course." He stared at his father. "She always sleeps on my bed."

Hearing her name, tri-colored Bonnie trotted into the kitchen, tail wagging, nails clicking on the tiled floor. She parked herself by Eddie's chair where he could reach her head easily, gazing up at him, adoration in her sad Basset eyes. Bonnie was trained as an assistant dog, fetching things for Eddie when he asked. A small cloth bag on the inside of the arm of his wheelchair held her favorite kind of dog biscuits. They'd all learned early on that Bonnie would do just about anything for treats.

Eddie wheeled his chair into his place at the table and flipped the napkin open to lay in his lap. "Are you home all day, Dad?"

"I'm not sure, why?"

"Well, I thought you might want to go out

84

and look at that property." He pointed to the ad now laying on the side of the tabletop.

"Eddie, why would I want — ?"

"We — I really want to see it too." Eddie shrugged. "Sorry, I interrupted you."

"What's wrong with this place? We have it just the way we like it."

"You know you said you need more office space if you are really going to run your business out of the house. Right?"

Gil stared at his son whose face wore such guilelessness he might have adopted it from the angels. "True." *This boy is going to make either a terrific attorney or a highly successful politician.*

"The lots are forty acres, plenty of room to build office space if you want, and only two miles from a major freeway. Plenty of room for my horse. Of course, we'll need a barn too, but not a big one." He forked scrambled eggs into his mouth from the plate Maria had set before him. "I'm thinking two horses."

"You need two horses to ride?"

"No, one is for you."

"Wait a minute. Who said I wanted to ride?"

"You said you wanted to spend more time with me, and you said I needed to be outside more so . . ."

"So is that why you bought the halter?"

Eddie took a long swallow of orange juice. "You think we could have a couple of orange trees too?"

"The halter?"

"Oh, remember you keep saying to write your goals down and then act as if you already have them?"

Gil nodded. Hung again by his own tongue. True, he listened to a lot of tapes and had been to many seminars on goal setting and success, the training he needed to be at the top of his field. Along the way he tried to impart the same knowledge to his son.

It looked like it was working.

"Do you have any idea what a place like that — if we actually liked the first one we saw, which is entirely not likely — will cost?"

"I think so. I went online and looked at houses. One site tells you what a house will cost in your area so I typed in our zip code." He leaned forward. "Did you know that building houses in California is more than twice as expensive as say, North Dakota?"

Gil looked at Maria whose face, just beginning to show lines, glowed with pride. Since she'd never married, Eddie was the son she'd never have. Looking from her to his son, he realized anew how much he owed this woman. Granted she'd come to him as an illegal from Venezuela, but at his prompting she'd taken advantage of the amnesty offered, studied and gotten her citizenship papers. It was at her insistence that he'd made the decision to move his office home. She'd been right. His son had been growing up without him. It was thanks to her that the boy was open to him at all. But the years of seventy-hour weeks had paid off, and now he could afford to relax a little.

"Would you want your office in the house or in a separate building?" Eddie's question broke into his father's thoughts.

"More coffee?" Maria stood next to Gil.

"Only if it's leaded. I need caffeine this morning to answer all his questions."

Marie studied his face for a moment, then brought the carafe over. "Just for today."

Gil looked heavenward as if praying for patience, but the slight smile made Eddie laugh.

"You might as well give up, she won't change her mind." He slipped a piece of his toast to Bonnie who'd been eyeing every bite that went into his mouth but never made a whimper. Wiping his mouth on his napkin, Eddie watched his father.

Gil picked up the advertisement. "Forty

acres, eh. I don't see that we need forty acres."

"They have some smaller ones, like twenty."

"Do you know how big twenty acres is?"

"Half of forty?" Eddie's eyes danced. "How long does it take to build a house?"

"Depends on the size, but usually six months to a year." Eddie had been a baby when he and his wife went through the construction of this house. Getting the house built took up a lot of Sandra's energy, but taking care of a baby who required repeated surgeries, only to finally realize their son would never be normal, was what really made her run.

Gil looked up to see Eddie watching him, one hand stroking his dog, the other tracing patterns on the place mat on the table. A sign that he was more concerned than he let on.

All he wants is a horse, for crying out loud. He's not asking for the moon. But what if he gets hurt?

That was the real question. While Gil had not been home much of the time, he made sure Eddie had everything he needed and was protected as much as possible. A gated community, a private school, all the gadgets any kid could desire, and now, his father's attention.

Guilt whispered, *His son didn't ask for much.*

Reason responded, *It isn't the money, it's the time. It's always been the time.*

"Get your backpack and I'll meet you at the car. Maria, you come too, please. But keep in mind, it takes a long time to find a house that you like. Don't get your hopes up."

They turned off the freeway at the designated road and followed the signs to Horse Country, entering under a squared arch of golden peeled logs. Local rock walls flared out to the sides with a bed of shrubs that hosted a rearing horse of bronze on each side. The paved road wound before them, going on either side of the guard shack in the middle. They stopped to greet the guard, and he handed them a map, showing the sales office with the already sold lots colored green. The developer had left many of the California oaks and Jefferson pine trees in place, clearing out the underbrush so it looked more like a park than a housing development. They headed back toward the entry and stopped at a model house with a Sales Office sign in a nicely landscaped yard. After Eddie wheeled out of the van, they made their way to the glass doors in what would eventually be the garage.

As they entered the office/house, a dark-haired woman motioned she'd be right with them, finished her phone call, and came around the desk with a smile as bright as the noonday sun. "I'm Francesca," she said, extending a well-manicured hand. "Welcome to Horse Country." Her voice was as smooth as her taupe pants, silk shirt, and modern art scarf.

Gil introduced himself, Eddie, and Maria and explained what their needs would be. "We drove around the development, and it seems all the level lots are already sold." As if twenty and forty acre parcels could be called lots.

"Strange that you should say that, as a house that might meet your requirements just came on the market today. The owners were transferred and have to sell their nearly finished home. Let me acquaint you with the amenities of Horse Country and then we'll go look at it."

As they left the building, Francesca got in her car and headed for the house. Eddie grinned up at his father. "She's hot, isn't she?"

"Eddie!"

"She likes you."

"Eddie. What do you know about some woman liking a man?"

"I watch television. My legs might not work but my eyes do."

"Yeah, well . . ." Gil shook his head. Whatever else would this kid come up with? "Don't go setting any dates up for me, all right?" Eddie had not asked about his mother in years. Perhaps it was time to talk about her. Most likely it was past time. He wondered what Maria had told the boy, other than the party line of they just didn't love each other any more and so they divorced. Never ever did he want Eddie to learn that his mother had deserted her son — and his father. He'd put all the safeguards in place. But they'd never been tested. At least not that he knew. Maybe moving was a good idea after all. "Now, let's go over this again. House hunting takes time. You have to see what you like about each house and then decide what you want. No hopes up on this being *the one,* okay?"

"Sure, Dad," Eddie said serenely.

They parked in the driveway of a single-story house with construction vehicles lined up along the curb. As Eddie's lift groaned into place, Gil studied the stucco exterior. The open double doors to the entry beckoned them. Three steps finished in slate

91

curved around the recessed doors. *We'd have to make a ramp,* he thought, although he was pleased with the entrance.

Francesca joined them and chatted with Gil while Eddie unloaded.

"How close to finished is it?"

"They're hanging the cabinets in the kitchen, fixtures need to be installed, perhaps some more painting, and of course the landscaping. While the footings are poured for the barn, they haven't begun the construction, and I don't think the pool is quite finished either." She waited while Gil backed Eddie's wheelchair up the stairs. "I think it would be easy to change one side of the steps into a ramp."

"It would." As they entered the house, the high ceilings of the great room caught Gil's attention. All on one level, no sunken living room. French doors on either side of the fireplace on the outer wall invited them outside.

"There are three bedrooms, each with a private bath, and a den."

Gil nodded and glanced at his son. The doors were wide enough for his wheelchair so even those wouldn't have to be changed. "What do you think, Eddie?"

"This one would be my room, right? And Maria could have the other."

"Or we could turn part of that monstrous garage into a private apartment for you, what do you think?" he asked Maria.

Maria nodded and shrugged at the same time. "What about your office?"

"The den would work until we could build a separate building."

They followed Francesca outside on an unfinished patio and backyard. "It needs to be fenced yet and will look so much better when the landscaping is in."

"How soon would we be able to move in?" Eddie's voice squeaked.

Francesca smiled at him. "It would take a month for escrow to clear."

"Title clearance is in place?" Gil heard himself ask, while at the same time he kept telling himself, *It takes a long time to find a house you want.*

"Of course."

"Could we move in before escrow cleared if we wanted to?" He could feel Eddie watching them, gazing back and forth, like he was watching a tennis tournament.

"That would be a possibility."

"Sprinkler systems are in?" Gil tried to think of all contingencies.

"I'd have to check on that."

"How big is the barn?" Eddie asked.

"I'm not sure, but I can show you the

plans back at the office."

"What are they asking?"

She told him and he nodded. The amount wasn't out of sight for this place. Under Eddie's scrutiny, he made plans to call the saleswoman tomorrow.

As they walked back to the car, Eddie turned his chair and looked back.

"What is it?"

"Just thinking what it will be like to live here."

Great. Gil watched the Realtor drive off. The sound of hammers and a drill motor came from the interior of the house, while a concrete saw whined from the backyard. *Up the street children laughed.* A car drove by. Ravens complained from the California oak trees scattered about the field. Twenty acres was a lot of land to fence. The three of them studied the property.

"The brochure said there were trails for riding." Eddie looked up at his father.

"The drive to school will be longer."

"Bonnie will have more room to sniff," Eddie countered.

Gil tried to think of all the minuses. "It will be farther to shopping, Maria."

"So I shop bigger at one time." She smiled at Eddie.

"No view like we have now."

"Eddie and his horses playing in the field is a good view to me."

Once they were ready to go, Eddie caught his dad's gaze in the mirror. "Did you like the swimming pool?"

"I guess. It's bigger than the one we have. Why?" He watched his son in the mirror. "Oh, you're thinking about getting in and out. Don't worry, we can fix that before it's finished."

"She said we could move in a month?" Eddie asked.

Before school started, but at least Eddie wouldn't be changing schools. He'd been enrolled in a private Christian school for prekindergarten and been there ever since. Gil had never regretted it. Although they weren't every Sunday in church, Gil made sure to contribute both time and money to the school — more time this last year than all the other years combined, but who was counting. Other than perhaps Eddie.

Gil cleared his throat. "I just want to remind you that this is totally out of the ordinary. Buyers never find a house this fast."

Eddie just grinned at him. Maria too.

Oh, Lord, in spite of all his warnings, he was going to buy the first house they saw.

Did God give a small boy's prayers precedence over those of his father?

Six

At the barn, Maggie stopped outside Breaking Free's stall and watched him come toward her. Ears forward, he hung his head over the door.

"Well, hello to you too." She dug a candy out of her pocket and palmed it for him. He sniffed it, lipped it, and then crunched. Mr. James had said that today they would turn him out in the corral while she cleaned his stall to see if he'd let himself be brought back in. She stroked his neck, still surprised he wasn't head shy. But he didn't like his ears to be touched, jerking away when her hand got too close to them.

Maggie checked to make sure the horse had water before heading over to the storage stall to get a couple flakes of hay.

"He let you pet him."

"I know." She nodded to Jules who had spoken, one who talked so rarely it caught her by surprise. The woman was forever sneaking up behind and watching Maggie. It was unnerving. "I never dreamed we could have such change so fast. But according to Mr. James, it often works that way."

"Can I watch you work with him?"

Maggie hesitated. "I don't know. Ask Mr. James."

"I — I . . ."

"He's one of the kindest men I think I've ever known, other than maybe my grandfather."

Maggie watched Jules struggle with the desire to confide in someone, all the while struggling with her own rule to stay out of other people's business. Then, with a look at Breaking Free, she knew she could do no less than what she expected of him: to try again to reenter life. She spoke softly. "You have to be the one to ask him. That's important."

Jules nodded and stared at the ground, finally raising doubtful eyes to Maggie. "You think?"

Maggie nodded. "I do." Her hand shook as she shoved it in her pants pocket. Jules was a lifer with nothing to lose if she didn't like Maggie's advice.

Breaking Free stood with his head over the stall door and snitched a bite of hay before she could open the door. "Back up, horse, and let me in." Jules moved away as silently as she'd arrived, and Maggie let out the breath she'd been holding. She dumped the hay in the rack and returned for a small serving of sweet feed, which he gobbled in a couple of bites.

Maggie dug a brush and a rubber curry out of the grooming bucket and started work on his shoulder. Her own spasmed when she raised her arm to groom his back. She'd been careful not to let anyone see the purple and green bruise that still bloomed like a flower on the front of her shoulder. By the time Breaking Free had finished eating, she'd finished brushing him, grateful she'd finally gotten the tangles out of his mane and tail. Leaving the wraps on his legs, she snapped a lead rope to his halter and led him out of the stall.

He stopped, raising his head to look around.

"He thinks he's the king," JJ called from the stall she was cleaning.

He looked in the direction of the speaker but paid no more attention. When one of the horses in the field whinnied, he answered, a loud blast that made Maggie's ears ring.

"Ow, you could warn me, you know." She tugged on his lead and took only two steps before he followed. No jerking on the lead, no chain over his nose. She led him to the round pen, opened the gate while he stood at her shoulder, and then walked him in.

When she unsnapped the lead, he walked forward to the center of the pen, his front legs buckled, and he groaned as he lay down.

"Is he sick?" Brandy and some of the other women walked up to the fence.

"No, watch."

Breaking Free kicked his feet until he rolled up on his back, then kicked and wriggled his back down in the dirt. Dust flew up around him.

"He's scratching his back, besides dust helps keep away flies and pests. All horses love to get down and roll, but racehorses are never given the freedom to do it."

They watched as he snorted and rolled over, then back the other way, all the while grunting and shaking. When he scrambled to his feet, head down, he shook all over, sending a cloud of dust skyward.

The spectators applauded. Maggie just watched. *Old boy, you're getting to be a horse, not a speed machine. Go for it.* She left him in the pen, enjoying the sunshine while she went back and cleaned out his stall.

Now for today's test. Would he let her bring him in? Back in she walked toward him and he turned to face her, then when she walked away, he followed. She stopped. He stopped. She trotted; he trotted, as if they were joined by invisible wires. When she stopped at the gate, his head was hanging even with his withers, right behind her shoulder. He was limping again, and she could feel his pain in her bones. She snapped the lead shank on his halter. Another test passed with flying colors. But would he be able to overcome his hatred of men before Warden Brundage came to evaluate their progress?

SEVEN

On the way home, Gil, Eddie, and Maria stopped for milk shakes to celebrate finding their new house.

While Eddie slurped his, he asked, "Dad?"

"Yes."

"Do you like Carly?"

"Yes, she's seems like a very caring person."

"She's pretty too."

"True. Why?" He watched his son's face.

Eddie shrugged. "Just thought I'd ask." He glanced out the window, then smiled at his father when he caught his eye in the mirror. "She's not married."

"Well, she's too old for you, sport."

"Daaad!"

Pulling into the driveway a short time later, they heard Bonnie's usual miss-you greeting. Her deep aroooohs echoed inside the house, and as soon as Eddie drove inside she skidded to a stop on the tiled floor beside his chair, wriggled furiously while he petted her head and ears, then tore down the hall, through the kitchen, sliding her long body around corners, up on the leather couch, off the other end, back to Eddie and off tearing around again. All the while barking and singing her ahroos.

"And that's the Basset Five Hundred." Eddie laughed along with his dog.

Gil stooped to pet her when she stopped, panting, in front of him, long black-spotted tongue lolling out the side of her mouth. "Bonnie, you are one crazy dog."

"I went online with that group of Basset Rescue people I told you about. Others write about their dogs doing the same thing. They say there's a basset-tude too." Eddie leaned over and scrunched her ears up in his hands, rubbing white nose to black, to get a slurpy kiss from chin to hairline.

"You talk to people you don't know?"

"You told me not to."

"I know. But that's not what I asked you. Do you go online to chat rooms and such?"

"Some."

"Some meaning what?" Sometimes being a father wasn't his favorite role.

"Well, I go on the Basset one, there's also a group for kids with spina bifida. I check out the therapeutic riding sites, like Rescue

Ranch, and then I look up stuff I'm curious about. Oh, and I found some horse rescue sites too."

"Near as I can tell, you are curious about most everything."

With a shrug, Eddie gave his chair a push and headed for his room. "I'm going swimming, you want to come?"

"I'll bring lunch out in an hour or so." Maria smiled at him from the arched entry to the kitchen.

Did he need to pursue this with Eddie now, or should they talk more about it later? Later sounded like a good idea, along with the pool. Sometimes Gil felt Eddie and Maria were in league together to keep him from working, and sometimes, like now, he was grateful. He knew he'd become a workaholic, saved only by the grace of a woman strong enough to stand against him and a son gentle enough to forgive. He whistled his way down the hall and into his bedroom to change into swimming trunks, ignoring the blinking light on the message machine, just like he'd turned off his cell phone on the drive to Horse Country.

"I have to work this afternoon," he announced after a lunch of BLTs on focaccia bread, fruit salad, and tall glasses of iced tea and lemon cookies.

"I know." Eddie looked up from slipping Bonnie a bite of bacon. "I'm going over to Arthur's to play video games." Eddie's best friend, Arthur, lived three houses over on the cul-de-sac. "His mom made caramel corn. You want me to bring you some?"

"That's a bit of an imposition."

"Nope, she makes extra, just for you. She said everyone needs at least one vice." Eddie laughed as he wheeled his way into the house to change out of his wet board shorts. His voice floated back. "Be neat to have a mom that did stuff like that."

A pang struck Gil. "Maria, how long since we've had the Owens over for dinner?"

"Not since . . ." she squinted her eyes in thought. "Couple months anyway."

"Okay, let's invite them for a pool party and barbecue on Saturday or Sunday, whichever they can make."

"Bueno. Anyone else?"

"We need to do more entertaining. Ask the Grandleys too. We'll do steaks, hot dogs, and hamburgers. And make a couple of pitchers of your special lemonade."

Gil heard Eddie whistle for Bonnie, and the two of them went out the door as he settled into his study to begin returning phone calls, starting with one to Amy, his secretary at the main office who wanted to know the progress of house hunting.

"I cannot believe I am buying the first and only house I looked at. It just isn't done."

"But if it is perfect, why question your judgment?"

"Good point." He shook his head. "I can't believe it."

They worked for several hours, e-mailing and faxing things back and forth, confirming his travel for the next few months. When he seemed to be overbooking himself, she reminded him of his commitment to stay at home more.

"I think you're all ganging up on me."

"That's what you pay me for."

He laughed at her teasing. "Thanks, Amy. Let me know on the convention in New York. That one I might take Maria and Eddie along with me."

That evening he and Eddie played chess and cleaned up the rest of the caramel corn. Eddie's comment about a mom who did stuff like caramel corn kept circling in his mind.

She is a beautiful woman, Gil thought the next afternoon when he took Eddie out for his riding lesson. Carly wore her shoulder length dark hair pulled back with a leather slide at the base of her skull. Today she was wearing a straw hat that had met with the dirt a time or two and perhaps had even been stepped on. But her dark eyes lit up when she greeted Eddie, and her smile softened a very square jaw. *Come on, Winters, you've not paid attention to her before — why now?* Of course he had paid attention to her, just not the male-female kind. Leave it to Eddie to stir things up.

The boy in question was not smiling today. His near fall during his previous lesson made his aides walk closer to the horse's sides, even with his stirrups, a real step down from his growing freedom. When one of the aides said something, Eddie smiled back. There would be no trotting today, a punishment in Eddie's opinion.

Carly strode to the center of the ring where three different students were circling the arena at the same time. Eddie was by far the more proficient rider. Two assistants were holding one little girl in place while a third led the small horse around. The third rider, an older teen, clung to the saddle horn, terror being the only visible emotion.

Eddie had been terrified at first too, but the way he'd blossomed in the nearly two years he'd been riding here was nothing short of miraculous. He was stronger, his balance much improved, but mostly his self-

107

confidence had him sitting straighter and willing to tackle obstacles in the rest of his life too. Not that he'd ever been an introvert, Maria had seen to that, but now he was independent too. Carly had added to that independence.

"Now, Eddie, I want you to circle the ring once, turn in to reverse, and go around the other way. Keep him at an even walk and paying attention."

"Yes, ma'am."

Gil made his way to the bleachers and took a seat halfway up so he could watch his son around the entire arena. He glanced over to the side when he heard someone crying. A little girl did not want to get off her horse, not an unusual situation.

Sure, just buy my son a horse. Carly'd made it sound so easy. Resentment tried to raise its sneaky head, but he squashed it like bashing pop-up critters in an amusement park. He knew letting thoughts like that get comfortable would take dynamite to get rid of them. And besides, resentment might bring along rage, and he'd beaten that one into oblivion more than once. He believed what he taught at his conferences. One could control one's thoughts and must, if you didn't want your thoughts to control you, but doing so took a lot of desire and practice.

Why was that easier on some days than others?

"There at the end, I finally rode all by myself again. Did you see, Dad?" Eddie popped a wheelie he was so excited.

"I sure did." Although his heart was in his mouth most of the time, he was not going to let on to Eddie that he felt that way. "You did really well. But I could sure tell you didn't like slowing down again."

"Carly said I recovered my confidence, and my balance is much better. I didn't tell her I was kinda scared at first."

"I'm really proud of you. Fear isn't easy to overcome, but you didn't let it stop you." *And now I can't let it stop me.* The thought made him catch his breath. How would he find someone to work with Eddie at home if and when they did buy a horse?

"I think I would like to enter a horse show."

Gil schooled his face into a smiling response. So many things could happen — a horse could get away, something could spook Eddie's horse. The list blew up in his face before he could shut it down. "We'll have to see."

"Oh." Eddie slumped. "You don't want me to."

Winters, get yourself under control. He doesn't need your fear to stop him. "Eddie, if and when Carly thinks you are ready for a horse show, I'll do everything in my power to make it happen." *But I don't have to like it.*

Gil found his mind full of questions and doubt. How would he find a horse that Eddie could handle? Buy the one he was riding? Would Carly be willing to help him find a horse and then train it for them? She'd said she would help find one, but she'd not mentioned training it. And bottom line, who would take care of the horse? Where would he find another gem like Maria?

"Thanks, Dad." But the exuberance had fled, leaving a pensive little boy behind.

Gil's cell phone rang twice on the way home, one of the numbers on the screen unknown to him, but he stayed by his rule to never talk on the phone with his son in the car, even though his curiosity plagued him.

He let down the ramp and followed his son into the house, returning the calls as he strolled. The first message was Amy with some last-minute questions on a client. He called her back, and then listened to the next message. The voice froze him at the first word.

EIGHT

"Do I get to do the horse whisperer thing today?" Kool Kat stopped beside Maggie, looking at Mr. James for permission several days later.

"Some call it natural horsemanship, others call it horse whispering, some call it understanding horses or ground training." A smile moved from his lips to his eyes. "Are you sure you want to do this? After all, you're the one who called them giants."

"Did I say that?" She glanced at Maggie.

"Don't ask me. I have enough trouble keeping track of what I say."

"Shoun't be hard, you hardly ever say anything."

Maggie felt her eyebrows go up. She sucked her bottom lip between her teeth. "That was a good one."

Kool Kat turned to go, but nailed Maggie with one slitted eye. "You almost laughed on that one."

"Bring your horse to the pen in half an hour," Mr. James said.

Kool Kat gave a shuffle leap. "Yes!"

"I never would have dreamed this of her." Maggie sighed after the woman moved away.

"As I said in the beginning, working with horses reveals who we are. No matter how hard we try to hide it."

Maggie turned back to begin cleaning Breaking Free's stall. Was he aiming that last comment at her?

She'd just dumped the final wheelbarrow of clean shavings in the stall when Kool Kat called, "You comin'?"

"I wasn't planning on it." She paused, caught by surprise. "You want me to?"

"Why you think I'm asking?"

Maggie leaned the wheelbarrow against the outside wall and unclipped Breaking Free. *She wants you to come, don't make her beg.* The horse might as well have been talking to her, the voice was so near. "I'll be right there." Giving her horse a pat on the neck, she unbuckled the halter and let it slide back over her arm. "Okay, fella, you're free. Now don't give me any flack when I come to get you again, all right?"

She rubbed his nose one last time and headed out of the stall, carefully latching the stall door behind her. She heard him follow her and turned to see his head hanging over the lower half of the door, ears pricked forward, watching her every move.

Her heart, so long merely a circulatory pump for her body, felt like it might burst with the thrill of it all.

Kool Kat had just led her horse into the round pen when she arrived. All the women were lined up, leaning on the top rail. Maggie shut the gate behind the horse and joined JJ and the others. DC was nowhere to be seen, which made Maggie want to keep watch over her shoulder.

"Now remember," Mr. James spoke loud enough for them all to hear. "This is about watching for the horse to tell you what he is feeling and thinking. So look for the signs we've talked about." He turned his attention to Kool Kat. "Okay, unsnap the lead and let him loose."

She did as Mr. James instructed. Halfway to the fence, the horse's head went down and his back feet shot for the sky, bucking and kicking. When he came to a stop after tearing around the perimeter, he stood with his rear toward the center of the pen. Maggie smothered a snort.

Kool Kat put her hands on her ample hips. "That horse be flipping me off."

"That's one way of describing it. So what

do you do?"

Kool Kat flipped the rope end of the lead shank and the horse took off running. When he slowed to a trot she flicked it again. He kept his head faced to the outside, not looking at her.

"I'm gettin' dizzy."

"Okay, keep your eye on him but walk in a bigger circle." For the next half hour, Mr. James led Kool Kat through the steps. "Keep your arms out, good, keep him moving. See, now he's looking at you." Soon, Mr. James issued the big statement. "Turn around and walk away."

Maggie wanted Kool Kat to feel what she'd felt that day Breaking Free had followed her. Would the big woman's horse oblige?

Sure enough, the horse, head hanging nice and easy, followed her across the pen.

Maggie watched Kool Kat's face go from face-splitting grin to a tear leaking down one cheek. The outside of a horse was truly good for the inside of a man — or woman.

Even the sight of DC ambling around the pen failed to dim Maggie's joy.

"All right, turn and pet him." Mr. James glanced around at the spectators. "Class in five. Bring your pencils."

"Hey, Mr. James, we all get to do this?" It was JJ.

"Those who want to. It's not required."

"I ain't gonna do that. My luck, the horse would run right over me," Brandy muttered as she walked away.

When they'd gathered for class, Mr. James handed out sheets of paper and, amid groans, asked them to write down their observations. A few moments later as they shared their answers, Maggie found herself nodding. If only she had known this stuff as a kid working with horses, she could have handled some problem animals differently. Think like the horse. Incredible.

As they finished their discussion, a low voice muttered, "If school had been like this, maybe I'd a stayed in."

DC. Her comment caught Maggie by surprise. School wasn't the only answer, but without some kind of an education or training, most of these girls would be back here. Maggie had heard the stats — they weren't good. But for her, once she was out, she'd not be back. Never touching liquor again seemed a small price to pay for freedom. She wasn't an alcoholic, but driving under the influence of alcohol had sent her to prison.

She jerked her mind back to the moment.

Why was not looking back getting harder? By now it should be easy.

"Mistah James, can I aks a personal question?" Kool Kat rocked her chair back on two legs.

"If I can retain the right not to answer." He nodded. "Go for it."

"Did you learn about horses this way, I mean like the ground training you teachin' us?"

Tossing the dry erase marker up and down, Mr. James leaned against the board and didn't answer for a moment. He seemed a long way away. "No, I'm sorry to say I didn't, but my father always handled horses gently, giving them the respect they deserve. He would have approved of this kind of training. I've been just as awed by it as all of you have."

Kool Kat and the others nodded. She thanked him and got a glint in her eye. "You married?"

"I stand on my right to remain silent." At his grin, they all burst out laughing.

He shuffled his papers into order as he continued, "Well done, all of you. Tomorrow we have two more horses coming in. That will bring us up to fifteen. Kool Kat, would you please set up the sprinklers in that west pasture? Brandy, you go along to help her. We have an hour until we leave. Any questions?"

"Who gets the new horses?" DC asked, shooting a dark glance at Maggie, whose insides flip-flopped. Kool Kat growled under her breath.

"I haven't decided yet. I want to know more about them first."

As the women filed out, Mr. James stopped Maggie. "Let's start working with Freebee on accepting a man in his life."

"That's what got most of us in trouble in de first place." Kool Kat tossed over her shoulder as she left the room.

Mr. James choked back a laugh. Kool Kat did it again.

That night the Bible study group met with Mrs. Worth, who'd been leading the group since long before Maggie was transferred to Los Lomas. Maggie slipped into the room during the opening prayer and waited to take a seat until the amen was said. She'd almost not come, but she had given her word to the petite woman who personified the love and forgiveness she taught. All through the study Maggie debated about asking the favor. She hated to ask for favors of any kind because in prison, favors cost you. And how she would pay this one back, she didn't know.

"You seemed distracted tonight," Mrs. Worth said softly after she excused the group and most of them shuffled out of the room.

Maggie nodded. Might as well get it out. "I have a favor to ask."

"Anything."

"You can't say that, you don't know what it is."

"Sure I can because anything that is in my power to do for you, I will." Her smile always made Maggie feel warmer.

"I-I need you to write me a letter of recommendation if you will, to give to the parole board."

"Of course. When do you need it by?"

"Whenever you can. I have another two and a half months before the hearing."

"I'll have it for you next week. I'll bring you a copy and make sure the original gets to the right hands."

"Thank you."

"Do you know what you're going to do when you get out?"

Maggie shook her head. "Get a job first thing. I'd like to work in a stable, something with horses."

"Racing?"

"No, a breeding farm or even a dude

ranch. Maybe a place like I worked when I was a teenager." She'd not realized that was her dream until she said it. Could she make enough to live on?

"I'll ask around. Have you talked with Mr. James about the places he knows?"

She hadn't thought of that. "No."

"They'll be more likely to grant your parole if you have a job to go to."

"I'll talk to him. Thanks."

"You're welcome. Anything else?"

"Um . . ." Say it! "Ah, could you pray for me tomorrow?"

"Of course, why?"

"It's my son's birthday."

"I didn't know you had a boy." The older woman's face softened into a smile.

"I don't . . . anymore." Maggie blinked several times and headed for the door.

NINE

The custody agreement said she was never to call or try to make contact.

Gil stared at the phone in his hand, the urge to fling it across a canyon so strong he had to unclench his fingers. Why did Sandra want him to call back? The question nagged until he stuffed the offending messenger in his pocket and strode up the walk. What did she want now, that was the real question? All he had to do was call his attorney and let him deal with it. But right now he had to put on his best acting face so his son wouldn't sense that something was wrong. Eddie had radar the government would envy when it came to his father.

"Maria!"

A crash sounded in the kitchen, and the woman streaked through the doorway. "Eddie? Is Eddie okay? What is wrong?"

Realizing his tone had again become clipped and taut, Gil forced himself to smile. "Sorry, Maria. Eddie is fine, but I don't want him answering the phone until I say it's okay."

She stared at him, concern wrinkling her broad forehead. "Sí."

"I'll tell you more later." He paused to watch Eddie outside playing with Bonnie. Teaching Bonnie to fetch had been fairly easy since she was already trained to pick things up for him. He threw the nylon bone that helped keep her teeth clean, and with ears flapping, she ran to get it. Bringing it back, she laid it in his hand and backed up to watch him throw it again. This time when she brought it back, she raced around his chair, once, twice, and then panting, gave him the bone.

Knowing Eddie would be occupied at least as long as Gil hoped the phone call to the attorney would take, he crossed to his office with long strides and had Ben Bowers on the phone in seconds. "Why do you suppose she's calling now? It's against the custody agreement, and she knows she loses big time."

"I don't know, but you can bet I'm going to find out."

"How will you locate her?"

"Didn't you see a phone number on your cell?"

"Unidentified caller."

"Then she'll call again."

Gil's tone sounded cold to his own ears. "Find her first and make sure she doesn't. I don't want Eddie learning about her this way."

"Then you'd better tell him." Ben never had been one to mince words.

Gil leaned back in his leather office chair, placing his stocking feet on the top of his desk. "I've never lied to him, but he's never asked many questions." He rubbed the top of his forehead where he used to have a widow's peak.

"He's getting older. He'll be, what — eleven next month?"

"Yes, in August. And she's not seen him since he was a year old; she left him in the crib at the hospital all alone for God's sake." The old rage slammed his feet back on the plastic mat that protected the carpet from the rollers of the chair.

"I know, I know. Leave it to me."

Gil had no doubt. His attorney had the well-earned reputation of being pit-bull tough. "Don't let me down." He set the phone back on the charger. *Don't underestimate her,* he ordered himself. *But what if she has changed? Yeah, like zebras change their stripes.* Sometimes he wondered how he had ever thought he loved her. She had been a looker, that was for sure. Sometimes he saw her in Eddie's dancing eyes or the way he smiled. What if Ben Bowers failed him and she found a way to get to Eddie? Gil's jaw tightened. He would do anything to protect his son.

The need to tell Eddie what he needed to know burned like a torch in his heart. But instead of Eddie, his only response was to call for Maria and ask how long until dinner. Some things could not be done on an empty stomach. Which he well knew was an excuse, he who told people to be honest with themselves and just get the hard stuff done. Sometimes he didn't like himself too much. Some would say that was an ordinary part of being human. Not a very palatable response.

TEN

"Dear God, just get me through this day."

Why was today so much worse than this same day a year ago or the year before that or . . . ? Granted the first year, the whole year, after her baby died, was pure hell. Guilt was an exhausting bedfellow, one who dogged her day and night. But she'd gotten through that. Along with other years. Just get through. But today crushed her so heavily, she couldn't force herself to get out of bed. If she wasn't in the head count line, they would come and get her, and she'd get demerits.

Demerits might mean no parole.

"Get up, get your back end out of bed — now!" She spoke to herself like a CO to one of the inmates caught fighting.

"Maggie?" A rap on the door. "You all right?"

Go away, Kool Kat. I didn't ask you to become my watcher. "I will be." With both feet on the floor she pulled her clothes on and grabbed her towel, washcloth, and toothbrush. Perhaps she could scrub it all away.

"You look like death on a rampage."

"Thanks." She started through the door and turned to grab her key. Not that she had that much in her room, but if it was left unlocked, it was her own fault if something came up missing.

"You got ten minutes."

Maggie nodded. She managed to get washed without having to talk with anyone else. But when she made the mistake of looking in the mirror, the tears burned anew. Her throat burned, draining salt tears bleeding it raw.

She picked at her breakfast; eating took too much energy.

On the bus over to the barns, she stared out the window, her shoulders hunched forward as if protecting her heart. The looks shot her way glanced off the shield she'd erected.

"You all right?" Mr. James asked when she left the bus.

The concern in his voice nearly undid her. Without looking at him, she half shrugged, half shook her head and kept on going, hands rammed in her pockets. Going about the business of caring for Breaking Free could be done by rote. He nickered as soon as he saw her. She tossed the flakes of hay in the rack and crumbled into the corner, burying the sound of her sobs in her arm.

Breaking Free stopped in front of her, head down, nuzzling her hair. He wuffled in her ear and when she didn't respond, nudged her crossed arms.

"Go 'way." She sniffed and dried her eyes with the hem of her shirt. When he licked her hand, she started to cry again, but this time the tears were silent, slipping down her face like raindrops down a windowpane. As she raised her hand toward him, he dropped his head to make her rubbing easier, breathing horse breath into her face. When she sighed at long last and pushed herself to her feet, he backed up and returned to pulling mouthfuls of hay from the rack. Maggie leaned against his shoulder, her knees weak and her head reeling. Who would have thought this horse who wanted to seriously wound her less than two weeks ago was now doing everything in his power to comfort her?

She took the bucket out of the frame and headed to the faucet to wash it out and refill it with clean water. DC bumped into her, sloshing water down her pant leg, but today she was too sad to care. Until she heard the whispered words, "Just wait. I'll get you." One more thing. How could DC always get away with so much? *If only I dared to report her.*

"You ready to help me work with him?" Mr. James asked, tilting his head toward Breaking Free's stall. He was either too male or too kind to mention that her eyes looked like boiled tomatoes.

"What do you want me to do?"

"We'll work in the pen. I'll come in while you lunge him and just wait by the gate until he settles down again. Then we'll push him a bit at a time to realize I won't do him any harm."

While waiting for Breaking Free, Mr. James conducted a round pen session for another of the women who wanted to try it. Maggie could hear the chatter but stayed in the stall and wrapped Breaking Free's legs. The swelling was going down; the joint didn't feel hot for a change. She applied the MSM liniment before wrapping and when she finished took out the brushes to groom him.

"You know, you're looking better every day."

His ears swiveled to keep track of her. "Wait until the warden sees you. He'll have to eat his words, ya know? Of course, you're going to have to let Mr. James come to you and realize he won't hurt you, not at all."

"You think he understand you?" Kool Kat filled the stall doorway.

Maggie started. What if it had been DC? She was letting her guard down too much. She took in a deep breath and answered, "He understands the tone. I know horses, or rather knew some, who had a pretty good vocabulary. Dogs can learn voice commands and so can horses. People call them dumb animals but that just shows who's the dumb one." Maggie ignored the desire to tell someone about Breaking Free comforting her. *How will I be able to leave him behind when I get out? Or let someone adopt him?* The thoughts, one on the tail of the other, nearly sent her to her knees again. *Don't think, don't feel, just get through. Brush the horse, clean the stall. Just get through. You have less than two and a half months to go.*

"Mr. James say to tell you he be ready when you are."

"Okay, we'll be right out. Are you taking Dancer out to graze?"

"Yeah. Hard to believe he the same horse came in."

"I know." *Oh, how well I know.*

When the other women had cleared away

from the pen, Maggie slipped the halter over Breaking Free's nose and buckled it, then snapped on the lead shank and led him out of the stall to the round pen. Once inside he followed her around the perimeter, letting her lead him from either side, stopping and starting, just like playing follow the leader. A children's song danced in her mind. When he saw Mr. James, Breaking Free snorted and stopped.

"Just look him over, he's not coming near you." She let him stand in one spot until he relaxed and then led him forward again. Reminded of her instructions, when he tensed she stopped and let him become accustomed again. When he pulled back, she turned and walked him in a tight circle. "Come on, get your mind off him. He's not bothering you."

"Okay, that's enough for now. He did well." Mr. James let himself out of the pen and leaned on the rail. "We'll do it again this afternoon. I have the vet coming this afternoon to check those legs and examine a couple of other horses. Good thing we have a lady vet."

"He needs to be reshod."

"The farrier is a man. You ever pulled shoes and trimmed feet before?"

"On a pony, in another lifetime."

"You use the clippers to cut off the crimp on the nail, then just pull them off."

"One's pretty loose."

"You use the nippers to pull them loose."

While they talked, Breaking Free finally dropped his head and scratched his nose against his knee.

"I've watched it done plenty of times. I can pick his feet with no problem now."

"Have you let anyone else hold him yet?"

"No, I don't think anyone wants to touch him and besides, the rules made him off limits."

"Ask either Kool Kat or JJ." He walked off, and Breaking Free watched him go.

Maggie got one front shoe off that morning before putting everything away to get back for roll call. Her back ached from bending over, his foot clamped between her knees. If she'd worked out in the weight room like some of the others, perhaps she wouldn't be in such a fix now.

"You walkin' like an old woman." Kool Kat fell into step beside her.

"Yeah, well, you pull the next one." Maggie thought she saw DC veer off. Had she been coming to stab in another threat?

"Hey, I got work to do."

"Right, holding that horse so I can pull

another shoe."

"Vet's comin'. I gets to hold Dancer and the others. She gonna check 'em all."

Maggie stiffened up even more during lunch, and by the time she got on the bus, she was wishing for some aspirin or the equivalent. But she'd have had to go to the infirmary for that and there just wasn't time. Besides, she'd never gone voluntarily in all the years she'd been locked up, other than at intake. Not even the time she'd been beat up.

"The vet will be here in half an hour," Mr. James announced as they reached the farm. He read off the list of horses that she would be checking. "If I called your horse's name, make sure you are ready with him haltered and either cross-tied or in a stall. Any questions?" He stepped to the ground and watched them file off the bus.

Maggie could feel him staring at her, but she refused to acknowledge any sympathy.

"You sure you can pull another?"

"I'll get the two front ones today. Surely the second one will be easier. I at least have a better idea what I'm doing now." She took borrowed leather gloves from a back jeans pocket and headed for the tack room to retrieve her bucket of tools. As soon as she pulled this shoe, she'd trim and rasp both front hooves. Having the vet here would give her someone to ask for advice.

When she entered the stall, Breaking Free lifted his nose from the water bucket and came to her, dripping water on her shirt. "You still like me at least, even if it took me an hour to get one shoe off."

She set the bucket down and cross-tied him in the stall. Next door Kool Kat was grooming her horse to show off for the vet. DC didn't usually come around Kool Kat so Maggie breathed a sigh of relief. Slipping her hands into the leather gloves, she pulled the nippers from the bucket, picked up his left front leg, and with her rear facing his head brought the foot up between her legs to clamp with her thighs and knees. One by one she cut off the bent-over shoeing nails, the crunch loud in the silent stall. With that finished, she set his foot down again and straightened her back, as if it would ever straighten again.

"How do farriers manage?" Even her grumble sounded pained.

"They build up their muscles over time." Dr. Harris leaned on the lower door.

Maggie turned with a greeting, wincing at even that motion. "Sorry."

"I hear this is the boy that came in ready to kill everyone in sight."

"True." Maggie took off her gloves and stuck them back in her pocket. "Come on in. Since you're female, he shouldn't mind."

"Unless he's had a bad experience with a vet and remembers the smell." Harris, who looked too slight to wrestle a cat down, opened the stall door and entered, keeping her attention on the horse whose ears had gone back. He raised his head as high as the cross ties would allow, nostrils flared.

"Hey, fella, easy, she's not going to hurt you." Maggie tugged on his halter to get his attention. She stroked his neck and scratched his cheek. As soon as he loosened up, nodded to the vet.

"You know I'd be able to see his legs better if we were outside."

"I know, I just thought the fewer distractions the better. I never know how he is going to respond."

"Okay. Inside it is. I read his history, and Trenton says he is responding well to the treatment." She stroked the horse's shoulder and along his back. When he didn't shift, she patted his rump and ran her hand down his leg. "Easy boy. You wrap him every day? Alternating hot packs and ice?"

"And I use the MSM."

"How's he on letting you pick up his feet?"

"Easy on the front, a bit touchy on the back."

"Hang on to him. I'd just as soon not end up in a pile back in that corner." She picked up his hoof. He took it away and set it down. She picked it up again, he pushed against her, she shifted to regain her balance, he set it down. "Okay, fella, let's quit playing games here," she said firmly. She picked up his foot again and tapped around the inside wall of the hoof. "Sound. I was afraid of thrush or rot." She probed the fetlock and up the pastern.

"It's not as swollen, and he can walk without limping but not for very long." Maggie watched everything the vet did while at the same time hanging on to Freebee's halter, one hand stroking his neck and cheek to keep him calm.

"Rest and what you are doing are the best treatment. What are you feeding him?"

Maggie told her, then asked, "How long will it take for the Equipoise to leave his system?"

"Any idea how long since he raced?"

"He's been here for a couple of weeks, and he'd been injured some time before they gave up and brought him here. Mr. James figured they gave up on him sooner because he was so difficult to handle. When we realized it was men he hated, not everyone, things began to improve. We left him in the stall by himself for several days." She didn't mention she'd been banged up by him at first.

"The rule of thumb is two months, but it depends on many things. I'd say you're getting close to that. We could test him, but I see no reason for that. Especially if he is settling down like you say."

Maggie nodded. That's about what she had figured too.

"Is he a biter?"

"Can be."

"Well, it's hard to believe this is the same horse I read about. He's a beauty, isn't he?"

"Grooming him helps a lot."

"Keep on with what you are doing, and you should be able to let him out in a small pen in a week or two. Don't give him enough space to really run or he may injure it again."

Maggie waited. Go ahead and ask. "You think he'll be one of those we can retrain for a pleasure horse?"

"Don't know why not. I doubt he would hold up for jumping or eventing, but regular riding shouldn't be a problem."

"Good."

"You're doing well with him, Maggie. I

know Trenton is really proud of what you've done."

"Really?"

"He doesn't say a lot to all of you most likely, but he brags about what's going on here."

"That's good to know. Thanks."

Dr. Harris stroked Breaking Free's shoulder and neck again and left the stall, on to the next one.

"Did you hear that, Freebee, he brags about us and our work here." She huffed out a sigh and brought back the tool bucket. "All right, let's get this shoe off and your toenails trimmed."

"You can trim more," Harris said when she checked back on her way out.

"I know, but I'm afraid of going too deep."

"Use the rasp then, with both hands. Across the hoof like this." She demonstrated how to hold the big-toothed file.

"I'll try again."

"Just takes practice. You're doing fine."

"Better me than having to put a twitch on his nose for the farrier."

"So true."

Maggie finished up both front hooves and contemplated starting the back ones when Mr. Creston called the time left.

"Tomorrow." She sat against the wall,

pushing her back into the wood, pulling the kinks out of neck and shoulders.

"You ready to go into business, shoein' horses? Mr. James say the pay is real good." Kool Kat gave her one of those half-sided looks that meant she was teasing.

"You pull the back ones tomorrow, and we'll talk about it then."

"Not me, not de back feet."

Maggie grunted as she stood upright. Not her either, but what was the choice?

ELEVEN

Like he'd always known, moving was the pits. August heat didn't help.

Gil watched the movers drive off. Even though they weren't going far, it had taken them twice as long as they said it would, and they were already over the cost estimate.

"You ready, Dad?" Eddie had Bonnie on a leash which seriously curtailed her sniffing of the grass along the driveway. She planted all four feet and leaned in the direction she desired to go. When he tugged on her leash, she turned her head to look at him as if he just didn't get it. There was something important to smell where she wanted to go. "Bonnie, come." With a put upon look that bassets had perfected through the ages, she turned and followed him to the van.

"You suppose that's what they mean by bassetude?" Gil asked.

"Better than flat basset. If she'd gone flat

basset, we might not have gotten her in the car for a while." Eddie handed the leash to Maria and rolled his chair onto the lift. As well trained as she was, even Bonnie hit a stubborn streak once in a while, and picking up a sixty-five pound lump of flat basset was not easy. Gil could attest to that.

Once everyone was loaded, Gil took a moment to stare back at the house. The cleaners would be in tomorrow, and as soon as the decorator brought rental furniture in for show, it was ready to be put on the market. His Realtor assured him he would get top dollar and an easy sale.

He tossed and caught his keys and climbed into the van, feeling absurdly adventurous, or, if he were realistic, crazy. They were heading to Bakersfield for a few hours to let the movers do their job, and then he'd hired someone to come in and make up the beds, unpacking enough so they could pick up their life again without the battle of the boxes.

Besides, they had to get back to normal quickly — he had a business conference in Chicago in two days, and he was the keynote speaker.

Late that afternoon when they arrived at their new home, the moving truck was gone and the beds were set up and made. The furniture was in the correct rooms, towels in the bathrooms, and the bare bones of the kitchen put together. While there were stacks of boxes in the garage, the house was livable.

Maria opened cupboards in the kitchen and shook her head. "Muy bueno. This is amazing. I will start dinner."

"No, check the fridge." Sure enough, the meals he'd ordered were in place. Hiring a moving specialist had indeed paid off. One of the perks of working too many hours.

"Is the swimming pool ready?" Eddie asked after zipping around the entire house, looking at everything.

"Sorry, it's not, but supposedly by next week." The barn wasn't finished either, but the fence around the yard was in place so Bonnie would be able to roam in a safe area. As he strolled through the house, Gil admired the views which would be far lovelier as the plants and trees grew and filled in the space. It would be a comfortable house. "Let's eat out on the deck," he suggested when he returned to the kitchen.

"Sí. Ten minutes. Tell Eddie to wash up."

"Where is he?"

She nodded to the door. "Out with Bonnie. They looking around."

Gil went through the French doors to the

redwood deck with steps down to the tiled pool area. One side of the deck now had a long sloping ramp, as did the front entrance. Bonnie and Eddie were playing on the lawn which had been sodded right after Gil signed the initial papers. Her bark rolled across the pasture. They had far more room to play here, and once the barn was finished and the path paved to it, it would open even more room. Space, he'd never owned so much space in his life. He'd never even dreamed of owning so much land. He heard a wild call from the sky and shaded his eyes to look for the hawk. He found it circling on the thermals to the west. Little more than a month ago he'd first started considering a horse for his son and already almost all was in place. Would you call it divine providence or the answers to a small boy's prayers — or both?

"Dinner's ready. Come get washed up."

Eddie waved and threw the ball one more time, then turned and propelled his chair up the slight grade to the ramp.

"We're eating outside?"

"Seemed like a good idea." He walked beside Eddie to the grouping of all-season wicker furniture. The umbrella shaded the place settings for three. Two tall blue pots held waving grasses and trailing flowers.

While they'd looked nice at the other house, they were spectacular here. Maybe he'd have a barbecue built in here. There was plenty of room.

A breeze cooled the air as the sun dropped behind the mountains. Bonnie snored under the table, waiting for her usual offerings from Eddie's plate. Rotisserie chicken, pasta salad, corn/black bean salad, and fresh rolls. Maria had made tall glasses of lemonade with wild berry syrup added and a sprig of mint on the glass rims.

Listening with one ear to Eddie talking to Maria, Gil's mind flitted back to the many moves his family had made as a child. His dad had a bad case of wanderlust until finally his mother got tired of all the moves and said that was it. If her husband wanted to see what was over the next hill, he'd find her right there in a little house with a fenced-in yard in a small town on the edge of the Sierra Nevada Mountains. And he better send money on a regular basis because his two children had to eat.

None of those moves went like this one today. And while his father had died during one of his frequent wanderings, his mother was now set up in a comfortable house in a retirement community where she played all the bingo and bridge her heart desired, along with making sure the other residents kept busy with volunteer work. He and Eddie went to see her once a month. He knew she'd like this new place, and as soon as he built an apartment for Maria so they had a guest room, he'd bring her to visit.

Eddie's question brought him back to the present.

"Sorry I was woolgathering, what did you say?"

"I asked when we might start looking for a horse."

"Not until the barn is finished. I thought we'd ask Carly to help us find a dependable one."

"She'll say build a round pen."

"A round pen?"

"An enclosed area where we can work the horse at first."

"I thought perhaps at first we'd stable him at Rescue Ranch so you could have plenty of time to get used to each other. I have to find someone around here to take care of him too."

"I was thinking that if I work with crutches and braces again, I could stand enough to groom most of him and feed and —"

"You want to do that?"

"I think so. It's just so much easier to get around in the wheelchair."

"As far as that goes, I can feed and such when I'm home, but I don't think Maria wants to take on a horse too."

Gil looked toward his housekeeper to see her shaking her head. "I know nothing about horses."

"I don't know much, but I'm sure we're going to learn."

"No problem, I'll teach you both."

"I'm sure you will." Gil took out his PDA and clicked to the calendar. "I'm flying the red-eye to Chicago tomorrow night so we need to make sure all is well here before I leave. Eddie, you have a dental appointment tomorrow at two forty-five. I can drop you off, run some errands, and pick you up. All right with that?" Gil had learned fairly recently that if he prepared Eddie for things in advance, his son handled them much better. Maria was the one to point that out, she'd learned it years ago. Sometimes he wondered how he would ever make up for all the years he was gone more than he was home.

"Just cleaning right?"

"Yes. Unless you want Maria there to wait with you?"

Eddie gave him an oh-dad look.

Gil raised his hands, palm out. "Just checking." When Maria got up to begin clearing the table, he helped her, carrying the tray into the house. "Thanks."

"I did nothing but set the table."

"Right. I hope you like your new kitchen."

She glanced around it, a half smile on her face. "It eez beautiful, how could I not like it?"

"If you want some things changed, just let me know."

"Sí. You could bring in some of those boxes marked kitchen."

"Done." He carried in three boxes and set them on the center island. "More?"

"Enough for now. Gracias."

"I'm going to be setting up my computer and such in the den if you need more."

"You go." She shooed him out of the kitchen with flapping hands.

Gil was under the desk connecting cables when he heard Bonnie's toenails and saw Eddie's wheels.

"Dad?"

"Here." He waved a hand above the desk. "Give me a minute."

"I have my computer ready for you to do the same."

"Okay." He checked to make sure the cables were all connected to the right ports and surge protectors and worked his way out from under the desk. "Now to see if it

145

all works." He pushed the start button and rechecked the cables to the printer and copy machines while he waited for the machine to boot up. When the proper images showed on the screen, he clicked to desktop and breathed a sigh of relief. No matter how many times he'd done this, he still feared a meltdown. "I think this room will work real well."

The U-shaped setup with the computer facing the wall and his desk clear to work on, all in rich ebony wood, took up a good part of the room, but no matter. Book-shelves would be built on both sides of the full wall section, and there was plenty of room left for the love seat and wing-backed chair around an ottoman that doubled as a table. The leather wingback with a good lamp beside it was his favorite reading chair. Although the room for Eddie to maneuver his wheelchair was tight, it was still manage-able.

"Okay, let's do yours." As he walked down the hall, he thought of the pictures and artwork he'd hung on the walls in years past. Pictures of Eddie when he was little, his mom and dad, aunt and uncle and cousins. The wedding photos of him and Sandra were stored in a box to be taken out some day or perhaps not. Although he knew if Eddie started pushing to know more about her, he'd bring out the pictures. Maybe he should have had them out all the time, just said they were divorced, irreconcilable differences. But then he'd have to tell him why his mother never came around — and he couldn't. He almost stopped. Come to think of it, his attorney hadn't gotten back to him this week like he said he would with a report on his finding of Sandra. Gil promised himself to call the man back tonight. This had gone too long.

"Looks pretty plain in here." He glanced around the walls that in the other house had been nearly hidden by Eddie's posters of sports heroes, shelves with books and games, a computer desk, and a bar along with hand weights for strengthening his arms. Eddie's tendencies toward neatness made use of baskets on shelves along with the old adage "a place for everything and everything in its place."

While Gil was neat by choice and effort, Eddie had inherited his near obsessiveness from his mother. Fortunately he hadn't inherited the judgment that went along with Sandra's views on perfection.

Gil checked to make sure all the cables were in place, then crawled under the desk to plug them in. "You did a good job."

"It doesn't take a rocket scientist, you know."

"True, but I know a lot of people who would panic at trying to set their whole system back up." Gil turned the desk and pushed it back against the wall. When he stepped away, he saw Eddie rubbing his head.

Immediately his heart rate picked up. "Something wrong?"

"Not much. I just have a headache, that's all."

"How long has it been going on?"

Eddie shrugged. "Awhile but I thought it would go away."

Gil crossed the room and laid the back of his hand on Eddie's forehead. "No temp."

"I'm not sick, I just have a headache." A touch of crankiness underlined his voice. Eddie hated getting attention for being sick.

Gil stared at the scar on his son's neck from where they had put in the shunt when he was an infant and had kept enlarging it as he grew. The shunt plugging up could indeed cause a headache. He scanned his memory. How long since it had been checked?

Eddie shrugged. "Don't make a big deal out of it. Lots of people get headaches."

Lots of people don't have spina bifida and

a shunt to drain the excess cerebral fluid off either.

TWELVE

At least he didn't attack.

Breaking Free stood at the far end of the round pen, ears flat back, staring at the man who had entered the pen. Trenton James stood perfectly still, just inside the gate, watching the horse. When the horse finally flicked his ears and shook his head, the man took two easy steps forward, stood and waited.

Maggie watched both horse and man, wondering at the patience of each to outdo the other. Before prison, she'd acted first and thought later, or, as her ex-husband Dennis described her, she was impulsive. Waiting for food, waiting to be counted, waiting . . . for freedom. She'd learned a lot about patience.

When the horse's ears shifted, the man took two more steps, but when the horse threw up his head, the man stepped back two steps. Breaking Free watched a moment, lowered his head, and played with his lower lip.

Mr. James nodded, backed up, and left the pen, the horse watching him all the while.

"Why did you quit?" Maggie asked.

"Because he now knows that men won't always chase him and hurt him. Leave him out there awhile before you bring him in. He can use some sunshine."

"Look at him."

Breaking Free had walked a few steps away from the fence and front knees buckling, rolled, on to one shoulder and over on his side. The horse grunted, rolled, and kicked before surging to his feet and giving a mighty shake.

"He's learning to be a horse, not a machine."

"I see that. I feel like a mother whose kid got up again and took three steps this time instead of one." A stinging pain pricked her stomach. Charlie had been eleven months when he took his first long "walk" — to Dennis. She'd snapped the photo, and it had resided under her mattress ever since she was incarcerated. Years ago, she'd forbidden herself to look at it anymore; it caused too much of the past to rise up, but at least she always knew it was there.

Sometimes she just put her hand under the mattress to feel the crinkle of it.

"Not a doubt in the world this horse is going to make it."

Maggie rolled her lips together, one of the tricks she'd learned to stem the burning behind her eyes. She'd cried enough in the last two days to last years. Even when she wasn't crying on the outside, the tears were still there and burning on the inside. Strange, since she'd managed these past years to hide the tears as she hid all of her emotions. What was the cause behind this ongoing eruption? Was it the horse program, like Mr. James had warned them?

"You think he'll go to the man who came in yesterday?"

"I doubt it. He wants a horse in his pasture and will enjoy caring for it, even knowing it'll never be ridden again."

"People do that?"

"Oh yeah, there's a man out in South Dakota who leases pasture from the BLM . . ."

"BLM?"

"Bureau of Land Management, government agency. He's adopted several Thoroughbreds and lets them be wild horses."

"I hope someday I can adopt a horse."

"I do too." He turned to her so she had to

look up at him. "You're going to make it on the outside, Maggie."

At the conviction in his voice, she could only nod. If she'd said something, anything, the soft glue holding her together would have precipitated a total washout.

He saved her by saying, "Go help JJ with the new horse, would you please?"

"Sure."

"Oh, and I'm assigning another horse to you. Breaking Free is coming along well enough."

She nodded and kept going. Good, she was beginning to feel like she wasn't pulling her weight in the program with only one horse to care for. But then who ever dreamed he'd come around so quickly?

That afternoon she saw Mr. James head back to the round pen where Breaking Free dozed in the sun. He repeated the dance of the morning, and the third time the horse settled down before the man exited the pen again.

"What he doin'?" Kool Kat asked nodding toward Mr. James.

"Getting Breaking Free to accept him and to not be afraid of men any longer."

"Well, I'll be d . . ." She glanced at Maggie. "Darned."

"You want to do the join up with your

other horse?"

"You bet. I read that book you said."

"Good for you." Maggie waited.

"Most of it anyways. That man live a pretty good life."

"True."

"So, you think someone like me can make a living working with horses?"

"Many do. That's what this training can help you do on the outside. Get you a job at a stable or a farm or even one of the racetracks."

"Never thought I'd want to work with horses."

Maggie clapped her on the shoulder. "You can do it." The action caught them both by surprise.

Kool Kat stiffened, then looked from her shoulder to Maggie, a grin deviling her widened eyes. "To quote my mother's mother, 'From your mouth to God's ear.'"

Maggie shook her head and headed for the tack room. If the overhanging fear of DC cooking up some revenge for being embarrassed by Kool Kat's intervention would go away, these final two months would be almost bearable, with Breaking Free doing so well and Kool Kat's humanity leaking out more and more each day.

After a wide turn of every corner and

several glances behind her, Maggie's shoulders lowered to normal. Time to do some lunging with Breaking Free and get him back in his stall so someone else could use the pen. Like Kool Kat.

The five days it took for Mr. James to approach Breaking Free and finally pat his shoulder seemed like forever with the impending warden's arrival only ten days away.

"Compared to other horses, he adapted pretty fast," James said when she commented. "You laid a good groundwork for me. Tomorrow I'll bring a saddle and bridle from home. We'll give it a go."

A deep swell of something she could barely remember rose in her. *Joy,* she thought. It had taken a hurting horse on a prison farm to bring back joy.

From the corner of her eye, she spied DC standing a short distance off, one hip jutted out and arms folded across her chest. The joy sputtered out. What a pity DC couldn't learn new things like Breaking Free — like terrorizing people wasn't necessary.

As soon as they saddled him the next morning, Breaking Free started to jig.

"Look at him, he thinks he's back at the track." Maggie slid the bit in his mouth and the headstall over his ears. "Come on, show-off, see if you like the round pen again."

"You goin' to ride him?"

"Nope, just lunge him. Get him used to a different kind of work."

"Bet he was somethin' on the track." Kool Kat, who now always seemed to get her work done and show up to watch Maggie and Mr. James work with Breaking Free, stroked the horse's shoulder and neck. "Look how red he is, sun on him looks like fire."

"I know." Maggie rubbed his ears and face. "Yet he's not the same horse. Not like when they brought him in."

Kool Kat looked over the paddocks of grazing horses and the bigger pasture where two of the Thoroughbreds were racing along a fence line. "None of them are the same."

You're not either, Maggie thought, but dared not say it. Despite the changes, Kool Kat was still Kool Kat.

After the first race around the pen, Breaking Free responded to Maggie and her commands of walk and trot. His initial run had scared her. What if he reinjured those back legs and never got their full use back?

Later when he let Mr. James pick up his feet, she felt like they'd won the whole war and not just the battles. Letting him loose in the grassy paddock was almost as bad as leaving her son at nursery school for the first time. The memory of that day rolled over her like an 18-wheeler in a skid. Charlie so excited to get there, walking into the room with a bunch of other little kids, some crying, some already playing with toys or in the playhouse. He'd been there before, but she always stayed to help.

"Bye, son, I'll be back later."

He waved and ran off to play. None of that clinging to Mom like some of the others. Out in the car, she'd cried, never sure if it was because he handled it so well or because she hadn't.

Now with her eyes still dry, she breathed in deep, letting the memory soak her instead of pushing it down. She propped her chin on her hands on the rail, watching Breaking Free sniff the ground, lay down and roll, get up and shake, fling his head in the air, whinny an announcement that he was there, and then take off in an easy canter. He made a round of the fences, sniffed noses with the two very interested fellows in the next pasture — one squealed, he snorted — then turn to look at her, like Charlie, as if to say, see I'm okay. Don't worry. She huffed a big sigh. Sniffing, she nodded. "You did it, big horse. You did it." Incredibly, so had she — lived through a Charlie memory without totally collapsing.

"You helped him." Mr. James leaned on the rail beside her. "Annie Forsythe, the director from the Association called last night. She wondered if we might have some horses ready for adoption fairly soon."

"Do we?"

"Possibly. A couple of them need lots of pasture time. No riding, but they might be ridden again eventually. Those that could be ridden will need to be retrained, and we're not set up to do that here. They will need to go to a training farm. Some could be adopted from the open house."

The term *open house* chilled Maggie. Open — as in people coming in to stare at the inmates and watch a freak show with horses. She couldn't do it. Nobody had said anything about the public being part of this program.

Mr. James, watching Breaking Free, continued. "We'll be inviting the public so they can become more aware of our program. Hopefully to adopt horses and/or support some of the ones who need extended care. Like old Ghost. He has too many health problems for someone to take him on, but he could be sponsored. I'm going to talk about this in class this afternoon, just thought I'd give you a head's up."

Maggie only half heard much of what he'd said. This new information felt much the same as DC's terrorizing.

"I'd like you to ride Breaking Free at the open house."

Her mind slipped into free fall. She'd dreamed of riding him. "You've cleared this with Warden Brundage?" To ride Freebee, she'd have to be at the open house. It only took a few moments of internal struggle. The big guy deserved to be shown off, impress someone enough to be adopted, and she was the likely one to do it. No matter it would rip out her heart. Her heart had been ripped out before.

He nodded. "This morning. Actually this all makes the prison, er, rather the correctional facility, look good. He's been doing a lot of PR for the programs here so that the funding isn't cut out from beneath them." He turned and leaned back against the board fence, watching the women as they went about their chores. "Now it's time for this program to prove itself like the beef and optometric programs have."

"You know it's been nearly twenty years since I've been on a horse."

"Would you say you were a good rider?"

"Y-yes." On a normal horse, not a racehorse. Not one like Breaking Free.

"That's enough for me. I'll see you in class."

She gulped. As soon as he left, Breaking Free ambled over to stand right in front of her. She rubbed his nose and up around his ears. "Hey, Freebee, we've got another big step to take together, you and me. I know you'll do fine. It's me I'm worried about." Brushing her too-long bangs out of her eyes, she wondered just what the general public would think of her. The jury of her peers hadn't thought much.

The next morning Breaking Free greeted her with a nicker when he saw her coming.

"Look at that." Kool Kat nudged Maggie with her elbow. "He sayin' good morning."

"I know." Maggie kept her eyes straight ahead. Kool Kat didn't need to see how close to the surface her tears were. These weeks with Breaking Free had flushed out more eye moisture than after the . . . the first months of her incarceration.

"First time Dancer greeted me like that I near busted out cryin'."

Maggie stopped and stared at the black woman. "You did?"

"You don't be telling no one, hear?" Hands in her rear pockets, Kool Kat shuffled her toe in the dirt. "They kinda get

160

to ya." She half snorted, half grinned. "Never thought I'd be like this." But when she looked Maggie fully in the face, she sobered. "So, how do you say goodbye when they leave?"

That was another subject Maggie didn't want to think about. She shrugged.

"Different for you, you get out on parole pretty soon, maybe you could find Breaking Free and visit him?"

"Who'd want an ex-con contacting them? There's probably rules against that." She changed the subject. "How much longer for you?"

"Two years, three months, and four days, unless I get out sooner for good behavior."

"Early parole?"

"Probably not, since this my second time in." Kool Kat shrugged. "Stupid twice, shame on me."

Maggie knew better than to answer that. She knew stupid. "We better get going. Hungry horses." Never had she asked one of the other women direct questions like that. Sure, she'd overheard lots of conversations, but she never took part. "Just getting through" had taken on a new meaning since the horses . . . the "just" seemed to be slipping.

Later when she climbed reluctantly once

more on the bus, thinking of the day when she would never get on a prison bus again and be counted, DC, who had taken over the seat behind Maggie, leaned forward and whispered just low enough to raise the hair on Maggie's neck. "You better watch your back." The chuckle that followed could only be called evil, strangling Maggie's stomach.

THIRTEEN

Do I go or stay home?

In twenty-four hours he was supposed to be keynoting the convention. Gil stared down at Eddie, sleeping now after the surgery. The ongoing struggle between good dad-bad dad tugged. They'd gone in and replaced the shunt that had grown nearly closed. Nothing new, and it would happen again, but it reminded Gil how temporary life with his son might be. To think his son had complained of a headache only a few hours ago.

"He'll be going home in the morning." The nurse checked Eddie's vitals again and smiled up at Gil. "He's off the oxygen, and we've removed the IVs." He'd stood to get out of her way when she came in. "You could go home and get some sleep."

"I know. But I think I'll just sleep in the chair."

"I'll get you a blanket and a pillow. That

chair kicks back, you know, into a recliner."

"Thanks." Sleep, however, didn't come, and about an hour later, he retrieved a newspaper from the lounge and sat near the doorway of Eddie's room, scanning it.

"Inmate program working with horses?" The article talked about an upcoming open house and adoptable horses. Dear Lord, he hoped Eddie never got wind of this. Who in his or her right mind would voluntarily go around inmates, much less trust a horse they'd trained?

He felt his cell phone vibrate in his pocket. It would be Maria. He headed down the hall and into the waiting room to return the call.

"He's sleeping, and the nurse said he could go home in the morning."

"Bueno. Can I bring you anything?"

"No thanks, you should have been asleep a long time ago."

"I sleep the sleep of the angels now."

Gil flipped the phone shut, returned the newspaper back to the table, and ambled back to Eddie's room, yawning. Something must have happened during the surgery for them to decide to keep him. Other times, as soon as he came out of the anesthesia they sent him home. Of course the other surgeries had been done during the daytime, not in a rush like this one. This doctor didn't let any grass grow under his feet that was for sure.

It only seemed like a few moments later that Eddie's voice woke him. "Hi, Dad." Even after anesthetic Eddie woke up looking as if he hadn't just been out for the count.

"Hi, yourself." Gil sat up, yawning. "How do you do that?"

"What?"

"Wake up so alert."

Eddie shrugged and tossed back the covers. He glared at the raised bars. "I gotta go."

"Just a minute." Gil jiggled the railing, pushed on it, and looked for a lock. No deal.

Eddie scrambled down the bed and around the rails.

Gil finally figured out how to operate the bed rails and lowered them. His son knew more about hospital beds than he did. It wasn't like he'd never been around through all those surgeries, but cribs were far different than real beds and Eddie had not had surgery for a long time. But when he got really honest with himself, Maria had done more bedside duty than him. Honesty might be the best policy, but it sure could be painful.

■ ■ ■ ■

After they were checked out and on their way back up the hills toward home, Eddie talked nonstop.

"I had a weird dream in the hospital, right before I woke up."

"Yeah?" Gil looked in the mirror.

"Yeah. My mom," here his voice trailed away for a moment; Gil's insides clenched and Sandra's phone call popped to the front of his mind, "or at least she looked like a mom, leaned over my bed and said my horse was waiting in the hallway to see me but the nurse wouldn't let it in. Crazy, huh?"

The all-knowing "they" of research said often we dream of things we yearn for, Gil knew. A mother would be tough to find since a wife came first, and he wasn't so great in his selection processes there, but a horse . . .

Eddie's voice again: "When are we going to look for a horse? Better not keep it waiting in the hall."

"Don't you think you'd better recover a little first?"

"Over what?"

"Um, a shunt replaced? Surgery?"

"No big deal." Eddie touched the bandage

166

on his neck with his fingertips.

If it were me, I'd be begging for pain pills. If this incision was anything like the last one, it was four inches long at least. Gil had cut his hand once requiring four stitches to close. All he could say was that it was a good thing he was healthy — pain and he were not a pretty picture.

"You know I'm supposed to be in Chicago tomorrow, but if you need me, I can stay home."

"Why? Maria's going to be there." He caught his father's mirror gaze. "Isn't she?"

Was that fear he saw in Eddie's eyes? *He's so used to you being gone that one more trip is no big deal . . . but the loss of Maria . . .* "She'll be there." What would he do without Maria?

A few miles later, Eddie switched from talking about Bonnie to a wife. "So, Dad, have you thought about getting married again?"

Gil, who'd been thinking about Sandra's phone call and needing to remind Maria about not answering the phone, twitched and the van swerved. Until his attorney eliminated the problem of Sandra, he must play it safe. "Hey, sport, remember I asked you not to answer the phone for a while?"

"Yeah. Why?"

"Why what?"

"Why can't I answer the phone? I do a good job."

"I know you do. This has — let's just say, ah, just do it, okay." Gil closed his eyes for a moment at a stop sign. He knew his voice had snapped, and the look on his son's face said the same thing. "Look, we'll start a horse search as soon as I get home, all right?"

Eddie nodded, said nothing until they pulled into the driveway. "So what about the wife thing, Dad?"

"Where's Eddie?" Gil asked that afternoon when he entered the kitchen from his office after reviewing the notes for his speech.

Maria turned from the refrigerator. "He said he was tired and went to bed."

"Is this usual?"

"Sí. He took the pain medicine."

Gil went to stand at the French doors looking over the deck and rubbed the back of his neck. "I don't see how I can cancel the conference tomorrow."

"Why do that?"

"Maybe I need to be here for Eddie."

"Why? He'll be fine in a day or so. If he need help, I call the doctor."

"He didn't tell me he was in pain."

"He not tell me either, I look at him and I know."

Gil studied the woman who went about her job so calmly. She ran his house, took care of his son, cooked, cleaned, and rarely asked for anything. Except for Eddie. When he needed something, she asked. Nothing for herself. She needed to know everything to protect his son.

"Maria, I had a phone call from Sandra."

"No." Her jaw tightened and her eyes narrowed. The string of Spanish included words he did not know, and he probably didn't want a translation. Maria had already been working for them when Sandra walked out. She had cared for the helpless infant, walked the floor with him when he couldn't sleep. She'd been the one at the hospital that day when Gil arrived after work to find Sandra had abandoned them.

"What *she* want?"

"I don't know. My attorney, Ben Bowers, is looking into it, but he hasn't been able to locate Sandra so far." He pursed his lips. "I'll transfer all calls to my cell phone. When I call home, I'll let it ring once, hang up, and call back. Then you can answer it immediately before it can switch over to call forwarding." He scrubbed restless hands through his hair. "Maybe I should stay home."

"You are big speaker, right?"

"Yes."

"They can find another?"

"Not easily." He knew he was the drawing card for many of the conferees, but . . . was this a sufficient family problem that he should stay home? He hated that it was still a question after all these years.

"You go. We'll be okay. You come back tomorrow night?"

"Yes." He'd be gone less than twenty-four hours. Red-eye there, lecture, do the Q & A, and catch the next flight home.

She was nodding. "Muy bueno."

"I'm going to look in on Eddie, and then I'll finish things in my office. Thanks, Maria."

"For what?"

"Just thanks." He felt like whistling as he walked down the hall. Bonnie lifted her head as he stepped into the dimmed room where Eddie lay on his side, one arm draped over the dog. His wheelchair sat by the bed, wheels locked in place. The light from the hall slid over his son's smooth skin, the bandage on his neck, his expression relaxed in sleep. Gil's jaw tightened. Sandra had walked out on a treasure, and she'd get no second chance.

Gil called home before his flight left and on his way to the hotel from O'Hare. He checked in, grateful he'd been able to sleep on the plane, took an hour's nap, showered, and was ready to face the crowd.

He dialed home just before leaving his room — letting it ring once, hanging up, then calling right back. Eight o'clock in the morning Pacific Time. "How are things?"

"Eddie is eating his breakfast. Bonnie chased a rabbit."

"Did she catch it?"

Maria laughed. "Way too slow." She lowered her voice. "No phone calls."

"Well, tell Eddie I said hi, and I'll see you both this evening."

"Sí. You tell them how to be big success."

"I will." He flipped the phone shut and briefcase in hand headed out the door.

After the presentation, waiting for his plane, he called Carly at Rescue Ranch. "Hi, this is Gil Winters."

"Well hello, Gil! How is Eddie?"

"Came through just fine. He should be back riding in a couple of days. The shunt was replaced and is working like it should again."

"I'm glad to hear that."

Silence. Gil, having heard her smooth, liquid tones, remembered Eddie's question about getting a new wife. Maybe it was time he put the bitterness of Sandra's betrayal behind and . . . what? Started looking? *Dating?* How would he even go about it?

"Gil?"

"Uh, I want you to start looking for a horse for Eddie."

Now it was her turn for silence. "I-I . . . that's wonderful. You caught me by surprise."

"I'm catching me by surprise too."

"This may take some time."

If it was anything like Eddie looking for a house, it wouldn't. "Our barn is not finished yet, and we've not built a round pen. I had the pastures overseeded, and we're watering to get it up." He paused a moment and inhaled. "I'll be home tonight. Is there any chance you could come look at our place in the next couple of days and see if you have any suggestions?"

"I'd love to." Her voice flowed with warmth through the cell phone.

"Good, I'll check with Maria's schedule when I get home, and we'll have dinner on the patio."

"Fine. Thanks for calling."

Gil hung up just as they announced the first boarding call, feeling like Good Dad, even if he was Good Dad half a country away. Eddie would have his horse. As he fell into the line, he mentally kicked himself. He'd not bought Eddie a present. After taking his seat in first class, he thought on what he'd like to buy. Something for his horse, but what? He smiled to himself at the blue nylon halter that now hung on a peg in Eddie's room. Like he always taught at his seminars. Preplay what you desire. Replay your successes. The halter was definitely preplaying on Eddie's part.

He leaned back, gratitude that he could afford to make Eddie's dream come true surging through him. Gratitude, another trait he had dwelt on in his presentations. Like Oprah, he kept a gratitude journal and wrote in it daily. Like right now. He pulled the leather-bound journal from his briefcase and listed five things he was grateful for today. The plane getting him home quickly. Eddie's recovery. Their new home. That he had a business that allowed him time to be with his son. He tapped the pen on his chin deciding on the next one, not that he couldn't keep writing if he so desired. That Carly would look for a horse for them. He thought a moment more. Hmm. Carly.

FOURTEEN

Could even heaven be better than this?

Maggie felt like she could see forever from the top of Breaking Free's back. The big gelding walked the perimeter of the round pen as if he owned it. Flat-footed, with a jig thrown in only once in a while, he had settled down within a couple of days. Not like the first time she rode him. He'd played with the bit, jigged sideways, and tried to bolt. Riding him then had felt like she was on a stick of dynamite with a short fuse. What she needed now was to get him used to a bigger arena. So far she'd not taken him faster than a trot. Not that she hadn't wanted to.

Teaching him to respond to leg aides, to stand for mount and dismount, to obey the reins and back up on command, all took time. Good thing he was a willing student. Each morning she and Mr. James laid out the plan for the day and after reviewing the earlier work, she'd start in. The day of the open house drew nearer.

"The warden plans on dropping by this morning," Mr. James had said just before they all filed off the bus. Everyone scurried around to make sure things were clean and put away. They cleaned stalls and groomed their horse as if the president of the United States were visiting.

Maggie asked her horse — oh, her nerve to call him hers — to back up again, not his favorite cue. He waited until she pulled firmly on the reins, then backed until she released the pressure. She patted his shoulder and up his neck. "You're ready for the warden, Freebee."

He heard the sound of the approaching vehicle before she did, raising his head and looking up the road.

"This is it, big boy, you better be on your best behavior." His ears flicked back to her voice and forward to the approaching car. Should she dismount and lead him over to greet the warden or keep on working? She opted for working and signaled him around the pen again, trotting diagonals, turns, and bending around her leg, slowly getting him back in shape and used to riding not racing.

"Maggie." Mr. James signaled her from the gate.

The warden shook his head as she dismounted. "This can't be that wild one."

"It is, sir. He's come a long way," Maggie said, sending up a quick prayer that Breaking Free wouldn't take some weird aversion to the warden's aftershave or something as she led the horse over to the two men.

Breaking Free tensed at the strange man but held his ground. Maggie could feel him tremble.

"You're the first man other than Mr. James to come near him. When we figured out it was men he hated, not humans in general, we were able to make more progress with him."

"Maggie made the progress," Mr. James said. "She is training him now as a riding horse, a far different kind of training than he has had in the past."

"So, he will be ready for adoption?" The warden looked to Maggie for the answer.

"Yes, sir."

"And he will be safe?"

"He will still need to receive more training, but it depends on his new owner as to what kind. The vet doesn't believe he'll be able to jump or do eventing, that his legs would break down again under that kind of pressure."

The warden turned to Mr. James. "These

kinds of things will be stipulated in the adoption contract?"

"Yes, and the foundation keeps track of the horses that are adopted to make sure they are properly cared for. The people who adopt cannot sell the horse to someone else. If they can't care for the animal any longer, it comes back to the foundation."

"I remember reading all that but seeing it in action makes more of an impact." Brundage nodded to Maggie. "You've done well."

She felt like she'd been knighted by the Queen of England.

Mr. James smiled. "Take Breaking Free through his paces, so Warden Brundage can see what we're talking about."

Maggie mounted again, praying that Freebee would stand still. He didn't always. But this time he did, and she breathed a sigh of relief. She walked and trotted him through the routine, so immersed in him and her together she never noticed the two men had left. "Guess we did all right, big boy." She leaned forward and wrapped her arms around his neck. *How will I ever be able to let you go?*

"Dad, look at this." Eddie held out a section of the local newspaper. "An open house for adopting retired racehorses. Inmates

177

worked with them . . . cool! And it's not far away."

Gil's heart sank. Had that much time passed? He took the paper, looking to stop this before his son took the bit in his teeth and ran with it. Purchasing a horse from a prison had never been in the plan. He read the article and looked at his son, focusing on anything but the word inmates. "Eddie, Thoroughbreds are huge. They know only how to run fast; it's bred into them."

"It's an open house, we could just go look, that wouldn't hurt anything. It would be a fun horse thing to do . . . you know, dad and son bonding." Eddie wore his most winsome and devastating smile. "Besides, it's been more than a week and Carly hasn't found me a horse yet."

I was hoping for something in the large pony size. Gil now knew, from Eddie's continual outpouring of horse info, that four inches equals a hand, the measurement used to calculate the size of a horse. A pony was usually under fourteen hands. Smaller sounded better in this case. But a Thoroughbred! He'd stood next to one when he attended the horse races at Santa Anita, a major track near Pasadena. The horses had not looked friendly and cozy like the one he pictured for his son to ride. They looked determined and high-spirited and — huge. In this case, handled by inmates. He wasn't sure having his tax dollars going toward inmates playing with horses set well with him. Those people were dangerous.

"Besides, if we go to the open house, we'd be helping a good cause."

"How do you figure?"

"Well, you can sponsor a horse there? It says in the article." He wheeled around to Gil's side.

"Eddie, it's at a prison."

"Girl prisoners, Dad. Not guys. Just girls." His son's tone was so matter-of-fact, Gil felt like a redneck, but it didn't change his mind. Girl prisoners stole things, lied, took drugs, and sometimes even killed people.

"Besides, you speak in prisons. You said you were trying to help."

Gil couldn't bear to look at his son. What could he say other than that things shifted when his son might be involved?

Gil glanced through the article again. Had his son memorized the whole thing?

"I just thought maybe we could do that sponsor thing. I'd put in half of my allowance."

"I thought you were saving for a saddle."

"I am but this seems more important."

Bonnie woofed at the door so Eddie let

her out. "They have rescues for bassets too. You know, like that group who has that Web site where I read about bassets."

"We're not getting another dog."

"They have a foster program where you take in a dog until they find a forever home for it."

"No, we're not getting another dog. Bonnie is plenty of dog for us."

"We should probably go to one of their events some time too. They have one over in Acton."

Gil stared at his son. Was this what Maria listened to day in and day out? He knew his son was not hard of hearing. Hard of listening at times was probably the more accurate diagnosis. Maybe that's why he and Bonnie got along so well. They both had an inside track on stubborn.

Eddie let Bonnie back in and returned to his dad. "You know . . ."

Gil knew he was about to get his own words back at him.

"You say we need to be generous to show our gratitude for all that we have."

"And your idea of being generous is to adopt horses and dogs?"

"Well, let's say choose to support."

Sometimes Gil had a hard time remembering that his son was only eleven years old. His reasoning power could sway a superior court judge, let alone his father.

Gil looked at the dates on the article again. "Eddie, I'm just not comfortable exposing you to people who've broken the law and been incarcerated. I'm sorry. Find another place for us to go."

That afternoon when he took Eddie to Rescue Ranch for his riding lesson, he wandered over to where Carly was working with a new student, this time an adult. The process was always tailored to the client's special needs. At least it was easier helping a child mount the first time.

"Good to see you." Her smile would melt a glacier. Nodding to one of her assistants to take over, she motioned Gil to walk with her. "I need to get over to the other arena to watch a new volunteer. You ever thought of volunteering out here?"

"To be honest with you, no. But let me know when you need money."

"You already give plenty of that. I just thought it might help you to keep up with Eddie."

He ignored her comment but returned her smile. "What do you know about the Thoroughbred Retirement Foundation?"

"Quite a bit actually. We have one of their horses here. I hear they put in a new facility up at the Los Lomas Women's Prison. And they are having an open house on Sunday." Her lovely face darkened into a frown. "Although I'm not sure of the wisdom of that."

"My thoughts exactly. Eddie thinks if they're girl prisoners they're harmless. You really have a retired Thoroughbred here, working with handicapped kids . . . people? A former racehorse?" He added that to clarify his mind more than hers. No way were he and Eddie going to the prison to see inmates . . . er, horses.

"Yes, his real name was High On Life, we call him Dandy. Easier for the clients to say. He's a real favorite. Eddie's on him now."

"What?!" Gil shook his head. "You're letting my son ride a racehorse?"

Placing a slim hand on his sleeve, her wide smile spread across her face. "Relax, Gil. He's been retrained. We're very thorough about our training, you know that."

"Still . . ."

"Horses have great affinity for people with special needs, they sense far more than we realize."

"Eddie is determined to go to the prison for their open house on Sunday."

"Like I said, the Thoroughbred program is excellent. I'm not sure I would take my child — if I had one — there. I'll find you a good horse for Eddie, Gil. It just takes time."

Gil chuckled and nodded. "I'll let you know how it goes. Eddie is bound and determined that we will join up to support one of the horses that can be a pasture ornament."

"They'd be better than a lawn mower."

"I don't mean to bring one home, just send money and go visit it occasionally."

She gave him a raised eyebrow look and waved at someone who'd called her name. "See you later."

He watched her walk away. The evening she spent at their house had been a real pleasure, so why hadn't he called her back and set up a real date?

FIFTEEN

Sunday morning. *The* Sunday morning.

Maggie woke with enough butterflies to lift her right out the window. The open house started at one. They'd finished painting the barn yesterday, the fences the day before. Halved whiskey barrels filled with blooming plants brought color to the place, and this morning a tent would be set up for the refreshments and tables and chairs. Now all they needed were guests. And for the horses to behave. And for DC to disappear into a poof of smoke, never to return.

The woman had escalated her sneak attacks on Maggie, and Maggie could do nothing about it. She refused to tell Kool Kat. DC wouldn't let Kool Kat stop her again; in fact, she would be clever enough to implicate Kool Kat and banish her from the program. Maggie's friend — and she guessed she truly was now — had progressed too far for defeat. Maggie had been tripped, backhanded with a hoe, slammed into hay bales, had her tools hidden, and once she'd come upon DC messing with Breaking Free's stall door. Everything happened below Mr. James' radar. If the other women knew, they were keeping their mouths shut for their own safety.

She bailed out of bed, wishing she could head right for the barn. Horses needed bathing and grooming and all the stalls needed to be cleaned out. They had several empty stalls now that more of the horses were well enough to be out in the pasture.

After returning from the showers, with no DC present, Maggie sat on her bed, sliding her hand under the mattress for the reassurance of Charlie's photo. She'd be riding in front of the guests. There would be men, women, and perhaps children around. How would Breaking Free handle all the excitement? Five other horses would be shown on leads. Since press releases had been sent to a lot of the media, there might be cameras and microphones there too.

Her fingers slipped deeper under the mattress, not feeling the paper yet. Her mind catalogued all the things that could go wrong. If only she'd gotten a decent hair cut. Or bought some makeup. A silly, girl thought. *Don't be stupid,* she chided herself.

They're not looking at you; they'll be looking at your horse. If they come. Would they come to a prison? Yes, some people would, if only to see the girl felons on horseback. She forced her attention back to Breaking Free. *He'll catch everyone's attention. And besides,* she reminded herself, *your riding helmet will cover your hair.*

Finally her fingers found paper . . . lots of paper. A rush of terror filled her lungs as she sprang off her bed and shoved the mattress to the floor. Laying on the steel platform of the bed were dozens of tiny pieces of Charlie. She reached for her keys. When had she left her room unlocked?

"You all right?" Kool Kat asked when they stood in line for breakfast.

The hot, red fog in Maggie's brain finally allowed her friend's question entrance. Maggie started to blow it off, but for some unknown reason said, "I have enough butterflies chasing each other to make me dizzy."

"Me too. Thought I was goin' to be sick." Kool Kat shook her head real slow. "This is near as bad as standing in court for sentencing."

They picked up their trays and found a table. "I din't hardly sleep last night. What

186

if someone adopts Dancer? What if they don't? Never thought I'd be sad to say good-bye to a horse. 'Course I never dreamed I'd know a horse enough to say good-bye or hello either. My mom think this the biggest joke ever."

"You've done a good job with the horses."

"Thanks."

"We always braided the horses for show day. I have to braid Freebee's mane and tail. Don't know if I remember how. Weave ribbons into the mane, but since we don't have ribbon, I'll have to do without." She recognized she was speaking in disjointed bits and pieces but couldn't seem to gather her mind enough to make sense. Charlie, her one contact with her son, was gone.

"I can braid real good if you want help."

Maggie glanced at the intricate braids that festooned Kool Kat's head. "It's different than braiding human hair."

"You telling Kool Kat she don't know braidin'?"

The morning shift flew by as everyone hurried to finish their chores and make sure their charges looked their best. The tent was up with the tables and chairs under its canopy. The caterer would finish setting up while the inmates were at lunch. Since only four of the inmates would be permitted to attend the open house, a security issue decided by the warden, several of those confined to the facility grumbled on the way back for head count and lunch.

"Don't worry, if there's any food left, you'll get to enjoy it during feed time," Mr. James promised.

The open house was going to be held from one to three so there would be time to feed the horses before the women had to be back for head count and dinner.

The thought of being around people from the outside sent Maggie's insides into a high dive. What if they looked at her like she was a freak? Had she become a freak? Would she remember how to be polite? Say the right words?

When had Gil stopped being the man in charge? The dad was supposed to put the kibosh on things, and when he did they stayed kiboshed. He pulled out of their driveway, checking both directions.

"We're going to be late," Eddie declared.

"No we're not. It's an open house. People come and go as they please." Prisoners. He was taking his son into a den of prisoners. Gil wished he had insisted Maria come along, but she had asked if she could go visit her sister. Since she so seldom asked for anything, what could he say? Not that Maria could defend Eddie against a prisoner. The picture of their short Maria with a death grip on a monster woman made an interesting thought. If Eddie were threatened, you'd be wise to bet Maria could fight off an inmate. A dozen inmates. *Get a grip, Gil.* He sighed. An hour later he said, "Read me the directions again, please."

"You turn off at the Los Lomas exit."

"Okay, last sign said that was two miles ahead. Good, there's the exit."

"Turn right on highway forty-six and go for three miles. The prison will be on the right side of the road. It says there is a sign."

"It's difficult to miss a prison, son."

"Minimum security, Dad," Eddie reminded him, like he'd been reminding him since the day of the newspaper ad. Somehow on the Internet Eddie had found out what kinds of prisoners were incarcerated at Los Lomas. He'd listed them in detail to Gil. Gil knew Eddie meant to reassure him. It didn't.

"The article said there would be signs to the open house."

Gil exited and began watching for the next turn. He jerked a look at Eddie. "Okay, quick review. Don't talk to anyone. Don't go off with anyone. Stay near me."

"Yes, Dad." Eddie sounded infinitely patient.

"And it's to sponsor a Thoroughbred, not adopt one. Got it?"

"Got it, Dad." More long-suffering sighs.

"I know you know, just checking." He followed a couple of cars to a field marked off for parking where a uniformed correctional officer directed people to the proper spaces. Gil thought about all those movies where the convicts drop a guard or two, exchange the officers' uniforms for their prison garb, and escape into the woods. After parking where instructed, Gil pushed the buttons so Eddie could exit the van.

"You need help?" the officer asked.

"Thanks, but we have it." Gil helped Eddie navigate over a stretch of bumpy dirt and dried grass, then let him go when he was rolling free. Unless he asked, Eddie hated someone pushing his chair.

They joined the people following each other into the tent, Eddie staring around as if to memorize everything he saw.

"Welcome to the Thoroughbred Retirement Foundation's open house here at Los Lomas," a woman, who appeared to still be in high school until they drew closer where Gil could see slight lines on her face, welcomed each of the visitors. Wearing khaki pants and a cotton sweater wasn't prison garb but still the question teased him. Was she an inmate or not? Surely those serving the food weren't — or were they? "This is the first time we've had a site at a women's correctional facility. Would you please sign our guest book?"

Gil glanced at her name badge. Bethany. "Thank you, we'll be glad to sign. I'm Gil Winters, and this is my son, Eddie."

"Hi Eddie, welcome."

"Hi, are you an inmate?"

Gil flinched and gave Bethany an apologetic look. Another rule to be firmly applied.

"No, Eddie. I'm a volunteer for the foundation."

"Oh. Where are the horses?"

"Some are in the pastures, some in the barn over that way." She pointed to the left. "We'll be having an introduction and a showing in twenty minutes or so. Can I get you something to eat?"

"No thanks, I'll help myself."

"Eddie," Gil hissed as he followed his son into the line for the buffet. "I'm adding to the rules. Don't ask women if they're inmates." The people milling around and in line seemed more like the business type than the horsey crowd he'd expected. A couple of teen girls were the only other children present, so far at least. He studied the brochure Bethany had handed him, information regarding the Thoroughbred Retirement Foundation. There was nothing about the program for the day here. He supposed they'd be told what to do, where to go.

Watching Eddie put only cheese and some fruit on his plate, he went lightly on his own serving. He knew what his son wanted — to see the horses. Time spent eating was way long on Eddie's list.

"Will there be people to tell us about the horses?"

"I'm sure there will be. Would you like something to drink?"

"If I can take it with me."

"You can stick a water bottle down in your chair."

"Okay."

After quickly consuming sliced ham and cheese on a roll, a spear of mixed fresh fruits, and a glass of iced tea, they headed for the barn. A black woman in green pants and shirt stood by one of the horses in a stall. She stood at least six feet tall; Gil had no question in his mind that she was an inmate. He hoped the shock didn't register on his face.

She pointed to Eddie. "Hey, you wanna meet my friend, Dancer?"

"Sure." Eddie smiled up at her. "Do you ride him?"

"No, we're not allowed to ride, 'cept for Maggie who you'll see later. We just take care of them. When he came here, you could count ever bone in his body he was so thin and look at him now."

The horse leaned his head over the stall door and sniffed Eddie's outstretched hand. "Will he be up for adoption?"

"Not yet, he goes to another farm for more training. All he knows to do now is race, and he can't do that no more."

"He was injured?"

"He jes broke down." She petted the horse's neck as she talked. Some other people gathered around behind them.

"Did he race a lot?"

She nodded. "But he weren't never a big winner. He too nice a guy." She pointed out the other horses in the stalls. "You go around that end of the barn and you'll see other horses out in the paddocks. Most of them really like peppermint candy." She dug in her pocket. "Here, you give Dancer this. You know how to feed a horse, proper like?"

Eddie nodded. "I've been riding for almost two years at Rescue Ranch."

Her eyes widened, taking in the wheelchair. "You been ridin'?"

He grinned at her. "I'm pretty good too. We have a retired and retrained Thoroughbred at our stable. I've even ridden him."

Gil noted the absence of the ultra-patient tone in Eddie's voice at this surprise of his riding ability. Usually he prickled like a porcupine.

"Well, I'll be . . ."

"See you. Oh, what's your name?"

"Kool Kat, and I never dreamed I'd be workin' with horses."

"I'm Eddie, and my dad says you have to dream it first to make it happen."

Shifting her gaze to Gil for the first time, the woman regarded him solemnly.

Gil gave the horse a pat and said, "Good job," immediately feeling like a genial overseer. Had she taken it as condescending? She could take him down in a second.

They wandered down the aisle, looking at the horses, and then on around the barn. Most of the horses had come up to the fences and were accepting the attention of the guests. One hung way back at the far corner.

"Why hasn't that one come up?" Eddie pointed to the loner.

"I have no idea." Gil shrugged his shoulder. "Why don't you ask?"

Eddie waited until the other group had

moved on. "Can I ask you a question?"

"That's what I'm here for." The girl was Latino and petite.

"How come that horse hasn't come up?"

"He's new here and pretty shy. These others are used to all the attention we give them so they have better manners."

"You teach them good manners?"

"Among other things."

"Which of the horses needs a sponsor?" Eddie had a buyer's look on his face. Gil groaned inside.

"Well, they all do for the time they're here and then some will need sponsors for life."

"Because they are injured too badly?"

"Right."

One of the horses nipped another and the two got in a scuffle. *I've had employees who did that,* Gil thought. Funny, he hadn't comprehended the different personalities of horses until now.

"All right, you two, break it up. They get to arguing over who got the most pets or treats," the woman confided to Eddie, as though he and she were the only ones present.

"Who's the boss?" Gil asked, now more interested than he thought he'd be.

"That dark bay over there; the one that looks almost black. When he gets fed up, everyone else leaves."

"Will all these be adopted some day?"

"I hope so. They deserve to have a good home and good care."

"What's that one's name?"

"We call him Strawberry. He's so tame, he could be a pet. Once he's your friend, he'll follow you around like a puppy dog." She grabbed the horse's halter and brought him closer to Eddie. "You can pet him if you like."

"We shoulda brought carrots, Dad," Eddie said over his shoulder to Gil. "Next time we come, we will."

Next time, buddy? I don't think so.

"I hate to tell you this, but most of these horses didn't know what a carrot or an apple was. No one ever gave them treats."

"I give the horse I ride carrots every time I ride. He slobbers carrot breath on me."

The two of them laughed. Gil was having trouble keeping his perception of inmates intact. What had each of these women done that warranted them losing their freedom, perhaps even their children? His hand tightened on the handle of Eddie's wheelchair.

A microphone announced the show in the round pen would begin in five minutes.

196

As they came out to the round pen, Gil surveyed the situation. Since the walls were solid, Eddie would not be able to see. Shame they hadn't set up some bleachers. People stood around the pen, visiting in groups.

"Yo, Eddie." Kool Kat was effortlessly pushing two hay bales in a wheelbarrow toward them. "If two ain't enough, we'll get more."

Eddie grinned up at his father.

She dumped the bales, and Gil helped lay them tight against each other. Together they lifted the wheelchair up and Eddie nodded. "I can see fine now, thank you."

Kool Kat high-fived the boy and nodded to Gil. "Cool."

Gil looked after her. He sighed. Such a waste. Surely someone as personable as she could make it on the outside.

Two men and a woman entered the pen and stopped in the middle, she with a microphone while one of the men carried a clipboard. "Welcome, everyone, to our first open house on the west coast for the Thoroughbred Retirement Foundation. You all received brochures about the Foundation so I won't bore you with what you can read. What I want to say is that we are committed to keeping as many Thoroughbreds out of the slaughterhouse as possible."

"You're kidding," Gil muttered spontaneously. Eddie shushed him.

"People in some parts of this world think horse meat is a delicacy — we think horses deserve to live out their lives serving and working with humans to make this world a better place."

One of the men took the mic the woman handed him, introduced himself and then the man in charge of the prison foundation program. "Mr. James teaches the women who volunteer for the program."

Gil regarded the man who wore his long sleeves rolled to his elbows, jeans that had seen many washings, and a smile both warm and confident at the same time. What passion for horse and human drove him to try something so . . . alternative?

"If they finish the training, the women will have an associate's certificate in stable management. The training will qualify them for a job on the outside. We believe that working with the horses is a benefit for both the humans and the animals. Mr. James."

Eddie was lost in the moment, Gil noted, as James began to speak.

"I'd like to share with you some of the histories of the horses we have here, introduce you to the kind of work we do. The

Thoroughbred is a very intelligent animal, not just a dumb jock that can run fast. We give them the chance for a new kind of life. I believe that everyone and everything deserves a second chance."

Gil's prejudice took another hit. That's what he taught when he spoke, so why was he having trouble applying it now?

"Or even a third or more if needed."

Gil wasn't sure about that part.

"In speaking of our workers, since our program is so new, only one of our workers has been released or paroled, but we all know of changes that are happening right before our eyes. Now," he turned. "Our first horse is Dancer's Delight led by Kool Kat, who had never met a horse in her entire life."

Someone opened the gate and Kool Kat walked in with the horse Eddie had fed the peppermint candy.

While she led him around the pen, Mr. James told more about the treatment and care the horse received. "Soon as the vet declares him sound, he will be released to a training facility and available for adoption from there. We will be taking applications, and there is a screening process so that we get the right horse with the right owner." He nodded at both the horse and woman.

"Thanks, Kool Kat."

The crowd applauded. Gil watched his son about as much as he watched the horses. Eddie had brought a small notebook along and was taking notes. Gil couldn't read them, he was too far away, but he'd bet anything Eddie was making lists of more questions to ask. Watching the next horse trotting around the pen at the insistence of his leader, he caught himself wondering what it would be like to ride one of these beautiful animals. Perhaps Carly would teach him to ride. That thought made him start to smile. But how would his small son without the use of his legs — or *with* use of his legs — even think of controlling one of them?

Then he heard Eddie suck in a breath. He looked to see where his son was looking and had about the same reaction. The sun set the horse on fire almost like sparks radiating from his hide. He had a braided black mane and tail, with one sparkling white sock halfway to his knee. The rider kept him turning in a small circle, waiting her turn in the pen. She was slender and wore the green uniform of an inmate, her face shaded by a black riding helmet.

"And for our final horse, Breaking Free, ridden by Maggie Roberts."

The two of them moved as one. Gil had read of that, but not seen it before. They said the Indians rode that way. She let the horse trot a straight line, his long legs reaching out, floating across the ground. When she brought him to a stop, she leaned forward and patted his long arched neck.

"Breaking Free." Eddie whispered the name and wrote something on his paper.

"Breaking Free came to us ready to maim anyone or anything he came in contact with. It took two big men to get him from the trailer into a stall, and they left with huge sighs of relief." Mr. James gave more of the horse's background and then said, "We discovered since it was men who had abused him, he hated men. Maggie took over and using all we know of what's called 'natural horsemanship,' brought him around."

She rode Breaking Free up to Mr. James for several pats and a cheek rub before trotting him around the pen.

"As you see, with extra work, we helped him get over his fear, and now our horseshoer — or farrier — who is a man said this horse is a dream to work with. Breaking Free will be available for adoption fairly soon so we are accepting applications for him."

Gil watched the woman back the horse,

turn first one way and then the other, trot a figure eight, and trot out the gate to the applause from those watching. How did a woman like that end up in prison?

Sixteen

Maggie collapsed in the saddle with her arms around her horse's neck.

"You did it, big boy, you did it." She sniffed and mopped under her eyes with her fingertips. "Freebee, you are one awesome horse!" She patted his neck again and sucked in a deep breath.

"That was awesome," JJ, who'd been her gate person, said. "You two were so beautiful out there. Maggie, I wish you could teach me to ride like that."

"I do too." She'd not been aware of the desire to teach until she heard herself say the words. A few months ago, she would have dismissed the thought out of hand. Now . . . was it possible? Could she convince someone she was capable of training horses? *Worthy?*

Breaking Free began a jig when he saw the boy in a wheelchair coming toward them so she dismounted and held her horse by the reins close to the bit. "You better stop there and let him get used to your chair."

The boy nodded and halted. "Sorry. My name is Eddie Winters."

"Hello, Eddie. I'm Maggie Roberts." She watched her horse as he studied the wheelchair then blew a soft breath. "All right, come a bit closer."

Eddie did as she told him and stopped again.

"Oops. Too close. He's getting uptight," the boy said, his eyes on Breaking Free.

She regarded the thin boy with the tanned arms. "How do you know that?"

"He raised his head real high, his nostrils flared, and he got stiff."

A quick lesson in not judging by appearances, she thought, chagrined that she of all people had viewed the wheelchair and not the horseman in it. She beckoned him to come forward again since Breaking Free had settled back down. He rolled a few feet closer.

"I've been riding at Rescue Ranch for two years. Well, almost." Eddie eased his chair forward, and Breaking Free lowered his head, reaching his nose to sniff and inspect the contraption. Eddie moved a couple of feet, stopped, and waited, intently watching the horse.

"Eddie, that's close enough. That horse doesn't know you."

Maggie met the gaze of the man who spoke. He stood behind the wheelchair and nodded briefly at her. He wasn't handsome, but he wore an air of confidence like a fine cashmere sweater. Kind might be a good word for him. But somehow she figured he wasn't the horseman his son was. And, by the way he averted his eyes from hers, he probably wasn't a fan of inmates mixing with the general public.

Eddie held out a hand and let Breaking Free sniff it.

"I'm Gil, Eddie's father. Do you suppose he knows the difference between male and female children?" the man asked hesitantly.

"Oh, he's not afraid of men anymore, and as long as all men treat him with gentleness, he should be fine."

"But if something happened, he might revert back to . . . his violent behavior."

Cautious, a cautious man who obviously loved his son. Probably treated his wife with the same cautious protection. A yearning lightly landed on her heart as she answered him. "I cannot promise that he wouldn't. Horses have to learn to trust their rider, like the rider must learn to trust the horse." She stroked Breaking Free with one hand while holding him with the other. "Come Breaking Free, give the boy a chance to pet you." The horse took the needed three steps forward and put his head down to the boy's hand.

Eddie stroked the red face, his own face one huge smile. "He is really a special horse, isn't he?"

"I think so, but I might be a bit prejudiced."

"How well is he trained for general riding?" Gil Winters kept one eye on the horse.

"He still needs a lot of work. We are rather restricted here on what we can do."

"I wish I had brought him and the others treats. I just didn't think of it." Eddie dug in the bag of dog treats by his hip. "You think he might like a dog biscuit?"

"Try him."

Eddie laid one on the palm of his hand and held it out. Breaking Free sniffed it and rolled his upper lip back. "I don't think he likes it." Eddie giggled and went back to petting the horse.

A woman standing behind Gil cleared her throat.

"Pardon us for monopolizing your time. There are others . . ." He turned to the woman behind him. "C'mon, Eddie."

"Thank you, Ms. Roberts. I hope I see you again," Eddie said.

Maggie kept her tears inside. Charlie would have been his age. She'd not seen any children for so long that she watched him like a starving woman as the two left, one walking, one wheeling, but talking together. Eddie looked back over his shoulder and waved.

She answered more questions, but couldn't remember about what. The loss of Charlie's photo returned to rob her of the joy of Breaking Free's debut. After walking Breaking Free back to his stall, she unsaddled him, taking care to put Mr. James' tack on the rack she'd built on the exterior stall wall. Letting her horse loose in the stall, she took out the brushes and gave him a good brush down. *The picture, why my picture?* Who knew about it? Had someone been watching Maggie in her cell, putting her hand under the mattress so many times? Who wanted to hurt Maggie most? Who? DC probably didn't even know what was there, she just wanted to destroy it because it was important to Maggie. It had to be DC.

Someone had already refilled Breaking Free's water bucket but when he drained half, she took the bucket for more water and brought back a small can of sweet feed.

"That was wonderful." JJ parked the wheelbarrow where it belonged. "I heard Mr. James say the open house was a resounding success. Eddie, the boy in the wheelchair, and his father signed up to sponsor Ghost. Guy has bucks. They paid a whole year in advance."

"That's great," Maggie replied tonelessly. She suddenly felt like she was a balloon and all the air had just escaped, leaving her zipping all over and then collapsing on the ground. She shut the lower stall door and gave Breaking Free one last pat as he sighed like he was worn out too. Now it was time to line up again, say good-bye to fresh air, and be counted.

Back on the bus to return to the prison, Maggie envisioned ways to get even with DC, even though she knew she would do nothing, could do nothing. DC kicked the seat a couple of times until Kool Kat slowly turned and glared at her. Maggie figured DC was letting her know she knew Maggie knew it was she who destroyed the photograph.

Mr. James stood in the door well and hanging on to the pole, smiled at each of them. "I am really proud of all that you have done. The work you are doing is going to make a difference in someone else's life down the road as these horses go out and join the world. Congratulations." He glanced at his clipboard. "Now, onward. Three horses will be shipped off to the trainers this week, and four new ones will be coming in."

As she rested her head against the window, Maggie felt waves of weariness wash over her. Now more than ever, she wanted out, and she wanted to work with horses when she got out. She carefully tucked away the thought of losing Breaking Free like the other women lost their three horses. The pain from the loss of her picture was more than she could handle already.

"I want Breaking Free, Dad." Eddie lay back in his bed, his hands behind his head.

Gil could feel his son's gaze boring into his back. He stood looking out the window, admiring the lights in the swimming pool. "He was beautiful, wasn't he? But huge, Eddie."

"He's not huge for a Thoroughbred, only a bit over sixteen hands." A pause stretched. "He liked me."

"Eddie."

"But Dad, he did."

"I hoped that sponsoring Ghost would be

enough, and Carly is looking for the perfect horse for you."

"We found the perfect horse." His son sounded so sure.

Gil kissed Eddie's forehead, patted Bonnie's head. "Good night, dog." As he left the room, Eddie called him back. "What?"

"I just thought you should know that I am praying for Breaking Free." There was the tiniest pause, then the young voice spoke from the darkened room. "Like I prayed for our new house."

After checking on Maria in the kitchen, Gil suggested she leave her fussing and go watch TV for a while. Anything other than working around the clock.

She laughed. "You want iced tea?"

"Thanks, I'll get it." Taking the pitcher out of the refrigerator, he poured himself a glass and held up the pitcher. "You want some?"

"Yes, but . . ."

"Maria, I know how to pour iced tea." He handed her a full glass.

"Eddie say he found his horse."

Gil groaned and leaned back against the counter, crossing his legs at the ankles. "The horse is huge, not well enough trained, and yet watching Eddie and that horse was like watching telepathy. I've never seen anything like it. Remember when he met Bonnie? They stared into each other's eyes, and the link was there. I don't get it."

"Gift from God?"

He shrugged and drained his glass, setting it in the sink. "I don't know, but I'm going to be working in my office for a while. By the way, have there been any unusual phone calls?"

"No." She paused. "Wait, someone call two, three times, only hang up."

It could have been anybody. "Thanks, good night."

"Buenas noches."

Gil wandered into his office, sat down at his desk, and pulled out a stack of cards to write thank you notes. That Eddie and that horse had connected was not in dispute. He'd seen it himself. He scribbled another card. He'd decided early on in his business that thank you notes to anyone who had helped make his trip more comfortable or more successful were mandatory. Usually he did them on the plane, but he'd only gotten about half of them done. With the stack ready to mail, he switched to updating his calendar on Outlook and syncing his PDA. Perhaps it was time to get one of the all-in-one jobs. Be one less thing to carry along.

Eddie and a huge red horse that used to hate men. Why was nothing easy with Eddie but loving him?

When the phone rang, he picked it up. "Gil Winters here." A silence made him add, "Hello?"

"Well, I finally reached you." Soft and sultry. The sound made the hairs on his neck stand at attention.

"Talk to my lawyer." He rattled off the number.

"Gil, please, just a minute. Is . . . is Eddie still alive?"

That she would think her son could be dead spoke volumes about what she didn't know about him. "Oh, please. As if you cared."

"You haven't given me any chance to care. He's my son too."

"Only in the biological sense. You signed away all rights to him, remember? And if you try to get to him, I'll have an injunction in place so fast you won't know what happened."

"Gil, it's been ten years. I was young and stupid then. I've changed, grown up."

He closed his eyes and clamped his jaw. *Hang up, call Ben. Let the attorneys duke this out.* "You realize that if you try to contact him without my permission, you will lose

212

your monthly allotment?"

"I hoped you would take pity on me and let me see him."

That would be a cold day in a hot spot. "You gave up all chances — both for pity and to see him. Don't call again. Goodbye." He set the phone back in the charger. "Blast." He'd not gotten her phone number. He picked up his phone to redial the number, but all he got was the dial tone.

He'd not handled this properly, he knew it, but then when had he ever handled things with Sandra properly?

SEVENTEEN

"Can we make recommendations to whom our horses go?" Maggie asked.

Mr. James gave her one of his assessing looks. "What do you mean?"

"The boy in the wheelchair? He connected with Freebee like I've never seen. It was like they'd known each other for a long time. They belong together."

Mr. James shook his head. "If only life were that simple."

"You think he could manage that much horse?"

"If they're both trained right."

"He said they have a retired Thoroughbred at the place he rides."

"Some horses have an affinity for serving the handicapped, some don't. Kind of like people." He looked directly into Maggie's eyes.

"Hey, Maggie!"

She waved at DC and turned back to Mr.

James. "If you talk with Annie about asking our opinion . . . well, you know. Anyway, I better go see what she wants." The thought of letting Breaking Free go warred with her trepidation about DC.

"Is there a problem between you and DC?" He nodded to where the other woman had been standing, but she had faded away.

"Ah . . ." Think fast. "Why?"

"Just a hunch. We'll talk later."

Maggie headed back to the barn, Freebee whinnying after her. A sense of foreboding ate at her mind, growing stronger when DC was nowhere to be found. Why did she call to her like that and where did she go?

After helping a new recruit catch her horse, she watched Kool Kat give another woman a lesson on grooming and picking feet. Such a gift Mr. James had with his "each one teach one" principles which were changing lives, including her own. As more horses moved to the freedom of pastures, he had upped the responsibility for the experienced inmates, assigning each a paddock, making it her job to check the horses in her paddock every day for health issues, see that no one was getting slighted in the feedings and no horse was being abused by another. Herd mentality meant that everyone had to get along after they settled the pecking order.

Maggie figured that people weren't much different.

When they returned to the prison for noon count and lunch, there was a message on her door to contact Mrs. Donelli. Glancing at the clock, she hoped she could at least set an appointment time if she hustled. Had she done something wrong? Not that she could think of. Could it be about her parole? *Less than two months to go.* Where she was going to go and what she was going to do hung heavy on her mind. But she knew the first thing was to meet with her lawyer and see how much money she had from the divorce settlement. Lawana Carlson said the settlement divided everything right down the middle. Not that they'd been wealthy, but the house had been worth something. The house she had so lovingly turned into a warm and comfortable home. *Don't think about that!*

All the things she'd refused to think about for all these years were now crowding in, demanding she pay attention. She knew there were some boxes of her personal belongings waiting for her at Lawana's office. Since she'd never answered any of her friends' letters, she wasn't sure if she had any friends any more. Perhaps it would be better not to go back at all, just start over somewhere new.

But one thing she had to do. And that door she slammed closed with all her might.

She set up the meeting with Mrs. Donelli for the next afternoon and returned to stand in the lunch line. If only there was a way to get back at DC. She remembered Mrs. Worth's talks on forgiveness. Well maybe not revenge but keep her from any more harassing — not only of Maggie but of the others who suffered too.

Images of the wheelchair-bound boy and Breaking Free slipped into her mind whenever she had a free moment. What special training would the horse need? Could she begin with it immediately? But what if they gave Freebee to someone else? She'd seen both interest and desire on more faces than just Eddie's.

"Carly said she hasn't found a horse yet." Eddie locked his wheelchair in place and laid his helmet in the box kept for his gear. He smiled at his dad in the rearview mirror. "So I asked her if she would go to Los Lomas and see Breaking Free."

Gil felt like banging his head on the steering wheel. Eddie would easily be voted President of the Persistence League. "And what did she say?"

"That she wants to look at another horse up there at the same time. For a schooling horse."

"When is she going?"

"Tomorrow. She knows the people who run the TRF."

"Thanks, I knew that." What he hadn't told Eddie was that he had talked with them too. They'd had four applicants for Breaking Free, but hadn't completed the adoption process for any of them.

"It wouldn't hurt to fill out one of those forms, would it? I mean, we wouldn't be committed or anything."

Gil watched his son try to be diplomatic, but his whole body sizzled with desire.

"Carly said she would train him."

Fear rode on Gil's shoulders, digging in with strangling fingers. *All I want is to keep him safe.* But he'd seen and read of other parents keeping their children so safe they never had a chance to grow and become independent. That was difficult enough with normal children, let alone one who could not use his legs. Carly was the only one he knew he could ask for advice, and she was so firmly in Eddie's camp, she might as well pitch her tent and stay there.

So, if Carly approved the horse and agreed

to train him, why was he holding back?

Because I'm his father, that's why. And there are too many ifs.

"I'll call her when we get home and talk this out with her. But don't go getting your hopes up. I did not agree to adopt him." Even he could hear the *yet* that filled the car and caused Eddie's face to burst into smiles.

The next day after dropping Eddie off for his first day of school, he picked Carly up and they made the trip to Los Lomas.

"Now if there is any doubt in your mind that this is not the horse for Eddie, you'll tell me honestly, right?"

Carly stared at him, a slight smile revealing more than her eyes hidden behind dark glasses. "I would never put Eddie in danger, Gil. Even if we brought the horse home and trained him and I had the slightest qualm, I'd back off."

Gil nodded. He'd trusted his son with her for nearly two years, this was taking that trust one step further. "Thank you." Now if he could just get his stomach to agree with his mind.

"Annie of TRF will be here at eleven so we are only a few minutes early. Since this is not a sanctioned prison visit, we won't be talking with the inmates today, although an inmate will be handling Breaking Free and the other horse for us to see," Carly explained.

"But we can talk with Mr. James?"

"Yes, he said he'd meet with us."

"You know Eddie is praying for this horse to be his."

"I know." She flashed him a quick grin. "And look at the house you have. Oh, that reminds me, is the barn finished yet?"

"Pretty much. They are putting up a round pen this afternoon. The wooden border fences are all in place." When another car drove up, they exited Gil's truck and greeted Annie as she got out of her car.

"Glad to see you back, Mr. Winters, and Carly, I'm thrilled you want another horse for your ranch. Mr. James says he has the perfect one for you." As they talked they headed for the round pen where a rider was already working a bloodred bay.

"Is that Breaking Free?" Carly asked.

Annie nodded. "Beautiful, isn't he?"

The three of them leaned against the fence and watched the team in action.

"She rides well."

"Yes, Maggie had a history with horses when she was a teen. Normally our horses aren't trained at this facility, but Mr. Brundage, the warden, is using Maggie and Breaking Free in some publicity for Los Lomas. Since this horse has been in the spotlight, he has had more adoption applications than usual."

Gil kept his attention on the horse and rider. You'd think they'd worked together for years. All that power collected. Could his son handle such an animal? He knew he couldn't, but then he wasn't a rider. Again he could hear the *yet* loud and clear.

"It's all about trust," Carly said, breaking into his reverie.

"Yeah, well, I'm having a hard time with that."

"You could look at other horses." Annie smiled up at him. "We have a few and will have more soon."

"Why couldn't Eddie have fallen in love with a nice, gentle, small horse?"

"Big horse, big heart?" Carly turned to greet Mr. James. "Is there any chance that I can work with Breaking Free?"

"Yes, while the inmates are at lunch." He faced Gil. "You do know that if a horse doesn't work out, you can always bring him back?"

Gil nodded. Yeah right, and break a small boy's heart?

"He's a great horse," Carly said on their

way home. She'd worked both Breaking Free and the other horse on a lunge line and handled them in the stall since prison rules forbade anyone else from riding.

Gil looked at the adoption papers he'd picked up. "You think I should fill these out?"

"Yes."

"I'd want him stabled at my house. Could you come there and train him?"

Carly blew out a breath. "I thought he'd be at Rescue Ranch so I could work with him in my spare time."

"Like you ever have spare time."

"That's beside the point." She worried her bottom lip between her teeth. "I'm going to have to think on this. I just don't know how I can work in the extra trips. Besides, I'm needed at the ranch, as you know. Today was a special treat for me."

"I understand." He glanced over to see her frowning. He knew she was always on the go. "And the other thing, I will need someone to take care of the horse."

"Both those issues would be solved if you stable him at my place." She shot him a half smile. "Finding good help is never easy, as you well know."

"But I would have to live at your place in order to care for the horse, and I don't want to do that. And I can't require Maria to do it either. Besides, if Eddie is to have a horse, he needs to be with his horse, doing what he can to care for him." Until this moment, Gil hadn't realized he'd already made some decisions.

Maggie loosed Breaking Free in his paddock and shut the gate before leaning on the fence. When he nuzzled her hand, she palmed the candy and watched him munch. Riding him was so much more than just a pleasure — the joy nearly overwhelmed her. She heard someone coming up behind her, but she ignored the presence and rubbed his ears until she sniffed herself back into control.

"He's goin' away and you won't never see him again." The voice reminded her of a hissing snake.

"Go away, DC." Maggie nearly choked when the words came from her mouth. She'd just been thinking them, or so she thought. A hard shove to her shoulder corrected that error.

"You wait, Miss Prissy white girlie. You gonna pay for that. Pay real bad, and Kool Kat won't be there to save you."

Shuddering inside, Maggie counted to three, then six, then ten. She sucked in a deep breath and turned to face her tormentor. Evil had eyes. Breaking Free tossed his head and jigged in place, his snort warm on the back of Maggie's neck. "Look, I'm tired of your games."

"What you gonna do? Fight back? Lose your parole?"

"Why are you out here anyway? You don't like the horses, nor those of us who do."

"How do you know what I like?" She leaned closer, fists balled. "You want a taste of what I like the most?" A fist slammed into Maggie's shoulder. Breaking Free shook his head, his whinny stopping DC from throwing another punch. Maggie staggered. Fight back! The scream in her head cocked her arm, clenched fist and teeth.

DC stared at the horse, who now had his ears pinned to his head. Taking a step back, she muttered, "Just wait till we get back to the yard."

"DC, in my office. Now!"

The woman spun on a heel and pushed past Kool Kat, who was coming toward them.

Maggie looked over her shoulder. Never had she heard Mr. James speak like that, his voice sharper than any whip snap. Had he seen what went on? Would he put her on report too? That was the rule if two people were fighting. But she'd not been fighting, at least not physically. Her roiling stomach reminded her that throwing a punch wasn't the only way to fight. Finally, she'd stood up for herself. And Breaking Free had backed her up.

Kool Kat stopped beside her. "Well if that ain't a kick in the pants." She glanced over her shoulder. "Might could be the end of DC here at Los Lomas. This time she done been caught."

That evening Gil filled out the application form, Eddie popping wheelies to let off his excitement.

"Breaking Free is my horse, my horse, my horse."

His soprano song finally got to his father.

"I'm just submitting the adoption application. Remember, you can't go getting your hopes up."

Eddie grinned at his dad and glanced around the room, all but shouting, I prayed for a house and look how God answered me.

Gil rolled his eyes and went back to the paperwork.

"The posts are in for the round pen." Eddie spun his chair in place, Bonnie's nails clicking on the tile as, ears flapping, she ran and skidded with him.

"I know."

"I spread the shavings in Breaking Free's stall. Maria pushed the wheelbarrow for me."

Gil nodded. "Listen, son . . ."

"I know, Dad, but I'm just doing what you always say. Act as if . . ."

"I know what I say, thank you, and I'm grateful you've been listening." He picked up the application and glanced at it again. "But . . ."

Eddie sat without moving, staring at his father. Finally he leaned forward. "Don't worry, Dad, I won't throw a fit if this doesn't happen. We'll look for another horse. You always say never never give up, and I won't."

"Oh, Eddie, that's not what's worrying me. You can throw ten fits if you want, you don't have to be all grown up yet." *After all, you're only eleven years old,* he added silently. *You've had so much sadness and struggle already in your young life, and I don't want to let more in.* As he got up from his desk and walked over to the fax machine, he ruffled his son's hair. "Don't you think it's time to take Bonnie out for her potty break?"

Bonnie looked up from where she'd

moved to the rug in front of the fireplace, out of the way of spinning wheels. Her thumping tail and raised ears showed she understood the suggestion as well as Eddie did.

As Eddie and dog headed for the arched doorway, he threw a comment over his shoulder. "Don't worry, Dad, everything is going to turn out all right."

Gil stared after his son. Shouldn't he be the one saying that?

Two days later Gil and Carly were on their way north again, this time towing a horse trailer to pick up her new schooling horse — and to discuss Breaking Free.

"So, what have you decided about bringing him to Rescue Ranch, if you get to adopt Breaking Free?"

"I want to have him stabled in my barn where Eddie can spend as much time with the horse as possible."

"I was afraid that would be your decision."

Gil waited for her to continue. If she said she couldn't make the time, on to plan B, whatever that was.

Carly blew out a sigh. "I'll ask around, see if I can find someone to help you."

"You'll be an advisor?"

Her nod gave him a brief moment of

security.

Annie, Mr. James, and Maggie were waiting for them at the prison stables.

"I just put in a call to Warden Brundage. He would like to talk with you," Mr. James said after the greeting.

"I see." Gil settled himself into waiting mode while Carly discussed the horse she was adopting with Annie. He watched Maggie try to stand still. He understood her jitters since his ear itched, his back twitched, and — he rammed his hands into his pockets and leaned against the right fender of his truck. "So, how's Breaking Free doing?"

Maggie glanced up at him, as if shocked he'd spoken to her. "Ah, fine. I mean good."

So much for that conversation. The warden's car coming up the driveway caught all of their attention. *Would someone just tell me if there's even a possibility that we get the horse or not?*

After more greetings, they all strolled to the paddock where Breaking Free grazed as if he'd never heard of a racetrack. Gil drew his hand from his pocket to stop the jingling of the coins.

Warden Brundage turned to Gil with a smile lighting his mocha face. "Mr. Winters . . ."

"Please, call me Gil."

"All right, Gil. I have a proposition for you, regarding Breaking Free."

"Yes, sir." Why did he feel like there was a two minute pause between each word?

"I believe you know that we've been using Breaking Free as a symbol of the good this program is doing here at Los Lomas. While your son's name is not the only one on the applications for this horse, there is great media potential here if we handle it right." When Gil started to say something, Brundage raised his hand. "Please, hear me out." At Gil's nod, he continued, "The horse is ready to be released and his groom and trainer, Maggie Roberts, has served much of her time and is being granted parole. What I propose is that you be allowed to adopt Breaking Free and that Maggie comes along to take care of the horse and continue his training to be a good mount for your son. In other words, to make this work for all of us." He paused, his dark eyes focused on Gil's face.

Gil hoped he wasn't showing the shock he felt. Maggie come along with the horse. An ex-con working with his son.

"So, do I understand that you are saying if we want the horse, we have to take the trainer too?"

"I'd rather not put it in those terms."

"May I say something here?" Annie took a step forward.

"Of course." Brundage nodded to her. "I didn't mean to take over this conversation."

No, of course not. Gil tried to corral his rampaging thoughts. A little inner sarcasm helped.

"We at TRF have the final say as to who will adopt this horse. Thanks to Maggie and what we have observed, we would love for Eddie to have Breaking Free. Our goal is always to fit horse and rider and let's face it, this is an unusual situation. But with more training, we believe this will be a good fit, and if we can boost the reputation of Los Lomas at the same time, we feel this is a win-win situation."

Are they all crazy? Recommending I take on a convict to coach my son? I'm out of here, folks. This is just not acceptable. But Eddie had his heart set on this horse. He said he could handle it, but . . . "I understand all that, but my concern is for my son." Gil shook his head. "No, this is just impossible."

"What is it you're worried about?" Brundage asked. "Ms. Roberts has served her time and has an exemplary record with us here."

"I don't care what her record is among the inmates. I'm concerned about the moral values of someone around my son, my home."

"I can vouch for the fact that Maggie Roberts is of the highest character. I would trust her with my son and daughter." Mr. James stared into Gil's eyes, never wavering.

Easy to say, you're not being asked to do this.

"Remember, if things don't work out, you can return the horse to us." Annie took a step forward. "We are giving you a special break here, you know."

Gil nodded. "I understand that." He closed his eyes for a moment, surprised that he caught himself beseeching the Almighty for wisdom. Taking a deep breath, he turned to Maggie and waited until she looked up at him, trapping her gaze. "Why should I hire you?" he asked, his voice soft but underlaid with steel ribbons.

Without blinking, she answered. "Because I can give your son the dream of his life."

If this was the way God was answering Eddie's prayer, Gil would not allow himself to stand in the way, but everything within him pleaded for more time, more choices. "What do I need to do?"

EIGHTEEN

"Ms. Roberts?" Eddie smiled from his locked-down wheelchair when she looked over her shoulder.

"You can call me Maggie," she said without thinking, then turned to the man driving the van. "If that's all right with you."

"I guess that would be all right." Gil nodded and glanced in the rearview mirror to see his son. The man didn't look at her.

Maggie watched everything Gil did and tried to see the scenery at the same time. She was free. Actually on parole, but out of the Los Lomas Correctional Facility. It had been Mr. James' idea that she accompany Breaking Free to help him get settled with his new owner and help train him. A temporary arrangement, at best, she thought. But it meant she didn't have to face filling out job applications right away and having to explain to every potential employer why she had a criminal record. Plus, she wouldn't have to say good-bye to Freebie, at least not for a while. Nevertheless, she had hesitated when Mrs. Donelli had told her the conditions of her probation and about the job they'd arranged. She liked Eddie, but she wasn't sure about his father. Gil Winters obviously wasn't thrilled about her working with his son, so why had he agreed to it? If their roles had been reversed, would she have done the same?

The gates had closed behind her for the last time. She was not just taking one of the daily rides to the horse barns but riding down the freeway, in a van with a young boy and his highly resistant father. What did she know about them, other than their names, that Gil made his living as a public speaker and corporate trainer, and that the board had approved their adoption of Breaking Free?

Her mind flipped back to the meeting in the visitor's room a few days before, the sober-to-the-point-of-unfriendly face across from her. Stopping the trembling in her hands took most of her concentration.

"I thought we should talk privately," he had said after an abrupt greeting.

"I see." Not at all, but that sounded polite.

"I got a copy of transcript of your trial."

He paused, perhaps waiting to see her response. When she just nodded, he continued. "It was pretty cut-and-dried. But I'm surprised that with no priors you received the full sentence."

She nodded again. They'd all been surprised, including her attorney. Another one of those memories she'd managed to bury deeply enough to ignore — most of the time. Dennis, her husband, had walked out. The divorce papers arrived a week later.

Mr. Winters stared into her eyes. "Are you an alcoholic?"

She shook her head. "Two drinks doesn't make me an alcoholic."

"Did you drink frequently?"

How do you define frequently? "Only when my husband and I went out to dinner or had guests or . . ."

"Or you got upset or angry or . . . ?"

Now he sounded like the prosecuting attorney, who'd tried to beat her into admitting a drinking problem. How many times had she wished she'd never had that second glass of wine? Oh, to be able to live that one moment over again, the one she'd paid for with seven years of her life. But the bottom line — two people had died that night. One of them her only child.

"Look, Mr. Winters, I've attended AA

meetings all these years . . ."

"And if you work for me, you will continue to attend meetings." He leaned forward and lowered his voice. "I have some other rules too."

She'd expected this, so why was it so unnerving? *I don't have to take this job, surely there are others. But I have to make sure Breaking Free makes it — and that little boy with a dream.* She'd not been able to help her son have dreams, but she could help Eddie. She straightened her shoulders. Nothing Gil Winters could dish out would even begin to compare with what she'd survived.

"You will not drive while Eddie is in the vehicle. You will not have guests on my property. You will train with Carly at Rescue Ranch so you know how to train the horse and teach my son properly."

"How will I get there? I don't have a car or a driver's license."

"Either myself or my housekeeper, Maria, will drive you. And just as a reminder, even when you get your license, you will not drive with my son in the car, under any circumstances."

"Anything else?"

"Not at the moment. I ordered a travel trailer set up by the barn for you. We're in the process of building my office, which will also have a small guest apartment. It won't be ready for another month at least — we didn't expect to need it right away."

"I see."

"If you will give Maria your grocery list, when she goes shopping, she'll fill it. Do you have any questions?"

She shook her head. No matter his rules, she would be free.

"Ms. Roberts, er, Maggie?" Eddie's voice brought her back to the present. "My dad bought a saddle for you and bridle for Breaking Free. We hope it is the right fit."

"Do you have one of those special saddles?"

"Not yet, I'm saving my money. Maybe by the time I can ride him, I'll have it."

She kept herself from glancing at the boy's father. Surely with all the money he had, he could afford a therapeutic saddle. But such a comment was not her place, she needed to remember that.

"I use one at Rescue Ranch where I ride." As though they were lit by candles, his eyes looked back at her. "I can't wait to ride Breaking Free."

"Well, Eddie, neither can I." To ride when she wanted, not just when allowed.

"My dad built a round pen for us to use."

Us, what a lovely word. *What had Mr. Winters said about riding? That's right, he said he didn't ride, wasn't a horseman.*

"Breaking Free arrived all right?"

"Last night. We left him inside his stall." Gil joined the conversation.

"He's still there," Eddie chimed in. "But Maria was going to check on him. I helped feed him this morning. Dad cleaned out his stall."

Maggie glanced at the man to catch his rolled eye look. "Have you ever cleaned out a stall before?"

"No, but I'm a fast learner. It's not exactly rocket science. What do people do with all that manure?"

"Depends on where you live. Some places compost it, some sell it, others just make a big pile until the neighbors complain."

"We have twenty acres and neighbors who would most likely complain sooner rather than later."

"Do they have horses?"

"Some do, some don't."

"We have fenced and cross-fenced pastures," Eddie joined the conversation again. "Bonnie, she's my service dog, likes to run in the pasture. Do you think Breaking Free and Bonnie will get along?"

"Most likely, unless she's afraid of him."

"Bonnie's not afraid of much, but we didn't let them meet yet. Dad says they need time to get used to each other."

Like we all need time, and for a change, I can pretty much be my own drummer. She wanted to stick her head out the window and let the wind blow her hair, blow all the prison smells out and away. Blow her last life away and let the new life begin.

Gil listened to their conversation, almost envying Eddie the ease with which he accepted Maggie. He'd debated warning his son about the dangers of hiring an ex-con but decided to just keep on eye on her himself. He had warned Maria however.

He heard her small intake of breath when they drove into the driveway. "We moved in a little over a month ago. This all happened so much faster than I figured it would." In his mind, it looked pretty chaotic.

"It-it's beautiful."

He tried to see it through her eyes. Although he knew she'd come from a middle class background, living in a cell for these years had to have changed her. He tried putting himself in her place and hit a stone wall. This mouse hugging the van's door didn't look anything like the confident woman riding Breaking Free at the open house. It made him wonder which one was the real Maggie Roberts.

Eddie pushed the button to the lift, and the door opened automatically. "I'll show you the barn." Excitement shot off him like sparks.

"Would you rather get your things settled in your new house or see Breaking Free's new home?" Gil tried reining in his son's exuberance.

"I'll just put my suitcase in my room, er trailer, if that is all right."

"Fine, I'll bring that, you walk with Eddie."

"No, I-I mean . . ." She clamped her mouth shut. And nodded.

"Can I get Bonnie?" Eddie asked.

"No, let's see how Breaking Free is first. He doesn't need one more distraction right now," Gil replied.

"What kind of dog is Bonnie?" Maggie stepped out of the car and shut the door behind her. She now understood what was meant by sensory overload. Grass so green it hurt her eyes, a breeze that while it cooled her skin, abraded it too, the fragrance of marigolds that lined the drive so strong she could taste them. If she followed her urges, she'd be curled in a fetal position back in the van seat. With a supreme act of will, she brought her attention back to Eddie.

"Bonnie is a Basset hound. She's trained as a service dog. That means she picks things up for me, brings me things." Eddie shot off the lift as soon as it touched down.

"I see." Maggie walked beside him on the smooth asphalted path. Sprinklers threw circles of crystal water drops on the pasture, everything looked brand new.

"That's your house for now." Eddie pointed at the travel trailer. "We hope you will eat with us like Maria does. But if you want to cook things, you can." He grinned up at her. "Maria is really a good cook."

Maggie wished she dared turn and look at the father; she could hear his steps behind them. Had he not informed his son of the rules he'd laid out for her at their meeting?

Eddie rolled into the dimness of the barn. With his head hanging over the stall door, Breaking Free nickered as soon as he saw her.

"He missed you."

"Not as much as I missed him." Maggie stroked the horse's neck and face, all the while inhaling the wonderful perfume of horse. "Hey, fella, did you like the ride?" His nose and upper lip quivered in a sound-less whicker as he leaned against her.

"Come pet him, Eddie. He'll be your friend forever."

Eddie rolled closer, then waited for the horse to relax again before stopping right beside Maggie. Breaking Free sniffed his hand then inspected his shirt and his head, snuffling and tickling. Eddie laughed and stroked the horse's face. "I can't wait to ride him."

"We'll let him settle in for a bit first. Get used to the place. Tomorrow we'll just walk around the pasture, see how he likes it." She checked his legs. "You never took off the wrappings."

"I didn't know we should," Gil said, a black shadow in the doorway behind them.

Was that a note of belligerence she detected in his voice? Outside her will, her mind flitted back to Los Lomas and the terror of her life, DC. Her voice always wore that tone. She swallowed the incipient fear. DC was no longer part of her life, now to drive her out of her dreams — or rather nightmares. "No problem, I'll take them off now." She opened the stall door and slipped inside. "Do you have brushes, curries, clean wrappings?"

"I'll get them." Eddie rolled away.

Gil leaned on the stall door and watched her unwrap the bandages and feel down

241

each leg. "Is he all right?"

"No swelling, feels fine." She gathered the bandages and slung them over the stall door.

"Over there is the tack room. I got a list of necessary supplies from Carly. You remember her; she was at the meeting with the warden. She's the owner of Rescue Ranch. We stored the supplies in the tack room, but feel free to redo that if you want. If you need more supplies, there's a pad on the wall." When he saw Eddie coming, he leaned closer and dropped his voice. "I have his special saddle on order. Should be here any time. He doesn't know it."

She backed away. "I see." She took the bucket of grooming supplies, everything brand new.

"If you need something, just ask."

"I'm sure . . ."

"We went shopping two days ago. I asked Mr. James what kind of feed and hay Breaking Free was used to."

"Feed's in the tack room too?"

"Yes. There is a phone in your trailer if you need to call the house. The number is right beside it. I left the key on the table. Maria put in some basic staples for you and something for dinner. I'm sure she'll be here to introduce herself in the morning." He nodded to his son. "Come along, Eddie, we'll let Maggie and Breaking Free settle in."

"But Dad . . ."

"Come on, Eddie." His voice took on that parental *now* tone.

"See you tomorrow, Eddie." Maggie nodded to the boy and watched the two of them walk out of the barn, Eddie sending her a wave over his shoulder. *Alone, I'm really alone.* "All by myself, except for you big horse." Breaking Free took a step closer so she could more easily reach his forehead. He lowered his head, another hint to his desires. Maggie complied, then picked up two soft brushes and beginning right behind the horse's ears, let herself relax into the rhythm. Grooming a horse was the same, no matter if at a prison barn or a fancy stable with only one finished stall and room for several others.

Maggie dropped the brushes in the bucket and leaned her forehead against her horse's shoulder. Not her horse, Eddie's horse. Somehow that distinction didn't bother her. She'd promised herself when she walked out the gates of Los Lomas to live in the moment and rejoice for every little thing. Like right now. Peace and freedom, what more could she want? "Let's take you out and walk out some of the kinks, what do you think?"

After a stroll through the soaked pastures, she tied him in the alleyway and found a wheelbarrow and fork. Cleaning the stall made her wonder about the women still at Los Lomas. They'd given her a good send off. Thank you cards and hugs. She'd never dreamed that leaving would be so hard. Hard because while she was being given the gift of a lifetime, fear ate at her insides. What if she couldn't do it? And now that she realized how far away from a town they lived, other questions arose. What if Gil Winters changed his mind and asked her to drive? She tossed more of the manure into the wheelbarrow. She'd never drive again.

Nineteen

"But why, Dad, why didn't you invite Maggie to come for dinner?"

Gil shook his head for the third time. No matter how he worded his excuses, that's exactly what they sounded like — excuses.

Eddie ignored Bonnie's vociferous greeting and concentrated on his father. "You tell me not to be rude." He stroked Bonnie's head with one hand. "And to always think of the other person."

"That's enough. Just leave it, okay?" The snap in his voice was nothing compared to the fire in his brain.

"Get washed for dinner, chico." Maria's soft voice was also more command than request.

Eddie glared from one adult to the other, spun his chair, and if he'd been able, would have laid tire tracks.

"Eddie, he is upset?"

"Yeah well, join the club." Gil raked stiff

fingers through his hair.

"Dinner in five minutes. I make pulled pork tacos."

I don't want dinner, I don't want more discussion with Eddie, and I don't want that woman on my property. "Fine, I'll go wash." Taking out his irritation on Maria would not benefit anyone. Maybe he should call Ben and see if he'd meet for a game of racquet ball. Surely if he slammed that hard little ball enough, he would feel more in control of things. He and Eddie returned to the table at the same time.

"Owner of the pool company call today. He say come by tonight, unless you say no." Maria set the steaming platter in front of him so he could begin serving.

"That's fine. Any idea what he wanted?"

She shook her head and returned to open the stainless steel door of the refrigerator to take out the salad. "Eddie, I made your favorite for tonight — sopapillas."

"Gracias." He sat stiffly, his voice matching his body. He had yet to look at his father.

Gil recognized the punishment but refused to succumb. If his son wanted to mete out the silent treatment, so be it.

Dinner was not a pleasant interlude.

Eddie laid his napkin on the table. "Sorry, Maria, I'm not very hungry. May I please be excused?"

Maria glanced at Gil, caught his nod, and agreed. "Do you have homework?"

"No, I did it already."

Gil watched his son roll his chair down the hallway to his room. Maybe swimming laps would be a substitute for racquet ball. Should he ask Eddie?

"More iced tea?" Maria held the pitcher.

"Thanks." He waited until the glass was full. "I'll be in the pool for a while. Call me fifteen minutes before my appointment arrives. We'll talk out by the pool."

A few minutes later Gil dove in the water and thrashed his way from one end to the other, flipping like he used to do on the swim team in college and pounding his way back. After four laps he settled into a steady crawl that after a mile or so left his heart hammering and his body limp. He hung on the edge of the pool with his arms crossed and let his breathing catch up with him. By swimming by himself, he'd not had to do the polite conversation gig a racquet ball match would have required. Ben would have wanted to know why he was killing the ball or who he wanted to destroy.

"Fifteen minutes," Maria called.

"Gracias." He hauled himself out of the pool, showered under the outside shower, and headed inside to dress. Knowing he should stop by Eddie's room was not the same as doing.

Coming back down the hall, he heard the doorbell and Maria hurrying to open the door. What caught him by surprise was the spate of Spanish and a squeal of delight with more rapid-fire words and laughter, both masculine and feminine. He met Maria, arm locked in that of a short man with a slight paunch, his hair shot with silver and a smile as wide as hers.

"You meet my friend, Enrico Jose Estrada." He'd never heard the giggle that followed.

Gil extended his hand. "I'm glad to meet you, Mr. Estrada."

"No, no, Enrico. I know Maria when she was little, back home in Guatemala. We live next door to her mama and papa. She my, what you say, dog love."

Gil stalled for a moment. "Oh, you mean puppy love. Like for kids. Come, let's go out on the patio and enjoy the sunset. What is it that brought you here?"

"Fate." He broke into a torrent of Spanish again, and Maria reached over and kissed his cheek.

She turned to Gil. "He say his wife died one year ago. They were happy together, now he is no longer sad."

Worry raised its ugly head. As far as he knew, Maria had never dated or had men friends since she came to his house. In fact, she had few friends outside of him and Eddie. She'd been back to visit her family only two or three times in all the years she'd worked for him. She and Enrico might have been puppy loves at one time, but who knew what had happened with him in the years since. He gestured for his guest to take a chair and pulled out another.

"Now, Mr. . . ."

"Enrico."

"Ah, yes, Enrico, what can I do for you?"

"This make me the most happiest man."

"I'm glad to hear that." He waited while the man took a paper from his pocket.

"Here, I have the figures for next year. I am so sorry to have to be raising my rates. You are a longtime good customer, so I want to tell you this in person. Not just on phone. My men do good job, yes?"

"Very good." Gil thought back all these years he had dealt with the foreman who sometimes checked on his crew. So strange he had never met Enrico before.

Enrico's smile slashed his tanned face. "This is God, eh? All these years Maria is working for you, and I not know it."

Maria returned with a tray of cookies and her famous lemonade. The two swapped more rapid-fire Spanish as she handed out the glasses and passed the plate of cookies. While Gil spoke Spanish, there was no way he could keep up with them, instead resigning himself to wait for them to finish. After he agreed to the new pricing schedule and Enrico left, he rose and headed for his office just in time to catch the ringing phone. Maria was singing in the kitchen.

"Hey, Ben, good to hear from you. Actually, about time."

"All right, old friend, what's wrong?"

"Why do you ask?"

"I just know."

Gil thought a moment, then threw caution in the wastebasket and told him the saga of getting Breaking Free. "But mostly I . . ." He paused, trying to find a way to say how he felt without sounding like a whiner.

"Just spit it out."

"I have never liked being manipulated."

"And that's how you're feeling about . . . ?"

"Being forced to take the girl, er woman, along with the horse." There, he'd said it. "I now have an ex-con living on my place to supposedly train my son and his horse."

"I see."

"And don't even suggest I can send the horse back because I refuse to break my Eddie's heart."

"I assume you've put all the safeguards in place."

"Of course. It's the drinking, Ben. Sandra is an alcoholic and here I am, saddled with another one."

"Wait a minute. Who's to say she's an alcoholic? Doesn't she deserve a second chance?"

"Now you sound like the do-gooders at Los Lomas."

"Gil Winters, I'm surprised at you."

"Me too, Ben, me too. But you made the mistake of asking, and I told you. Now, what did you call for?"

"You're not going to like this any better than hiring your new horse trainer, but I think you should see Sandra, Gil."

Gil held the phone away from his ear and stared at it. "Did you just say what I think you said?" *And I'm paying you for this kind of advice?*

"I know. But we were discussing the situation here at the office and the consensus is that if she takes this to court and can prove she is now a fit mother, well, you know they often decide in the mother's favor."

"Ben, she left. Walked out. Demanded money. All that is duly recorded. How can she have a leg to stand on?"

"What makes you so sure she hasn't changed? People do, you know. Look at yourself."

Gil was forced to admit the truth in that statement. Through his speeches and coaching he had helped people change pieces of their lives all the time. That was what he did. When he came right down to it, Sandra's leaving had forced him to change, to seek help to make growth happen — her leaving and the fact he needed money to give his poor little baby some kind of life. Lots of money since the insurance company fought against some of the surgeries and medical care Eddie needed, claiming they were experimental treatments.

He'd put the principles he learned to practice and now here he was, arguing about letting the mother of his son see her boy. Would a judge say she had the right to that?

"Have you posed this situation to any of your judge friends, hypothetically of course?"

"No, but I can. You know they'll say circumstances vary and without having all the facts will give lukewarm advice."

Gil left his chair and paced the room. "So, what are you suggesting? We just give in?"

"No, but I don't know what's best either."

"You could put a tail on her. Find out if she's clean and sober. That would tell us a lot right there. First she'll ask just to see him. Then she'll want him to come visit her."

"Perhaps."

No she won't. She'll be so put off by his wheelchair and the extra help he needs that she'll have built his hopes up and abandon him again. "Ben, get all the facts that you can. Until I know more, I can't make a decision."

Gil stared out the window to see the lights were still on at the trailer. "What did you say?"

"I said I will find out what I can. She's played a real low profile. Been married twice I think."

"Twice besides to me?"

"That's what has made her hard to trace."

"Let me know what you find. In the meantime if she calls here again, I will give her your number."

"Thanks a lot."

"That's what I pay you big bucks for." Gil heard Bonnie greeting Maria. "I gotta go. Talk with you soon."

A bit later Maria brought him the contract he'd signed with Enrico. "Something wrong?"

Gil shook his head, working his bottom lip with his teeth. "Sandra."

"She call?"

"No, I talked with Ben. He says I should see her."

Maria paused, staring out the window. "She no change. She want something."

"But what?"

"Money."

"But I pay her every month. I've always paid her."

Maria motioned to include the house and everything. "She want more."

Gil stared at her. "Of course." Of course Sandra wanted more. Obviously she had kept track of him, even though he'd not kept track of her. He'd sent the check to the same bank all these years and figured since he'd kept his part of the bargain, she'd keep hers. How stupid could he get? What would ever be enough for her?

The bottom line: was she still drinking or using? The thought of her meeting with Eddie when she was either drunk or stoned made him leave his desk and pace the room. From his conversation with Ben, a court order might be the only deterrent, and there was no proof that Sandra was still up to her old habits.

Just because you teach people tools for change, you expect that everyone will change. You didn't know this stuff when you were married to her. But why did she turn to alcohol? He knew the question was rhetorical. She'd always liked her cocktail in the evening and wasn't willing to give that up even when she knew she was pregnant. Short of locking her in a room, he'd not known what to do. When she'd realized her baby had a hole in his spine and would need many surgeries and might never be normal, she'd asked the doctor for antidepressants. Then for sleeping pills and . . . the list went on and on, and he'd not been able to stop her. Thank God for Maria.

The more he thought about it, the more he paced; the more he paced, the more furious he grew.

TWENTY

Maggie stared at the door handle of the travel trailer. Her hand refused to reach for it. She sucked in a deep breath and, scolding herself for being a coward, concentrated on lifting her hand, inserting her fingers behind the lever, and pulling. The door swung open inviting her in. She inhaled, not quite a new car smell but close. Mounting the steps she stopped in the doorway and looked around. Kitchen with stove, sink, and refrigerator, a nook with two benches for dining, bedroom to the front, and bathroom to the back, all done in milk-washed wood tones and neutral sands and creams with a touch of turquoise in the bedspread and valances. Turquoise throw pillows colored the bed and sofa.

It looked huge.

When she stepped inside, she inhaled again. So much loveliness, it was hard to believe it was for her. She sat down on the queen-sized bed and then flopped back, spreading arms and legs wide, reveling in the silky feel of the fabric. Would she get lost in a bed this size? Her clothes — two pairs of jeans, three T-shirts, and a cotton jacket — wouldn't begin to fill the closet. Staring at the ceiling, she inhaled deeply again, letting her air out on a gentle whoosh. How long would it take to get all the oxygen cells of the prison out of her body? The memories would most likely remain forever.

She sat up and took six steps to the kitchen. A list on the refrigerator door informed her what was hidden within. Homemade chicken rice soup, salad fixings, fried chicken with mashed potatoes and gravy. She opened the door to see all the condiments she might desire plus milk, cottage cheese, cheddar cheese, and sliced ham and beef for sandwiches. Picking up speed she checked the cupboards, all stocked, including a coffee pot, pots and pans, a microwave, toaster. Towels in the bathroom along with shampoo and a hair dryer. She stared in the mirror. As if her prison shag needed drying. Toothpaste and soap in the cabinet, toilet paper underneath.

She sank down on the sofa and stared at a bowl flowered in bright primary colors centered on the table that held apples, oranges, bananas, and grapes. Maria, the housekeeper, must have done all this — for her, a woman she'd never met and one who had a prison record. Maggie picked off a couple of grapes and nibbled them while she studied her new home some more. She'd thought a dingy apartment somewhere would be her new home — nothing like this. Shaking her head in disbelief, she hefted her duffel bag onto the bed and within three minutes was all unpacked, her things stowed in the closet and drawers.

Taking a couple slices of cheese and ham, she sat on the steps and watched the sunset flaming the cloud ribbons until the clouds faded to gold, then silver, and the evening star winked at her. A dog barked from some other house, a chill seeped into her shoulders, but still she sat there. A donkey brayed, catching her by surprise. No one could tell her to go in, to eat, to sleep, to get up. She hadn't even noticed a clock in her new home.

When the stars grew beyond her ability to count, she stood and stretched, then opened the door and stepped back into her house. Alone, she was all alone. She opened the fridge door again and tried to decide what to fix. Soup? No. Fried chicken, maybe. She shut the door and sank down on the nook bench. She couldn't decide. She'd not had to make decisions like this for nearly eight years.

"Just put something in the microwave and eat, for crying out loud." Her voice sounded loud in the stillness. She opened cupboards again and found a plastic container with homemade chocolate chip cookies. She took out two and closed the container carefully before setting it back on the shelf. Next to it sat peanut butter, extra crunchy. How had Maria known she liked extra crunchy? How would she ever tell the woman thank you enough? She twisted off the lid, peeled back the seal, and inhaled fresh peanut butter. They could make a perfume with that fragrance. Taking a spoon from the drawer, she dug into the peanut butter and alternately munched the cookies and the crunchy treat.

A small television waited on a corner shelf, but she didn't bother to turn it on, just undressed and stepped into the shower. She could have stayed there longer, but the water changed to cold so she turned it off, dried, and promising herself a nightshirt when she went shopping, donned a T-shirt and crawled into brand new sheets on a huge bed and no bars anywhere.

Day one of her new life already flown by.

Maggie turned over and thumped her pillow — high loft after the years of flat. She stroked cotton fabric of the thread count she'd forgotten. So many contrasts it was more sensory overload than she ever dreamed. When she finally slipped into sleep, nightmares chased memory dreams, jerking her awake but not enough to let them all go. Finally she got up and sat at the table, staring at the bowl of fruit. She plucked a few grapes and ate them, then leaned over and pulled the blinds closed. Too much space, too much to see, too much living to catch up on.

She was out in the barn when the birds grumbled at each other in the trees and the dawn was still caught in indecision. Though the barn was dark, she didn't turn on a light for fear that Mr. Winters — er, Gil — would think something was wrong. She slipped inside Breaking Free's stall and waited for him to come to her, his warm presence a reassurance they were living a new reality. She sat down in the corner by the hay rack and stroked his face when he lowered his head.

"I think you're adjusting better than I am, Freebee. If I think my life simple, all I need to do is look at yours and see real simplicity. Hay, feed, water, a place to run, a good brushing, a good friend or two. Did you have bad dreams too? You should see all the choices I had in there. Overload, that's what it is, but I'll get used to this life — you can bet your whiskers I will."

Gil found her sound asleep in the corner of the stall when he came out to check on her. He brought several flakes of hay and dropped them in the hay rack, the noise of it making her blink and stretch.

"Did you sleep out here all night?"

Maggie shook her head, pulling bits of straw out of her hair. "Dawn was coming." Staggering to her feet, she yawned and stretched again. Was there a law against sleeping in a horse's stall? Not that she'd ever done such a thing before. When he returned with a full water bucket, she bit her lip. "I'll do that."

"See that you do then."

"Is there a certain time schedule I need to follow?" Why was he being so grumpy? She didn't remember him being like this at Los Lomas. In fact his good humor at the open house was one of the things that made her willing to try living here. But he'd been curt yesterday too.

"No. But you weren't in your trailer and I . . ."

"You thought I'd taken off?"

261

"The thought entered my mind."

"And leave Breaking Free and Eddie? Do you think I would break my word to him?" She crammed her hands into her pockets to keep them from shaking. "And parole? You think I'm nuts or something?"

Gil stopped and stared at her. "The thought entered my mind."

"Well, get rid of it. Unless you kick me out, I'm here for the duration or until Eddie no longer needs me." She swallowed at the thought of her outburst. *Maggie Roberts, what has gotten into you?* She wasn't where she should have been. Her thoughts warred between apologizing and getting more frustrated. She sucked in a deep breath and exhaled. "Look, just because I'm an ex-con doesn't mean I don't keep my word or that I can't be trusted. I did not willfully go out and commit a crime, and I have paid for the crime I did commit. Now all I want to do is get on with my life and right now that means taking care of this horse and helping your son . . ." She nearly stumbled at the pang that stabbed her heart. Catching her breath, she finished with . . . "Helping your son and this horse become the kind of partners that can make both their lives better." *And yours too,* but she didn't add that.

"Words are easy."

"Not necessarily." She held his stare until Breaking Free nudged her for an extra pat.

Gil finally exhaled a sigh and turned away. "We'll see."

We'll see what? If I do my job? If I split? She shrugged it off. "What time does Eddie get home from school?"

"About three. He rides at Rescue Ranch today. Would you like to go along?"

"Yes, I would. I need to make arrangements with Carly for my own training."

"Maria will be driving today. I have a meeting. They will leave about three thirty." He left the stall, and she could hear him walking out of the barn. Shaking her head, she leaned against Breaking Free's shoulder. "Well, round one is over. I wonder who won."

Once she'd cleaned out the stall, she brushed Breaking Free and tacked him up. "Time for the round pen, fella." She led him out and into the pen, shutting the gate before mounting him and adjusting her stirrups. He snorted and she sighed. How beautiful everything looked from the back of the horse. The house with the French doors leading to the patio and pool area, green fields crisscrossed by white board fences, green lawns, some trees turning the reds and oranges of fall, all the pieces of her new life laid out before her. She clucked Breaking Free forward and walked him around the pen to loosen up, always making sure that she spoke the commands that went along with the signals she sent him with her legs and hands.

All the while she rode, she tried to figure out how Eddie would ride, how to build the trust between horse and handicapped rider. She reminded herself to ask Carly if there were any books for training horses to be used this way. Her stomach grumbled that she'd not eaten, so she dismounted and removed the saddle and bridle, then let Breaking Free loose in the round pen. Some workmen had arrived and were working on the frame of a building that Maggie assumed would be the office/apartment Gil had mentioned. She watched Breaking Free, but the men and the noise didn't seem to bother him. Maggie wondered if she'd still be there when it was finished as she made her way to her trailer.

Just inhaling the freshly dripped coffee was a spiritual experience. Wheat toast right out of the toaster, spread with peanut butter and a sliced banana, eaten on the steps of her new home with the sun hot on her face. All by herself. She cradled the cup in her hands and alternately sipped and sniffed. Such simple things. She'd promised herself to consciously enjoy every act of her new life. Real life, not just marking time, not just getting through. Making her bed and putting the breakfast things away took all of five minutes. She eyed the phone. Calling her attorney should be next on her to-do list.

Hearing a voice, she stepped to the door. A dark haired woman and a basset that could only be Bonnie were nearing the trailer. Maggie stepped to the ground. "Hi, you must be Maria." Maggie extended her hand. "I cannot thank you enough for all you did here for me."

"You are welcome. This is Bonnie." Maria smiled and squeezed Maggie's hand again. "I am glad you are here." She waved to the pen where Breaking Free stood with his head over the railing, watching them. "He is a beautiful horse."

"That he is. And this Bonnie is a beautiful dog." She extended a hand to be sniffed, then squatted down to rub the dog's ears. "How are you, girl? What a beauty you are."

"She misses Eddie when he at school."

"I made coffee a few minutes ago, would you like some?" How strange it felt, to be offering someone coffee like this, like a normal woman would.

"Sí, with sugar please."

"Come inside." Maggie held open the screen door. "Bonnie, you too."

"We bring you some chairs for outside?"

"That would be wonderful." Maggie poured the coffee and set the cups, sugar, and spoon on the table. Nose to the floor, Bonnie gave everything the sniff test. Taking the cookie container out of the cupboard, Maggie offered Maria one and then took one for herself. "Is Bonnie allowed people food?"

"Sí, Eddie slips her treats all the time." Maria picked up her cup. "You tell me what you need, and I get it."

"Is it all right if I ride to Eddie's lesson with you?" Maggie took a bite of her cookie. *I could bake cookies.* The thought made her nod. Other than caring for Breaking Free, her time was her own. "And could I go shopping with you sometime if you don't mind?"

"I go before I pick up Eddie at school. You want to come?"

Maggie hesitated and then nodded. "I'll make a list." She sipped her coffee. "Is there somewhere I can buy clothes?"

"At Kmart."

"Could we go there?" Maggie thought of

her cash situation. She'd had fifty dollars saved in her account at Los Lomas. That wouldn't go far.

When they finished their coffee, Maria and Bonnie returned to the house and Maggie took Breaking Free for a walk along all the fences that divided the field into smaller pastures. She let him stop and graze in one spot where the grass was fetlock high, mentally making her list as she looked up at the hills that blended into more hills. In other parts of the country these hills might be called mountains, here they were all part of the Tehachapi Mountain range, covered in pine and oak trees. She could just stay here forever.

Later in the store, she forced herself to move from item to item when her temptation was to look at everything, but the variety, the colors and textures quickly overwhelmed her. She checked out with only a few of the things on her list and a driving need to get back outside. She waited by the car until Maria returned.

"You okay?" Maria asked.

Maggie nodded. She was now — the shaking had stopped.

Back at her trailer, the thought of getting in the car again and going to Rescue Ranch seemed as difficult as climbing a rock face — barefoot. But after talking it over with Freebee from the safety of the corner of his stall, she patted him good-bye and joined Eddie and Maria in the van. She'd expected Eddie to come to the barn to see Breaking Free before leaving but decided not to ask why he didn't.

"How was school?" she asked when he'd finished buckling in.

"Okay." He shrugged. "How is Breaking Free?" His eyes lit up.

"He likes the pasture, the round pen and the new saddle fit him fine."

"You rode him? Wow!"

"Gave him a good workout. He is settling in well. Will you be feeding him tonight?"

Eddie glanced at Maria who nodded. "Yes. And grooming him."

"Good. I'm thinking we need to build a ramp for you, to get you higher."

"I've been working with crutches again. I'll try those."

"Your braces too small." Maria shook her head, all the while keeping her eyes on the road.

"I'll use them anyway."

Maggie detected a tone of defiance in his voice. What was going on?

When they arrived at Rescue Ranch, she

learned Carly wasn't there. So she and Maria made their way to the bleachers to watch the lessons in progress in the arena. Maggie wasn't surprised to see that Eddie was a favorite with the aides as they laughed and teased him, getting the same right back.

"Eddie one of the best kid riders," Maria volunteered.

"He sure looks happy."

"He loves to ride."

Maggie thought a bit, then asked, "Why didn't he come down to see Breaking Free after school? I expected him to be so excited." She watched as Maria studied the actions in the arena.

"I too busy to come." She paused, bit her lip. "I-I had a phone call."

"Excuse me?" Then it dawned on her. Mr. Winters' rules. Eddie was not to be alone with her. She huffed her disgust. Well, the man would have to learn. *No,* her inner voice chided her. *You will have to earn his trust. Like you did with Breaking Free.*

Eddie vibrated with excitement as he wheeled back and forth. "Did you see me trot all by myself?"

"I-we did." Maggie included Maria. Once the wheelchair was back in the car and everyone's seat belts fastened, Maggie turned to glance at Eddie who grinned back at her.

"Hey, Maria, did Enrico call you today?"

Maggie glanced at Maria. Was that a blush she saw? Who was Enrico? Did that dip of the chin mean Maria had a man friend? Leave it to Eddie to fill her in.

"Enrico and Maria were friends in Guatemala, and he owns the company that cleans our pool. They just met again a couple of days ago. He likes her, I can tell."

"Eddie!" Maria failed to trap the giggle that lent truth to Eddie's burst of information.

Maggie changed the subject. "What verbal commands do you use with the horse you were riding, Eddie?"

Maria shot her a glance chock-full of gratitude. Maggie nodded. This would be between them, after all there was no one for her to tell anyway. Surely Mr. Winters already knew about it.

"I tell him to walk, to back, to trot, stop, and over. Since I can use the reins — some of the riders can't you know — I don't have to use left and right and not really halt either, unless he is backing up."

"When you first started riding . . ."

"The aides had to hold me on." He shook his head. "But not anymore. Carly says I am one of her best riders."

"You have good posture and balance."

"Sometimes my balance isn't so good. I almost fell off not long ago. I was careless."

Maggie admired the way he didn't try to blame anyone else or the horse for his near accident. This was an unusual boy for sure. Would Charlie have been this brave? She pushed the thought away, knowing that one of these days she was going to have to take out all these buried thoughts and memories and deal with them.

"Can Bonnie come with us to the barn?" Eddie asked as they parked in the driveway.

"Let me check on dinner. Then we go down." Maria smiled at Maggie. "We not be long."

Maggie strolled to the barn, hands in her pockets, enjoying the air that hinted at the crisp feel of autumn. While September clung to summer, the nights welcomed the coming change.

After greeting Breaking Free, she set the wheelbarrow in front of the stall and forked out the manure, then emptied the wheelbarrow, talking with the horse all the time. She leaned the wheelbarrow against the stall wall and turned to Breaking Free, who was watching the trio, Eddie in his chair, his father and dog, with forward pricked ears.

"Easy, fella, they are friends." She stroked his bloodred neck and patted his shoulder.

Gil and Bonnie stopped when the horse snorted.

"Just give him time. He had a hard time with some men, and sometimes he still over-reacts. Next time bring him treats. He loves carrots, apples, and hard peppermint candies."

"Peppermint candies?"

"I know, but he likes the sweetness and the crunch."

"I told you, Dad." Eddie dug in his dog treat bag and palmed a candy for Breaking Free, who took it without taking his gaze from the dog.

"Something like you, eh Bonnie." Gil leaned down and petted the dog who sat right beside him. Bonnie and the horse stared at each other, both extending their noses and sniffing the air.

Both horse and dog leaned forward, Breaking Free taking first one step and then another. Bonnie looked up at Gil and whined, her tail swishing the hard-packed dirt aisle.

"Bring her closer, let's see how they do." Maggie clamped a hand on the halter snapped to the cross ties.

Bonnie kept her attention on the horse as

she moved closer, her black nose quivering as she sorted through all the scents in the barn.

"Bonnie, sit." Eddie spoke gently and Bonnie planted her butt on the ground, her tail sweeping away bits of hay and shavings.

Maggie watched the horse. "He must have had a dog friend before. Look at the way he's acting." She patted Breaking Free's neck. "Will she come if I tell her to?"

"I don't know, ask her."

"Bonnie, come." Maggie said.

Bonnie looked over her shoulder to Gil, and when he told her to go, she walked up to Maggie and stopped right in front of the horse. Breaking Free lowered his head and sniffed the dog. Nose to nose, the two sniffed. When the horse raised his head, Bonnie sat up on her haunches, her nose still reaching toward the horse.

"She can sit up? I didn't know bassets could sit up."

"She's a member of the sitter-upper club. Taught herself just because she is so curious. Like right now." Eddie's laugh made Bonnie give him a quick look, then her head turned back to the horse.

Breaking Free lowered his head again, and Bonnie gave his nose a quick lick. The horse snorted, and the dog shook her head.

"See, Dad, I told you they'd be friends."

"He had to have known a dog, that's all." Maggie leaned down and patted Bonnie. "You two are something else." She unsnapped the lead shanks and led Breaking Free back into his clean stall and slid the hasp in place. "That was amazing."

Twenty-One

A rerun of the pacing and discussion with the attorney over Sandra and Maggie had continued through his dreams right on into his waking. Instead of dissipating, the anger had dug in, taking up residence.

"Dad?"

He whirled around at the sound of his son's voice. "Hey, sport, good morning."

"Is something wrong?"

He sighed. He needed to work off his frustration away from the house. "Nothing that you need to be concerned about. Is breakfast ready?"

"Yeah, Maria said to call you."

Gil crossed the room and ruffled his son's hair. "Let's go eat then." At least Eddie seemed to be over his bad temper. One out of two was a good start.

As soon as he'd eaten, Eddie headed for the door.

Gil laid his paper down. "Where are you going?"

"To the barn to see Breaking Free."

"Wait until I finish."

"But then we have to leave for school."

Tell him. Sometimes his thoughts got in the way. He heaved a sigh. "Eddie, remember I said I don't want you going to the barn alone."

"But Maggie is there."

That's the whole point. How to explain this without sounding like a total ogre. "I know. But until she's been here longer, I want either Maria or me to be with you."

Eddie narrowed his eyes and glared at his father. "This is more of that last night stuff, isn't it?"

"Give me a break, Eddie. I've got a lot of stuff I have to work out." What he meant to sound like a plea came out as a growl.

Eddie glared again. "Do you mind if I take Bonnie out?"

Gil rubbed his forehead. "No, go right ahead."

"Does she have to stay away from the barn too?"

"Yes." His tone snapped, and Eddie spun his wheelchair and out the door he went, Bonnie right at his wheels.

Sensing Maria's displeasure, he looked up

to catch a frown. "You know the rules."

"I know. Eddie not to be alone with Maggie. But you tell him why?"

"No, and right now I don't plan to." *Like I don't plan to tell him about his mother and both these things are likely to come back and bite me on the behind, but I don't know what else to do at the moment.* He shoved his chair back and grabbed his car keys from the counter. "I'll get the car out." He figured he should probably turn on the heater for the drive to school since the temperature in the van was definitely frigid.

When they reached the school parking lot and Eddie had lowered himself to the sidewalk, Gil handed him his backpack. "Have a good day, Eddie." *And please cut your dad some slack.*

"Yeah, you too." But the glare said Eddie wished him anything but.

That afternoon Gil watched Maggie working with Breaking Free and Eddie, teaching him how to groom his horse from his wheelchair, not that Eddie could reach very high. But she made Breaking Free lower his head so Eddie could brush his face and forelock. Seeing his son laughing and happy brought such joy to his heart that it felt like bursting, especially after the grumpy morning. While Eddie loved riding at Rescue Ranch, he was right here, in his own home, with his own horse. And a woman who seemed to bring out the best in both of them. When Maggie handed out carrots, she gave one to Bonnie too.

"Dad, did you know Maria is going on a date with Enrico?" Eddie asked during dinner, which was served inside the kitchen instead of on the patio since the evening had chilled off when the sun went down.

"No, I knew she was going out." Gil turned to smile at Maria as she brought her famous enchiladas to the table. "So, you have a date?"

"No, no, just two friends going to a movie." She motioned for Eddie to pass his plate, but she didn't look him in the eye and the blush showed even in her dusky skin.

"Two *old* friends?" Gil and Eddie swapped teasing grins.

"You no want me to go?" A few words in Spanish followed.

"Now, did I say that? Maria, of course I want you to go, but I think I should give you some advice. As your employer, you know?" He had to bite back a laugh at the consternation on her face.

He glanced at his watch. "First, you should be home by ten."

Maria arched an eyebrow. With the dimple showing in her right cheek, he knew she was on to his game. "You want me to take along a duenna?"

"Well, perhaps that —"

A spate of Spanish too fast for him to translate made Eddie laugh. "What did she say?"

Eddie had learned Spanish along with his breakfast cereal. "She said she is forty-one years old and has never been on a date so if you want to go along, she will find a sitter for me."

Gil looked up at Maria as she laid his plate in front of him. "Very good, Maria. It is hard to get one on you."

"No more advice?"

Guard your heart? "You want me to run a background check on him, make sure he is honorable in his dealings?"

Maria shook her head, rolled her eyes, and sat down with her plate. "Please pass the guacamole."

After Maria left, he and Eddie played a game on the Xbox where Eddie beat him soundly. While helping his son get ready for bed, he ran his new rules through his head. How to say them without sounding like a jerk was the problem.

With Eddie in bed, he sat on the edge. "Eddie, I'm having trouble figuring out how to say some things, so please be patient with me, all right?"

"About Maggie?"

Gil nodded. "I know I'm repeating myself, but I don't want you at the barn without Maria or me along. Not for forever but until we see how this whole situation is going to work out." He watched his son's face tighten. "Please."

"Maggie wouldn't hurt me."

I hope you're right, but I'm not taking any chances. Gil sighed. "And secondly, please don't answer the phone until I tell you it is all right." He held up his hands. "It is not that you've not done a good job with the phone. But I've gotten some strange calls lately and . . ."

"Obscene?"

"No. But two rules aren't a lot, you know." *And please don't ask me for more information.*

"All right. But you said . . ."

"I know what I've said, and I know what I'm saying. Promise?"

"I promise, but I don't like it." Eddie clamped both arms across his chest.

"That's good enough." Gil leaned forward

and kissed his son's forehead. "Good night."

"We didn't say prayers."

"Oh, sorry." He listened while Eddie thanked God for Breaking Free and blessed his family.

"And please take care of Maria, amen."

Lord, yes, please take care of Maria and all the rest of this mess. "Night."

Later that night he was about to leave his office and head for an hour of reading in bed when the phone rang.

"Gil Winters."

"Whatever happened to hello?"

He recognized the voice immediately, sucked in a deep and calming breath, and forced himself to answer politely. "Hello, Sandra."

"I hoped we could chat a bit about our son."

"Our son? You signed away all rights to my son years ago, or perhaps you've forgotten."

"No, Gil, I've never forgotten. I've lived to regret that decision every day of my life."

Was that true regret he heard in her voice? Sorrow? "You've never regretted cashing the checks I send every month."

"Please, please don't be nasty. I know I've not been a good mother, but I would like to make amends. You lecture on the value of making amends and I — I was hoping you could extend that graciousness to me."

"How do you know what I lecture on?"

"A friend of mine gave me one of your tape sets. Hearing you speak like that, about making changes in one's life, gave me the courage to call you."

He leaned back and stared at the ceiling. What could he say?

"All I want to do is see Eddie, get to know him, and let him get to know me. Surely you can afford to allow me that little privilege." Her voice sounded so sincere. Was he wrong in prohibiting contact with her? "Haven't I paid enough for my youthful mistakes?"

Gil sighed. "Let me think on this, and I'll get back to you in a couple of days."

"Oh, Gil, you'll never regret it. Thank you."

After he hung up the phone he stared at the framed picture of Eddie on the wall. They'd taken it shortly after Bonnie came to live with them. She had her front paws on the seat of the wheelchair and was kissing Eddie's chin. You could hear his laughter just by looking at the picture. What would be the best for his son? That was all that mattered.

Twenty-Two

The next morning Maggie started her training at Rescue Ranch. After a tour of the two arenas, the round pen, the horse barn, and viewing the corrals and pastures, Carly showed her the specialized tack, mounting blocks, and other aids developed for the benefit of disabled people of all ages who rode to gain or regain far more than just physical agility.

"The very action of the walking horse works muscle groups that are not used by most sedentary people," Carly explained. "And the more the body improves, the more the mental and emotional facets of our riders improve. They learn that they can do something physical but even beyond that, there is a gentleness and caring from the horses themselves that brings out the best in both our riders and our volunteers. Horses have a healing quality about them."

"I realized that at Los Lomas when the

women started working with the Thorough-breds. The horses came to us for care, and through it we received healing. I saw one hard-core woman sobbing on the neck of her horse. She'd never ever felt as accepted as she did with him, and when he followed her around the round pen after the joining up exercise, she lit up like a torch. I felt the same way when Breaking Free came to me."

Carly nodded and smiled. "Horses break down barriers that people don't even realize they've put up." She walked toward the clos-est arena where two horses were being walked, one person leading, one riding, and two on either side. "All of our volunteers take classroom training to be able to recog-nize when a person who can't talk is in distress and how to help the rider mount, get firmly seated, and dismount. They get to know the personalities of each horse. They learn about order, a routine, all those things that people with handicaps need to succeed."

"Do you assign the horses and volun-teers?"

"I do and I supervise, as does my as-sistant. Now I know you already know the basics of horsemanship, grooming, and tacking up, so today I'd like you to observe the riders in the arena. By the way, some of the clients will ride double — I mean have an aide riding with them until they gain some balance and confidence. Watch to see how the volunteers react with their riders."

"Thank you. I'm hoping you'll teach me how to train Breaking Free for Eddie too."

"Oh I will, but today just observe. You might want to take notes. You need paper and pen?"

"No, I have them in my backpack."

"Good, I'll come by to answer your questions and point out things after I get this new client taken care of."

Maggie took a seat on the bleachers and drew out her notebook and pen. While the commands given the riders were too soft for her to hear most of the time, she watched one adult straighten her back and legs. It appeared she'd had a stroke with partial paralysis on her left side so using her whole body on the horse strengthened muscles that otherwise would atrophy. A little girl rode in front of a volunteer, her smile wide, her helmeted head supported by the volunteer's chest. The little girl cried when it was time to dismount.

While it appeared the horses did nothing more than plod around the arena, they also stood perfectly still while people mounted or dismounted, took treats daintily, and let both small and large hands rub their faces and ears.

When Carly sat down beside her, Maggie turned half sideways so she could watch the riders and Carly at the same time. "You do this seven days a week?"

"No, we usually have Sundays off, unless there is a special event like the horse show coming up. We are also forced to do a lot of fund-raisers. This is an expensive operation as you can guess. That's a lot of my job, meeting and greeting, begging and pleading. If we can get people out here to see what we really do, usually they want to help on some level."

"Strange, but before today, I thought this was mostly for children."

"Physical and occupational therapists are realizing the benefits of therapeutic riding for all ages. So many muscular and neurological disorders and injuries can be helped here. Look around you, wouldn't you rather exercise here than in some gym?"

"No contest."

"About training Eddie's horse. It'll need to learn voice commands. Since Eddie has no leg strength, the regular leg aids won't work. Eddie will use the reins for some signals, turning, stopping, and backing up. So when you are riding the horse, when you would use your legs, say the command at the same time. 'Forward', 'stop', etc."

"All right. I've already started some of that, and Breaking Free is a quick learner."

"Eddie knows many of the commands from working here so let him teach you too. That will really boost his confidence."

Maggie saw Maria drive into the parking lot. "I need to get going. See you tomorrow?"

"Yes, be ready to work in the arena."

"I will." Maggie stuck her notebook and pen in her backpack and slung it over one shoulder. Tomorrow she would wear her baseball cap for sure. Already her nose felt tight, a sure sign of sunburn.

"Thanks for the ride, Maria," Maggie said back at the house.

"You are welcome. Do you need more groceries?"

"No thanks, you stocked my cupboards with plenty. And your enchiladas are fantastic." Maggie waved as she took the path to her trailer, passing the work site where they were installing the windows in Gil's future office.

The morning had given her plenty to think about. After eating the remaining enchiladas and rinsing her dishes, she headed for the barn to saddle Breaking Free. Training him to voice commands would take a lot of repetition, no matter how smart he was. Two hours later she saw the car go out again; Maria on her way to pick up Eddie from school. He'd be out here by three thirty. She gave the horse a break, cantering him across the pasture. While the horse snorted and played with the bit, he didn't grab it and try to run away with her, which made her think how best to train him for the horse show. They needed another horse or horses in the ring to practice for the Rescue Ranch fund-raiser. If Eddie wasn't ready to participate this time, he would be for a later event. Breaking Free had to learn that he didn't need to race or outdistance any of the other horses but obey the commands he was told.

Maggie had just returned with Breaking Free to the barn when she saw Gil strolling over with Eddie zipping ahead of him.

"Hey, Maggie, did you ride him today?" Eddie's smile added sun to his words.

"I sure did. He's learning." She watched as Bonnie and Breaking Free did their nose touching greeting and the big horse snuffled Eddie's hair, making the boy giggle and reach with both hands to pat the sides of Breaking Free's nose.

"You are the best horse. Pretty soon I'll get to ride you." He dug carrot pieces out of his pouch and handed one to the horse and one to the dog.

She glanced over to see Gil watching her instead of the tableau. What was he thinking with his face so somber?

"Today after grooming Breaking Free I want you to lead him around the pen, then you can take him out to graze before you feed him and put him away in his stall."

"Do I have to clean the stall too?"

"No, I've already done that." Maggie had already decided that Eddie needed to learn and do as much of the care of his horse as he was able. "Now, snap a lead rope on his halter first and then unsnap the two cross ties. Never leave your horse without a way to restrain him." She demonstrated, then watched Eddie copy her actions. Together they left the barn with Eddie holding the lead rope in one hand while at the same time using both hands to propel his chair forward. The temptation to help him made her stick her thumbs in her pockets. But Breaking Free surprised her by not minding the alternate tightening and slacking of the rope.

"Okay, turn him around and return to the barn. You always need to be thinking ahead as to what could happen. What if Breaking

Free spooks at something, what would you do?"

"Why would he spook?"

"Say a cat leaped out and frightened him."

"Is he afraid of cats?"

She heard Gil's snort behind them.

"I don't know, but horses sometimes spook at shadows or anything unusual, like a paper blowing in front of them."

"Would he run away?"

"He might."

"Then I'd hang on tight to the rope."

"What if it tipped over your wheelchair?"

Eddie stopped the chair and drew in the lead shank so Breaking Free's head was even with the boy's shoulder. He turned the chair and reached up to rub his horse's nose. Breaking Free lowered his head. "You won't tip me over, will you, Freebee?" Eddie laid his cheek against his horse's nose, then turned back to Maggie. "I'd have to let go of the lead shank, but if I holler halt, he will stop."

There's another good reason for voice training. Maggie nodded. "That's a very good answer, Eddie. I'm working on teaching Breaking Free to respond to your commands." She heard Gil clear his throat and turned to see the man swallowing and sniffing. He nodded to her and the trio beside her. A long-eared dog with front paws on the wheelchair seat, a big red horse standing quietly beside it, and Eddie a hand on each — a trio bathed in light and love. She would capture this moment and keep it, a memory for a lifetime.

By the time Eddie shut the stall door behind him and slid the hasp home, shadows filled the barn. "I did it all," he said, a note of satisfaction in his voice.

"Yes, you did." His father nodded and ruffled his son's hair. "I'm proud of you." He turned to Maggie. "Thank you."

"You're welcome. Have a good night." She walked with them out the door and turned to her trailer. That night she cried herself to sleep. Were they tears of sorrow for her losses or joy for the present? Most likely some of each.

Two days later, Gil stunned her with an invitation to come up to the house for dinner, said he had a surprise. "Maria said come at six."

Maggie nodded. That would give her time to get cleaned up first. She put on the clothes she'd bought at Kmart for the first time, khaki pants and a royal blue T-shirt with a collar, and slid her feet into the scuffs. She had begun to wonder if she would ever have an opportunity to wear them. She stared into the mirror in the tiny bathroom. Hair gel or mousse would help, even hair spray, but she had none so she simply combed her hair, knowing that only wearing her baseball cap would help. Stepping outside was a sure answer — the wind picked up strands of hair and blew it wherever it so desired. So much for looking tidy.

The need to return to her hideaway grabbed her around the shoulders, fighting to drag her back. She shoved her hands into her back pockets and stared at the lights from the windows of the house. Welcoming lights that pulled her forward, gave her the strength to ignore the burrowing instinct and stroll up the walk, through the gate into the backyard, bypassing the lighted blue swimming pool, and up the slate ramp to the French doors. She sucked in a lung-expanding breath and knocked on the door.

Bonnie's announcement of the visitor could surely be heard two houses away. Gil opened the door and stepped back, motioning for her to enter. She nodded and in spite of shaking knees, stepped through the door. Bonnie yipped and wagged so hard her whole body wiggled. Petting the dog was an easy way to catch her breath and glance around. The exterior of the house only hinted at the beauty of the inside. The rock fireplace led her gaze to the vaulted tongue and groove ceiling of the great room finished in the same light oak as the floor. Leather sofas and chairs, rust and orange chrysanthemums spilled over a copper bowl on the massive slate coffee table, matching another pot on the table behind one of the sofas. Color everywhere, from the original paintings on the walls to the stack of throw pillows next to the hearth.

"This is lovely." She nodded to Gil who smiled back.

Maria brought her a tall glass with a sprig of mint leaf on the edge. "Welcome."

"That's Maria's famous lemonade." Eddie rolled his chair closer to her. "You look nice."

"Thank you." Maggie took a sip of the drink in order to cover her discomfort. Other than her trailer, this was the first home she'd been in for those long years. And home was the best word to describe Gil's house. Beautiful, yes, but more than that — welcoming and comfortable. *Someday,* she promised herself, *I will have a lovely house again.* People had praised the home she'd made for Dennis and Charlie, and she would do that once more.

"Eddie said you made him work at the

barn. That is very good." Maria spoke from behind the chair-high countertop that marked off the cooking area. At one end of the counter an arrangement of miniature pumpkins and curious gourds spilled from a basket tipped on its side. Another sign that this was truly a home.

"He did well."

"Eddie always do well." Maria's statement made Eddie roll his eyes.

Maggie watched the byplay and caught a look of pride on Gil's face. What was the story behind this family? No mother, no trace of a wife in the pictures on the mantel or the tabletops.

Everyone might know all about her, at least Gil did, but Maggie had nothing to go on. Other than what she'd seen and heard.

"Wash up," Maria ordered as she set a plate of various cheeses and crackers on the low counter, followed by veggies and dip. "Dinner in fifteen minutes."

While Maggie took part in the dinner conversation, she never initiated a topic, preferring to watch the interaction between the three family members, for Maria was a real part of the family, in spite of her title as housekeeper. Eddie teased his dad about the surprise; Maria made a comment that set them to laughing, and Gil caught Maggie's gaze every so often, sending a tendril of warmth twining around her heart. When he was at his most gracious and spontaneous, like tonight, he could charm the birds out of the trees.

The apple crisp Maria served with vanilla ice cream reminded Maggie of her mother's recipe and therefore one of hers; a recipe hopefully locked safely away in one of the boxes being held for her at her attorney's. Perhaps it was indeed time to make contact with her former life.

When they'd finished eating, Gil brought in a big cardboard box and set it beside Eddie's chair.

"For me?" Eddie asked, eyes shining.

"Well, I didn't offer it to Maria."

"Knife, please." Eddie took his father's pocketknife and slit open the tape. Pulling back the flaps, he stared into the box. "A saddle! My own saddle! Bonnie, look, a Thornhill therapeutic saddle. See it's special for me." The dog put her front paws up on the edge of the box and peered in, her tail whipping from side to side.

"I bought saddle soap and a pad too." Gil pulled the saddle from its nest of Styrofoam peanuts. "It's all yours, son."

"Thank you, thank you. Now I can ride Breaking Free." He grinned at his father and then at Maggie. "I can, can't I?"

"Tomorrow when you get home from school." Gil glanced at Maggie to make sure she agreed. At her nod, Eddie spun his wheelchair in a circle, making Bonnie bark and chase him. Her antics made Gil laugh which made Bonnie, always the clown, bounce even more, her ears flopping, tail waving, a wide grin with tongue lolling in the basset way.

Maggie lowered her gaze to stop the burning in her eyes. Would Charlie have been exuberant like Eddie? Between the dog and the boy all she saw was pure joy. Sometimes joy hurt.

"Thank you for dinner," Maggie said as she excused herself after helping Eddie inspect every inch of his new saddle.

"You are most welcome." Gil's gaze caught hers and held it. "Thank you."

Maggie nodded and stepped out the French doors. Stars, like crystal bits of light, pinned the azure heavens in place. She'd not noticed before what warm eyes he had.

The next afternoon Eddie's wheelchair sprouted wings as he rushed from the house to the barn. Both his father and Maria followed him.

"How was school?" Maggie asked.

"Fine, good. Can I ride now?"

"Grooming comes first."

Like any kid, Eddie groaned.

"But today I will take pity on you, I have already groomed him, and he likes his new saddle. It fits him perfectly."

"I didn't think about the horse when I bought the saddle, only about Eddie." Gil shook his head as he walked up behind his son's chair. "So much to learn."

"Horses can get sore backs from saddles that pinch or rub, and like anyone with an achy back, they get cranky. I read about one dude ranch where all the horses had back problems so the wranglers tried all the saddles on all the horses and found the perfect fit for each, labeling them with the horse's name to keep it all straight."

"Did it help?" Gil asked.

"Sure did. The horses improved immediately and everyone was happy."

Eddie wheeled his chair up to the stall, where Breaking Free greeted him with a nicker. The horse then leaned his head down for a nose lick from Bonnie who sat up to deliver it.

"I cannot believe that horse and dog. Who would have dreamed they'd become such good friends?" Hands in the back pockets of his denim jeans, Gil stared at the scene.

"It's a threesome: horse, dog, and boy. You read about these things, but when they happen right before your eyes, it makes you wonder." Maggie chewed on the inside of her lower lip.

Gil turned to her. "Wonder about what?"

She stared back. "It's just a phrase, you know." She thought a moment. "No, it's more than that. Mrs. Worth, who led our Bible study, often said, 'It's a God thing.'" This most assuredly was, this whole scenario, her here doing what she loved most instead of waiting on tables or running a cash register. Business people didn't just hire ex-cons like Gil did. While she knew she would have a few financial resources, still she had feared life on the outside; rampant among the inmates were horror stories of no jobs, no friends, and no life once you left prison.

"Eddie says God is answering his prayers."

"Then I am sure Eddie is right." She pressed her lips together and nodded before turning to Gil. "I'll need help to get him mounted so the sooner we can have a mounting block built like the one over at Rescue Ranch, the easier it will be on all of us." She stopped and blinked at what she'd said. More like ordering than asking. She caught her lip between her teeth and turned to face him. "I'm sorry for talking like that." Her fingers knit together all by themselves.

"That's okay. We do need a mounting ramp built. I'll get the construction crew on it tomorrow."

"Thank you."

Eddie was feeding carrot pieces to his friends, one for the horse, one for the dog; horse gets impatient, dog woofs, boy laughs, and they start all over again. If only she had a camcorder other than the one running in her head to record all these memories; good memories to overlay the prison years and all the despair that accompanied them.

"Okay, let's saddle him up and your dad and I will get you mounted and you can ride." Maggie paused. "One thing, you'll be on the lunge line for a while but today your father and I will be your walking aides."

"Did you hear that, Freebee? We get to go riding."

The horse nuzzled the boy's shirt pocket looking for more treats, then found the pouch attached inside the arm of the wheel-chair.

"Oh no you don't." Eddie pushed him away before he could help himself.

Maggie cross-tied Breaking Free in the aisle then saddled and bridled him, all the while answering Eddie's many questions with all the patience in the world. A cool breeze drifted through the barn, inviting them to come out and play. She nodded to Gil. "We're ready."

Gil lifted his son into the saddle and Maggie secured the Velcro leg wraps that would keep the boy's feet in the stirrups. She adjusted both stirrup leathers and looked up at Eddie.

"Are you comfortable?" At his nod, she continued. "Riding Breaking Free will be different than the schooling horse at Rescue Ranch so be prepared." She checked the position of his hands on the reins, his posture, his seat in the saddle. "You ready?"

He stared down at her, a grin splitting his face, his riding helmet shading his eyes. "Yes, ma'am."

"Okay, here we go. Gil, will you please walk beside him on the other side, then do the honors and open the gate to the round pen?"

"Be delighted to." He smiled up at his son. "And here I thought a small horse would be a good thing, instead you are up on a giant."

Eddie leaned forward and patted Breaking Free's neck. "He's not a giant, he's my legs."

"Right."

When they'd circled the round pen once

with one adult on either side, she reminded Eddie that he needed to be in charge and give the verbal commands.

"Okay." The boy took in a deep breath. "Forward, Breaking Free." They practiced walk and stop-reverse-walk and stop, all the while staying on the edge of the pen since Breaking Free had a tendency to pull toward its center.

"Check your body." Maggie nodded when she looked up at him.

Eddie gave her a verbal rundown. "Shoulders back, back straight, head up, hands even."

"Where are your eyes?"

"In my head?" He grinned down at her. "I know, look between his ears. Look toward where I want to go. And concentrate."

"Very good. Don't let him go to sleep now."

Eddie giggled. "How can he sleep and walk at the same time?" But he did what she said, and they continued working.

After half an hour, Maggie called a halt. "Are you tired?"

"No, I'm good."

"You sure are, you're better than good." But she could see his shoulders beginning to droop. "One more round." Once that was completed, she led them back to the barn.

Gil snapped the cross ties in place and after loosening the braces helped his son dismount.

"You did great, Eddie. Amazing, in fact." He set his son in the wheelchair then leaned over and laid his cheek on Eddie's head. "I am so proud of you I could . . ." He looked to Maggie and nodded again. "You too."

Maggie felt warmth steal around her heart. "Thanks."

Bonnie yipped and did her wiggly butt dance of excitement then sniffed Eddie all over to make sure nothing was wrong. Assured that all was well, she gave his cheek, chin, and hands a good cleaning.

"You'd think he was one of her pups." Gil smiled at Maggie as they watched the demonstration.

"She takes her job of caring for him very seriously." But when Maggie saw Bonnie sit up to beg for more carrots, she felt something strange rising within. Could it be laughter? How long had it been since she had laughed? She made a face and went to unsaddle the horse and help Eddie brush him down. While he'd not worked up even a drop of sweat, she needed to keep her hands busy and nothing was more calming than grooming a horse.

When she picked the horse's feet, she felt

that one of his shoes was loose. "See that?" She wiggled the shoe. "Loose."

"So what do we do?" Gil leaned closer to see what she was talking about.

"I thought I heard it when he walked on the asphalt. I can pull them if you could get me a nipper and a rasp, or we call a farrier."

"You mean you could get his shoes off?"

She nodded. "That's what I said, but I'd need the tools to do the job."

"But what if he kicked you?"

She sent him a puzzled look. "Why would he do that?"

"Well, I don't know, but . . ."

"You've seen me pick his feet. Pulling the shoes is not that different, just takes more time, and I've been trained to do it." She concentrated on keeping patience in her tone. Why was he making such a big deal of this? She glanced over to see Eddie still brushing his horse, as high up as he could reach.

"In prison?"

"Yes."

He watched her for a long moment. "Which do you prefer?"

"Well, it would be cheaper to let me do it, but like I said, I'd need a nipper and a rasp."

"Cheaper isn't the issue here. What's best in the long run for all of you?" He motioned to her, the horse, and life in general.

"Look, if you don't want me to do it, call a farrier." At the slight tightening around his eyes she realized she'd sounded pushed. "Or I'll call one."

"You know one?" His eyes narrowed.

"Guess we could use the same man that Carly uses at Rescue Ranch."

"I'll call him tomorrow." He sounded like an executive giving orders.

"Suit yourself." She turned on her heel and headed for the tack room. Didn't he even trust her to call a farrier? Once the horse was fed, she could return to the sanctuary of her little house on wheels. Why did the discussion leave a bad taste in her mouth? After all, the horse did belong to him, or rather Eddie. But Gil paid the bills. So what if he was rich as Croesus, she'd only offered because — she thought for a moment — just because. Why did he have to mar a wonderful afternoon by being snappy? Was every discussion of caring for the horse going to turn into an argument?

Twenty-Three

"You'd think they'd been friends for years," Gil muttered. Bonnie gazed up at him, her ears on alert, eyes seeking understanding. He watched from a distance as Eddie chattered away and Maggie nodded in some spots and listened intently in others. While he wanted his son to relate well to adults, actually to everyone, he was a bit surprised at Eddie's reaction to her. Maggie did not seem that open and friendly to him.

He watched the carpenters put the finishing touches on the mounting block and ramp so Eddie could be more independent down here too. One of these days the boy's arms would be strong enough for him to swing his body from the chair into the saddle. Gil had seen a man do that over at Rescue Ranch. Several wounded war veterans rode there, one without the use of his legs.

Spending so much of his time like this was

getting to be a pain. It wasn't that he didn't enjoy watching Eddie's enjoyment, but he needed this time to get his own work done. All he had to do was renounce his edict that Eddie could not be alone with Maggie. It had made perfect sense a week ago when Maggie came. He moved to the plastic chair in front of the barn and tipped his face up to get the full rays of the sun, since it no longer had the heat of summer. While he couldn't hear everything, he still felt like a Peeping, or in this case, eavesdropping, Tom.

"So where are your mother and father?" Eddie asked.

"They died several years ago. First my father with a heart attack and then Mom from cancer." Maggie was more than grateful that they hadn't been around for the accident and its repercussions.

"So you don't have anybody?"

"Well, not exactly. I have a brother somewhere."

"My mother died too, when I was really little. She got real sick, you know. But I think she is in heaven and watching out for me."

Gil sat upright. Where had Eddie gotten that idea? Ben's admonitions came back to him. "You have to tell Eddie about his mother." Yeah, well, it sounded like it was way past time. He should have done so years ago. But how do you tell a little boy that his mother couldn't handle her baby's diagnosis and split? That she accepted monthly payments in lieu of living with and loving her son? Gil felt like banging his head against the barn wall. Bonnie laid her chin on his knee and stared at him. At least he could make the dog happy. He rubbed her ears and around the bump on the rear of her skull. Her eyelids drifted down, and she fell over on her side, the universal invitation to a belly rub. Leaning over to comply, he tried to decide when he and Eddie would have this talk that was likely to blow their relationship into tiny bits that scattered all over their twenty acres.

That night after dinner he invited Eddie to walk with him.

"Sure, Dad. Right now?" At his father's nod, Eddie headed for the front door. "Can Bonnie come?"

"I guess." Gil waited while Eddie put the leash on his dog and received a slurpy nose kiss for the effort.

Was walking best or sitting in the office? Gil followed his son out the door. Dusk had tiptoed in while they had been eating. This would have to be quick. He caught up with his son's wheelchair, and they headed down the driveway to the sidewalk.

"Eddie, you never ask about your mother, how come?"

Eddie grimaced, screwing his mouth from one side to the other. "You don't like me to."

"Yeah, well, I'd like to change that right now." Inhaling a deep breath, he continued. "Your mother is alive. Her name is Sandra. When she was young, she was very beautiful."

"I thought she was dead since you never talked about her." He peered up at his father. "Isn't she beautiful now?"

"I don't know. I haven't seen her in a long time."

"How come?"

"That's neither here nor there." *Be honest,* again Ben's words. How come he could teach people about being honest and up front with others and with themselves and yet fail so miserably right here and now? "We had some very serious disagreements."

"So you got a divorce?"

"Yes."

"So she got divorced from me too?"

"Something like that."

"Jenny's mom and dad got a divorce, and

she lives part-time with her mom and part-time with her dad."

"I know, lots of families do it that way nowadays, but ten, eleven years ago that wasn't so much the process."

"Can I see her?"

The question he'd been dreading and yet knew would come. "I don't know, sport. Wouldn't it be better to leave it as is? I mean you are growing up just fine and . . ."

"She doesn't want to see me."

Gil squatted by Eddie's chair and took hold of his son's hand. If he were a praying man, now would be a good time for it. But since he wasn't, he cleared his throat and said softly, "Yes, she does."

Eddie studied his father, thoughts and feelings flitting across his face like clouds before a capricious wind. "But you don't want me to see her?" He narrowed his eyes and withdrew his hand. "That's why you haven't told me before." He spun his wheelchair, jerking Bonnie and making her yip.

"Eddie, son, I only want what's best for you." *I don't want you to be wounded by a woman who can think of no one but herself.* Her soft voice came back to him. "Can't you believe that I have changed?" No, he couldn't.

"You don't want what's best for me; you

want what's best for you." Eddie's shout came back over his shoulder as he wheeled furiously for home.

Gil followed, hands in his pockets, despair a two ton weight punishing his shoulders and smashing his heart. When he walked in the door, Maria glared at him from the arch into the great room.

"You and Ben both agreed I should tell him about his mother. I did, and now I have no idea what to do next."

"Eddie's in his room."

"I figured as much."

"You go talk to him?"

Gil shook his head. "You know Eddie; he has to think things through."

"I know Eddie. He is a little boy with a broken heart, and he need his father."

You know how to help him more than I do! He needs a mother's love, and he won't get it from Sandra. "You've always been a mother to him."

"I know, but now he need you."

Gil shook his head. "We'll talk later." He made his way down the hall and tapped on Eddie's closed door. No answer. "Eddie? I . . ."

"I don't want to talk with you — ever!" Something slammed against the door.

Gil tried the doorknob. Locked. He'd

been meaning to take the lock off the door, just in case something happened to Eddie and he needed to get to him. But he'd not done that either, just like he'd not told Eddie the truth before.

What else had he done or not done that was going to come back and bite him on the rear?

The next morning's drive to school passed in absolute silence, but for the humming of the car.

"Have a good day, sport," did nothing to cure the stranglehold of tension.

Eddie wheeled away without even a glance at his father. Gil stared after him. Now he knew what being invisible felt like — and he didn't like it.

Back home he wandered over to the barn where Maggie was just dumping the last wheelbarrow of dirty straw and shavings.

"I'll be ready as soon as I wash up."

"Take your time."

Maggie paused. Who was this man, and what happened to the real Gil Winters? *So, do I ignore this and go on about my business or . . . ?*" "Will you be home this morning? I'd like to leave Breaking Free out in the pasture."

He responded with only a nod, staring —

at what? She followed his gaze to see nothing but a blank barn wall.

"G-Gil, ah, is something wrong?" She still
stumbled over his name.

The pain in his eyes caught her in the
midsection with a one-two punch.

"Do you want to talk?" *What I really mean
is do you need to talk.*

He stared at her, but she wasn't sure he
was even seeing her. His voice came hesitantly, stumbling over his sorrow. "What
would you do if you broke your son's
heart?"

She thought of a flip answer but agony
stopped it. *Ah, Charlie . . .* She fought off
the panic that sought to strangle her and
answered instead. "I-I guess I would want
to help it heal."

"How would you do that?"

Oh, Lord, give me wisdom. "I-I can't — I
mean, I don't know enough. In general
I'd . . ."

"I finally told him his mother is alive and
wants to see him." The words came in a
rush, like blood from a severed artery.

Maggie sank down on a bench. "You realized Eddie had created his own life
story. . . ."

"And finally took a friend's advice and
cleared up the misconceptions." Gil joined

her on the bench and propped his head in his hands. "I thought keeping it simple would help. I cannot tell him that his mother couldn't tolerate her infant son's medical problems, that she resorted to drugs and alcohol, and finally one day left him in the hospital and split. Her next communication was a request for a divorce. I've not seen her since that final day in the judge's chambers." All this was spoken in a monotone that only emphasized his despair.

She glanced at him. The frozen look on his face matched his tone. An overwhelming urge to put her arms around him and hope he could cry on her shoulder forced Maggie to stuff her hands in her pockets. Oh, the secrets that slashed and burned when they finally erupted. "And now Eddie wants to see her?"

"How did you know?" He shook his head. "Why isn't he so furious with her that he would swear to never hear her name? I would be."

"But Eddie doesn't know all the details."

"No. So he thinks that I have kept her away. All because I told him she wants to see him and that I didn't think it was in his best interests." He tipped his head back and squeezed his eyes closed. "She could destroy my son." The words fell separately, each clothed in anguish.

Sometimes silence is the best answer. Maggie had learned that early in her prison stay. She rested her elbows on her knees and locked her hands together, staring at her ragged thumbnails. The patience to wait she'd also learned.

"So, what do you think I should do?"

She could feel his gaze on the side of her face. "What are your options?" Don't look at him. Another lesson. Talking was easier sometimes without eye contact.

"Set up a meeting with Sandra for him. Or ignore this all, let it go away."

"You think it will?"

"He'll give me the silent treatment for a time, but eventually he'll start talking again. At least that's the pattern." She started to say something, but he held up his hand. "I know. What if this time he doesn't follow the pattern?"

She nodded. "The thought had crossed my mind."

"So, I force him to talk to me?" He shook his head. "That'll just make things worse." He scrubbed his fingers through his hair. "How do I set up safeguards if she does see him?"

"What are you afraid of?" She who lived with fear could smell it miles away.

"I'm not a —" He stopped midword. "I'm afraid she will come into his life, not be able to handle it, and take off again. Only this time he will know about it, and it will break his heart."

"Eddie has a pretty sturdy heart. He would be wounded, but he would recover. Breaking Free will help him do that."

Gil stopped pulling out his hair and turned to look at her. "You honestly believe that?"

"Yes. Yes, I do. Your son has inner strength far beyond his age." *Lord, let me say the right words.* "And he has a deep faith that will help him get through. Look what it and you have done for him so far."

"Maria is the one to be lauded for that. She has raised him while I traveled around, building a business to provide the income to make life comfortable for him."

"To make up for the crummy hand life has dealt him?"

"You could put it that way. Maria insisted that I had to spend time with him now or there never would be time. A wise woman is our Maria." He locked his hands together, his elbows resting on his knees. He blew out a sigh and then another, his shoulders dropping with the expelled air. "So, it looks to me like the question is — where and when do they meet? Which is safer, a restaurant or a park or here at home?"

"What about a supervised phone call first?" Where that idea came from was beyond her.

"What if he asks her questions she doesn't want to answer?"

"Isn't that her problem, not yours?"

Gil turned his head to stare at her. "How did you get so smart?"

"Seven plus years in the pen teaches you all kinds of things."

He nodded, slowly as if her ideas were taking time to sink in. "I'll take you over to Rescue Ranch now, if that is all right with you."

"I'm good."

"Yes, you are. I'll be at the truck."

Maggie watched him walk off. At least his shoulders had straightened. How could a mother do that to her child? *Who are you to talk?* That inner voice that caused her so much despair spoke louder. *You killed your son.*

TWENTY-FOUR

"Eddie, I've set up a time for you to talk with your mother." Gil waited beside the lift for the wheelchair to reach the ground.

Eddie stared up at his father. "On the phone?"

"Yes, and I must tell you that I will be on the phone too." *Please don't fight me on this. I have to have protections in place somehow.*

"Does she want to talk with me?"

"Very much." But has she really changed? That was the question that dogged him day and night. His son looked mighty somber. Maybe he'd been having second thoughts too. Knowing Eddie, he'd mulled over every syllable of their conversation. "Do you want to talk with her?"

Eddie nodded but without a lot of force. "I-I think so."

Gil squatted down in front of the chair so he and Eddie were eye to eye. "You don't have to, do you understand that?" At his son's slight nod, Gil added, "I did this only because you seemed to want it so badly."

"I-I know that." Eddie had his elbows propped on the arms of his chair, rubbing his fingers together. When he looked up at his father, confusion darkened his eyes. "I'm sorry I was a brat."

"Oh, Eddie." Gil put his arms around his son and held him close. Eddie's arms circled his father's neck. "I really don't like it when you do the silent treatment, but I sure understood why you were upset. Please forgive me for . . . for handling this so poorly." *Lord, thank you for healing my mistakes.* "Eddie, I know I say this often, but please understand that I truly want to do what is best for you and me, our family."

Eddie nodded and wiped his eyes on his father's sweater-covered shoulder. "So, when do I talk with her?"

"I figured Saturday would be a good time."

"But Maggie and I are giving Breaking Free a bath that day."

"It'll be in the evening."

They turned as the front door opened and Bonnie charged down the ramp and up to the chair, woofing and yipping her delight, wriggling all over and making sure both her men got drooly greetings.

Gil stood and wiped his cheek with his handkerchief and then extended the cloth to Eddie who mopped up, giggling all the while.

"Let's go ride, huh, Bonnie?" He headed for the ramp to the house, leaving Gil to reset the lift and close the van doors. And be grateful.

By the time Gil got to the barn, he was ready to rip into both Eddie and Maggie for not minding the rule. But he stopped when he heard Eddie mention a phone call. He paused in the doorway, not intentionally eavesdropping but hesitating to interrupt as his curiosity got the better of him.

"So I get to talk to her tomorrow night." Eddie paused. "So what do you say to your mother when you are eleven years old and you don't remember ever seeing her?"

Good question, son. Gil rubbed the back of his neck. Did Eddie not trust him well enough to ask him that question?

"Good question." She paused. "I don't know, Eddie, I mean . . ." Another pause stretched before she began again. "I guess if it were me, I-I'd make a list of the things I wanted to know. I always used to make a lot of lists."

Was that pain he heard in her hesitating voice? When he gave himself a moment to think on what he knew of her past . . . how could she talk so gently with his persistent son?

"Way cool. I hope she doesn't get all mushy."

Gil nearly chuckled. He hoped so too, for Eddie's sake. Maybe he should warn Sandra. He shook his head, no way. She asked for this, let her deal with her forthright son. He strolled up to them.

Maggie nodded a greeting and handed him a brush. "Here, you need to learn how to groom a horse too."

Her business-like tone didn't match the clouds in her eyes. He nodded. "Thanks, I guess."

"For when you own one." Eddie grinned at his father, lifting one eyebrow and wiggling it, a trick he'd practiced until he perfected it.

"Who said I was going to get another horse?" He watched how Eddie brushed the horse's coat and did the same.

"Always go with the direction of the hair," Eddie advised and then added, "Well, we could go riding together and if you didn't want to ride all the time, Maggie could go with me."

"Since when are you ready for trail riding?"

"I will be."

When Gil glanced at her, Maggie looked the other way. He knew she was enjoying this conversation and yet — he realized something. Maggie never smiled. What would it take to make Maggie smile?

"Okay, so if we got another horse and you note, I said if. A big if." Eddie kept brushing, so Gil continued, "What kind of horse should we possibly, maybe, perhaps, think about?"

"You could always get another Thoroughbred at Los Lomas." Maggie dumped her brush in the bucket and motioned for her two helpers to do the same. "How about you learn to saddle a horse today too?"

"Everything in one day?"

Eddie hooted. Bonnie yipped, and he could swear Breaking Free was laughing too. But while Maggie's eyes glinted, her mouth remained . . . what, frozen? Surely she had a sense of humor in there somewhere.

Step by step she showed him what to do then stood back and let him do it. Pad first, stirrups crossed over the seat, make sure the saddle is exactly in the right place, then buckle the girth and let the stirrups down.

"Good job." Maggie looped the bridle over her arm and proceeded to do the same procedure. "Remember when you take the halter off to buckle it around his neck so he is never left unrestrained."

He remembered the lesson from the other day regarding the proper method of tying and untying a horse.

With Breaking Free tacked up, they helped Eddie mount, and she had Gil lead the horse out of the barn and to the round pen where they repeated the lessons from the day before with both Gil and Maggie working as escorts. Keeping his full concentration on his son was not easy. Thoughts of Maggie kept slipping under his guard. At one point they stopped and he listened as she asked Eddie what other verbal commands she should be teaching Breaking Free. His son proved again how knowledgeable he had become, making Gil's chest puff in pride.

"How about coming to the house for dinner?" he asked when they were putting Breaking Free out in the pasture.

"All right, thank you."

"Good, maybe you can play Xbox with me." Eddie slapped his hands on the chair arms.

"Xbox?"

"You'll be sorry," Gil murmured.

She glanced from father to son. "Is this some rite of passage or something?"

"You'll sec."

Later after dinner, Eddie rolled into the kitchen where Maggie was helping Maria clean up the kitchen. "You ready for Xbox?"

Maggie stared at him a moment. "I guess."

"Come on. We can play on the one in the family room."

Maria leaned closer. "He beat your socks off. Be careful."

What have I gotten myself into? Maggie wondered as she followed the wheelchair into the family room. Sitting on the floor in front of the large television, Eddie handed her a controller.

"This is what you use to move around on the screen to attack and keep from getting shot out of the game."

"This sounds pretty bloodthirsty."

"It's good for eye/hand coordination."

She looked at him and shook her head, then stared at the thing in her hand. While she'd played earlier versions of video games when she was a teen, she knew the world of gaming had changed a lot in the years in between. "Couldn't we read a book instead?"

"Two people can't read a book at the same time."

"Sure they can if one reads to the other."

"Easier to listen to the book on audio." He pushed a button on his controller and an action game showed up on the screen.

She tried to listen as he explained the story and the rules, but her mind flipped back through the years to playing Candy Land and LEGOs with Charlie. He loved building towers and then smashing them. And he loved to be read to, enthralled with the pictures from the beginning with board books and as he grew older chanting the rhyming couplets after a few times through.

"Okay, you ready?"

Maggie came back to the room at the question and nodded.

Maria was right. Eddie beat her so badly that she vowed never to play again.

"How can you get good then?"

"What if I don't really care much about video games?"

"Well, Arthur can't come over often enough and Maria and Dad got tired of losing. Guess I'll just have to play by myself." Eddie assumed a doleful look that closely resembled Bonnie's, who as usual was lying right next to Eddie's chair, snoring away.

"Sorry, but I'd rather read a book." Would Charlie have become a master gamesman like Eddie? "I need to head home. Thanks for trying to teach me. Remember if the weather is warm, we're giving Freebee a bath."

"I know." He spun away from the television. "Maybe Dad will help."

Oh, I'm sure he's going to love that. But Maggie followed the chair back into the great room where Gil sat reading the paper.

He glanced up. "I warned you."

"I know. This is pretty hard on the ego."

"Don't let it bother you. He's beaten experts." Gil smiled at his son.

Maggie paused on her way to the door. "I have a favor to ask."

"What do you need?"

She cocked her head at the guarded tone but continued, "I'd like to research spina bifida. Do you have a computer I could borrow?"

"I'll see about a computer, but here . . ." He rose and went into his office, returning in a few minutes with an armful of books and pamphlets. He handed them to her. "You want a bag?"

"No, this is fine. Thanks." She nodded. "See you in the morning. After riding, you want to help us give Freebec a bath?"

"If it's warm enough," Eddie added.

Gil caught his breath along with the challenge in her eyes. "Ah, of course."

Bathing a horse was not Gil's first choice for a Saturday afternoon activity, but after the workout of the morning and lunch on the patio, he joined Maggie and Eddie at the barn.

"Putting a hot water tank out here was a good move," Maggie said as she unwound the hose she'd already attached to the faucet in the room next to the tack room. She'd set up the wash area on the gravel at the back of the barn.

"Thank Carly for all the right things in right places down here. She made me a list with instructions, then checked to make sure everything met her approval."

With Breaking Free cross-tied between two posts, Maggie handed Eddie the hose. "You soak him down and then we'll all soap him."

Bonnie backed out of the way as soon as the water spurted from the hose and went to lie in the shade. Eddie got as wet as the horse, and before they were done everyone needed dry clothes. Hearing Eddie laugh and tease made Gil's day.

"He enjoys this?" Gil inclined his head toward Breaking Free, all the while looking at Maggie.

"Of course he does. All this attention and the rubbing and scrubbing, it all feels great. Think how much you enjoy having your hair washed."

"You mean when someone else washes it?" Gil caught himself in a not really proper thought — he'd seen Maggie washing his hair in his mind's eye. Her strong fingers massaging his scalp would feel mighty good. Good thing she wasn't a mind reader.

She handed Eddie the hose. "Okay, let's rinse him off, then we use the scrapers to dry him." She handed Gil a tool that looked the same as a window squeegee. "You spray the horse, not the humans," she reminded Eddie as she and Gil wiped water off their faces.

"It was an accident." But the boy's eyes danced.

Maggie took the hose and rinsed off the horse's rump and along his topline since Eddie couldn't reach that high. "There now, scrape away. Eddie, let us do the top first, then you get the sides and legs."

"How come we don't use towels?" Eddie asked, waiting his turn.

"How many do you think it would take?"

"Oh, lots."

"Would you like to wash all those towels?"

"He'd let Maria do it." Gil's comment made Eddie giggle again.

When they were done, she unfolded the horse sheet and buckled it around Breaking Free. "That'll finish him off. Later we'll let him out in the pasture."

"So he can roll?" Eddie asked.

"But he'll get dirty again." Gil kept on coiling the hose and hung it over the rack on the wall.

"That's the way it goes."

Gil looked down at his wet clothes. "Come on, sport, let's go change."

By evening he could tell Eddie was getting more apprehensive by the minute. Instead of playing with Bonnie, he sat in his chair, staring out over the pasture. "You want to beat me at Xbox?" Gil asked.

"No thanks."

"Are you worried?"

Eddie nodded and then wrote something in his spiral-bound notebook.

At six-thirty, as arranged, Gil dialed the number and handed the phone to Eddie. "You can say good-bye any time you want to."

"I know." Eddie took the phone. When she answered, he said, "Hello, Mother" in the gravest tone.

Gil held the other phone to his ear.

"Oh, Eddie, I am so happy to be actually talking with you. How are you?"

"Fine." Eddie glanced down at the list. "Where do you live?"

"In Santa Barbara. Do you know where that is?"

"Yes, west of us, out at the beach."

"Why yes." She sounded surprised at his answer.

Gil turned his back so he could smile. She had no idea what a bright and articulate young man she was talking with.

"Do you have any other children?"

"No, I'm sorry to say I don't. Do you have other brothers or sisters?"

"No."

"You mean your dad never remarried?"

"No." He looked down at his list again after a glance at his father. "Do you like dogs?"

"Ah, well, I guess they're all right."

"Do you like horses?"

"I don't know, I've never had one, but they're awfully big."

Gil rolled his lips together. Unless she'd changed in that area too, Sandra had not been an animal lover.

"Do you have a cat?"

"No."

329

"A husband?"

"Yes, a very good man named Frank." A slight pause seemed longer. "Eddie, I would like to come and see you."

"I-I'll ask my dad."

You pushed him, Sandra, not a good move. Gil watched his son's face. A frown creased his forehead, under the lock of hair that insisted on flopping forward.

"Good-bye." Eddie set the phone down.

"Eddie?" Sandra sighed and hung up.

Gil set both phones back in their cradles and leaning against his desk watched his son.

Eddie rolled over to the window and sat looking out, his chin propped on one hand. When Bonnie laid her head on his knees, he stroked her head with his free hand. "I wanted to ask her why she left me, but I chickened out."

Gil felt his heart clench. If only she hadn't called and set all this in motion, bringing her son more hurt. For this wasn't a joyful reunion as far as he could see. "Do you want to see her?"

"Maybe." Eddie sighed. "It might be best." He turned and looked at his father. "She doesn't like dogs. And maybe not horses."

TWENTY-FIVE

"I talked to my mother on the phone last night." Eddie tossed the flakes of hay into Breaking Free's hay rack.

When he drove out of the stall, Maggie asked, "How did it go?"

"She doesn't like dogs."

Maggie looked from Eddie to Bonnie. That could indeed be a problem. "She hasn't met Bonnie yet." How could anyone not love Bonnie?

"And she said horses are awfully big. I don't think she likes horses either."

His matter-of-fact tone caught on Maggie's heart. "Did you ask her your questions?"

"Some. She doesn't have any other kids, lives in Santa Barbara, and is married to a man named Frank." Eddie stroked Bonnie's head. "She wants to see me."

Maggie turned off the water from filling the water bucket. "That's not surprising."

She fought to stay noncommittal when she wanted to call the woman up and give her an earful. At least she had the possibility of seeing her son. Sandra had chosen to leave her baby, not had him torn away from her. Deliberate versus accident. Either way they were both the losers.

"Here you are." Gil walked in wearing a frown. "I thought I told you to let me know when you were ready to come down here?"

"But you were busy on the phone, and I didn't want to interrupt you."

"Then you could have waited." His abrupt tone caused his son to look down and Maggie to send a hard look his way.

And here she thought he was beginning to loosen up. Ah well, she should have sent Eddie back, but the thought hadn't entered her head. All had been free and fun when they gave Freebee his bath. She glanced at the horse and saw his ears go back. A man was in the area with a harsh voice. "Ah . . ."

Gil turned to her. "What?"

She motioned to the horse who'd started twitching his tail. "He is reacting to your tone. Remember, men probably yelled at him. He's come a long way, but right now . . ."

"Eddie, get away from the stall." Gil didn't soften his voice.

Maggie gave him a nasty look and went to the stall door to take the horse's halter and murmur soothing words to him, stroking his neck all the while.

"See, this is one of the things I worry about. That horse is not dependable. That is why I don't want you down here alone."

"I wasn't alone, Maggie and Bonnie were here and we were fine until you growled."

"That's enough, Eddie."

Eddie spun his chair and headed out of the barn, Bonnie sending a reproachful glance over her shoulder as she went with him.

"What is the matter with you?" Maggie fought to keep her voice even and soft.

"I set up rules in the beginning, and I want them followed, that's all."

"Can we talk outside? There's no sense reminding Breaking Free that he doesn't trust men." *Or like them for that matter and right now I understand why.* She led the way out to see a glorious sunset gilding the tops of the hills and reflecting pink off the clouds straight above them. "Oh, isn't that beautiful?" Her voice reflected her awe at the way the sun tinged the western clouds in scarlet.

Gil rammed his hands in his back pockets.

Maggie drank in the peace of the moment before turning to Gil. "All right, we weren't careful about the rule. If it happens again, I will send Eddie back to the house for either you or Maria. Will that solve the problem?"

Gil stared at her for what seemed like a long moment, shook his head, and headed for the house.

"Tell Eddie I'll finish taking care of Breaking Free."

He waved a hand to signal he heard her and kept on pounding the walkway.

"I feel sorry for whatever thorn got stuck in that lion's paw." Maggie stared after him, shaking her head. Back in the barn she dug out a carrot from the fridge, broke it into pieces, and fed them to the horse, all the while continuing to stroke his neck and face. "I don't get it, fella. I just don't. But there's no sense in being angry at him you know, he's the boss."

Maggie retired to her trailer and after fixing something to eat propped the pillows up on her bed and picked a book off the stack on her nightstand — books on spina bifida, horse training, novels Maria had loaned her, and her Bible where the psalms calmed her in the night when she couldn't sleep. Tonight might be one of those nights, thanks to Gil Winters.

Too restless to read, she took out paper and pen and began the letter she'd been meaning to write.

Dear Kool Kat,

I'm sorry I've taken so long to write. I guess life is finally calming down so I can believe it is real. Breaking Free is making great progress. He and Eddie have become best buds, along with Bonnie, a basset hound assistant dog. She fetches and picks things up for Eddie, more a companion than a helper.

I live in a travel trailer by the barn, brand new, both trailer and barn. I cannot begin to describe the peace and comfort of quiet and freedom. I know you dream of this too, and I believe that somewhere there is a place for you working with horses. So learn all you can. I'll include a list of books that I've enjoyed and perhaps Mr. James can find some of them and add them to his bookshelf.

She went on to describe her average day, rejoicing again in the simplicity of it.

I've attended two AA meetings now. Maria takes me to a noon meeting and to see my parole officer, Mark Gillespie. He's a good guy. Greet the horses and Mr. James for me. I would enjoy hearing from you.

Your friend,
Maggie.

She made a list of books, reading down the spines of those on her nightstand, folded the two sheets of paper, and addressed the envelope. After fixing herself a cup of tea, she made herself comfortable again on the bed and immersed herself in a mystery. The ringing phone made her jump and be grateful her cup was empty or it would have been all over the bed.

"Hello?"

"Maggie, I'm sorry."

She held the receiver away from her ear and stared at it. Was she really hearing Gil Winters' voice?

"Maggie?"

"I'm here."

"You didn't answer."

"What did you want me to say?"

"That I'm forgiven would be good."

"You better ask for that from your son." *Whoa girl, you do have your dander up.* She must have been thinking about Kool Kat too much.

"What happened to the silent woman I brought back from Los Lomas?"

"She's breaking free."

His voice had changed back to the usual deep, slow timber. "I was a jerk."

"You'll get no argument from me."

"Eddie forgave me."

"Good. He sets a fine example."

"Is Breaking Free all right?"

"Bring lots of carrots and peppermint candies next time you come down to see him." Maggie slid down against her pillows. Did she dare ask what set him off or be content with the apology?

"I will. Sorry to bother you."

"No problem."

"Good night."

She responded in kind and hung up the phone. Talk about a weird evening.

The next morning when Maria took her to Rescue Ranch, Maggie got up the courage to ask for help.

"Sí, what do you need?"

"Next time before you go shopping, will you tell me who to call for an appointment to get my hair styled? Maybe next time you go to Bakersfield?"

"I go to Bakersfield on Friday, that be soon enough? But you get hair cut up here. I get the number for you."

"Thank you." Maggie lifted her cap and ran her fingers through her hair. "This needs help."

"We could go before I pick up Eddie at school. I call."

The next afternoon, Maggie kept wanting to look in the mirror on the van's visor when they joined the queue of mothers waiting to pick up their children at school. After a good conditioning and a decent cut, she couldn't believe the difference. She'd left the shop armed with hair care products and a tube of lipstick. Feathered back on the sides and moussed for body on top, her hair felt strange to even touch.

Eddie grinned when he saw her. "Look at you, Maggie. Like, wow."

She could feel the heat rising from her neck. When she'd looked in the mirror she'd seen vestiges of the young woman she had been before the night that changed her entire life in one instant.

"Wait until Dad sees you. He'll be impressed."

"Thanks, Eddie. You think Breaking Free will like it?"

His hoot made Maria chuckle too.

Maggie left her ball cap in the trailer and leaned against the fence, watching Breaking Free graze. As soon as he saw her he wandered over to the fence to snuffle her, but when he sniffed her hair, he backed up, rolled his lips back, mouth open in horsey signal of yuck.

"What's he doing?" Eddie called, rolling toward her as fast as he was able.

"He doesn't like my hair." Surely that feeling rising in her chest was plain old laughter, but it didn't make it all the way to her mouth. She paused. "Where's your dad?"

"He's coming." Eddie looked over his shoulder. No dad.

"You better go back."

Eddie rolled his eyes and still laughing, wheeled back toward the house where Gil was just coming out the door. "Dad, you missed Breaking Free. He made a funny face." He spun his chair. "Can you make him do it again, Maggie?"

Maggie shrugged and held out a carrot chunk. When Breaking Free came close, she bent her neck so he could sniff her hair, but he only took the carrot and ignored her. "Guess not."

Gil joined Eddie at the fence, but kept his gaze on Maggie. "I like your hair that way."

"Freebee didn't," Eddie replied.

"Thank you." Maggie kept from touching her hair by a swift order to keep still.

"You ready to ride, sport? I need to get back to work."

"You could always watch from the patio."

"No, he needs to be here as an aide." As they walked toward the barn, Breaking Free followed them to the gate and hung his head over the metal bars to greet first Bonnie, then Eddie.

With the three of them grooming him, it didn't take long. The dust rising made Eddie sneeze. "See, I told you he would roll and get all dirty again."

"That's a horse for you." Maggie agreed.

While the lesson went well, she could tell Gil was impatient to get back to the house so she said she'd do the night chores.

"But I . . ." Eddie caught a look from his father, patted his horse's face, and dolefully wheeled away.

Gil stopped and turned. "I'd better tell you. I'll be away for the next three days so you and Maria will have to work things out. And Sandra, Eddie's mother, is coming for a visit at lunchtime on Saturday. You have my cell number on the pad in your trailer."

"Have a good trip."

The next day Maggie and Eddie were grooming Breaking Free and Maria was planting rust and yellow chrysanthemums in a half barrel in front of the barn to celebrate October. Maggie mentioned how calm he was now compared to how wild he had been.

"So what did you do?" Eddie stopped brushing.

"I spent a lot of time with him. The warden said he'd be put down if he couldn't learn to behave so we worked really hard. The day that I got him to follow me in the round pen, we were doing a drill called joining up or natural horsemanship."

"So what happened?"

"He came to me and followed me around like Bonnie does you."

"I want to do that. Can I?"

Maggie paused. Did natural horsemanship take a person with two good legs or could Eddie do it? "Well, you're good with your wheelchair, but you can't flick a rope and turn at the same time. But you could turn, pause, and then flick." She narrowed her eyes. Did she dare let Eddie try this? It wasn't as if they were working with a wild horse. Nor a fear-crazed one like Breaking Free was in the beginning. But wasn't life like that, take away the fear and everything worked better?

"Please, Maggie." Eddie's desire made her chew on her bottom lip.

"Let me think on it some more, and if I can figure out a way, we'll give it a try."

The shine in his eyes and the grin that stretched his cheeks were all the impetus she needed. But the question remained, would he be safe?

The next afternoon she took Eddie into the round pen and had him practice turning his wheelchair and flicking the rope. "You have to keep your attention on the horse at all times, so I'll be the horse and you keep doing the turn and flick." She trotted around the pen and when she slowed, he flicked the rope.

"Now you have to watch Breaking Free closely; he'll give you the signals to tell you when he is ready to join up with you. When he hangs his head and he licks his lips, he's getting ready. You'll need to watch his eyes and when he starts throwing you glances, you lower your arms. When he comes toward you, turn away and let him follow." By the time they had finished the trial exercise, both she and Eddie were exhausted.

Maggie fought with herself during the night over the wisdom of offering Eddie this chance. If it worked, his confidence would soar. If it didn't, he could get hurt.

That afternoon Eddie raced up to the barn. "I'm ready."

She led Breaking Free out and with Maria along they headed for the round pen. They could hear Bonnie's plaintive howl from the house. She did not like being locked up and left behind. With Eddie and the rope in the center of the pen, Maggie walked Breaking Free to the rails and let him go. When she waved her arms, the horse tossed his head and broke into a trot, then a canter. When he turned to the center, Eddie flicked the rope at him, and the action sent him back to the rails. The circular dance continued for three rounds before the horse started looking at Eddie, then slowed and sure enough licked his lips. At Maggie's quiet command Eddie quit flicking the rope, and Breaking Free turned to look at him. He took three steps forward so Eddie turned his chair and rolled a few paces away. Breaking Free followed.

When Eddie stopped, the horse stopped. The boy turned and offered Breaking Free a carrot chunk and then rubbed between his eyes and under the black forelock.

"You like me, huh, big horse?" He raised his arms, and Breaking Free allowed himself to be hugged by a small boy in a wheelchair.

Maggie didn't bother to fight the tears, especially when she saw Maria's tear-streaked face.

"You mean I could do this with any horse?" Eddie asked when she saddled up for his riding time.

"I don't know why not. Although Freebee already was your friend, so other horses might not respond so quickly."

"I want my dad to do this when he gets his horse."

"That would be good." *Please, Eddie, don't go getting your hopes up too much. But then, when this kid prays for something, it seems to happen. Perhaps there is a lesson there for me.*

"Thank you, Maggie." He looked away, then bent his head. "I wish you were my mom."

Twenty-Six

Saturday morning Gil met Maggie at the barn, without his son.

Uh oh, Eddie told him about joining up. "Good morning, did you have a good trip?" Maggie kept cleaning the stall.

"I did. But I have a question for you."

"Oh."

"Why did you choose to do the joining up exercise when I wasn't here?"

Maggie knew this was coming. Why hadn't she waited? "I went with it because it was something that would bolster Eddie's confidence, and he wanted to do it so badly I couldn't say no."

"Even if it could have injured him?" His eyes narrowed and his tone bit.

"I knew it was safe and it was. He already has such a good relationship with Breaking Free that this was more for his benefit than for the horse's." She leaned her fork against the wall and trundled the wheelbarrow past him. "Gil, if you want me to help your son the best I can, you have to learn to trust my judgment." *Even if I am an ex-con.*

He was gone when she returned to the barn.

She stared toward the house and watched him lean down to pat Bonnie before striding through the door. Well, I'll be . . . either he was too angry to talk with her, or he wanted to think on it, or he had decided to trust her. Now if he'd only do the same with The Rule, as she'd come to call it.

Bonnie whined at the gate, then yipped. Maggie heard Eddie call her into the house. All the normal morning noises. Eddie would be down to ride pretty soon. She figured Maria would be making something special for the big lunch. But not a normal Saturday morning, that was for sure. Maybe she'd just take Breaking Free out for a ride on the horse trail.

Later when he was mounted, Eddie looked down at Maggie. "I want to ride by myself." The set of his chin told her he was in a bulldog mood. She'd seen it happen only once before.

"Eddie." Gil's voice also wore an undertone of — what? Stress? Anger at her? Or most likely, he dreaded Sandra's visit as much as Eddie did.

Play it cool, Roberts. "Look, I have an idea. Instead of riding in the round pen today, why don't we go out in the pasture? I'll lead and your dad can be the aide." *Please agree, Gil. We can diffuse some of the tension here before it gets to the horse too.*

"Can we?" Eddie's smile came back. He grinned at Maggie and looked toward his father.

"I guess so, if Maggie believes it is safe."

Surely Eddie wouldn't notice the slightly sarcastic tone in his voice, Maggie thought. "Good, let me go get a lead shank and that way you can continue to hold the reins."

Walking in the pasture did indeed make a difference. Breaking Free nodded along with his nose by her shoulder. Maggie didn't dare turn around to see how Gil was doing. Why was it she could sense his feelings so easily? Like she had special Gil Winters radar. Breaking Free pricked his ears at kids playing ball in a field one over from theirs and stopped to look at a cat strolling along the top of the board fence. Maggie gave him plenty of time to look.

She looked up at Eddie. "See, when he reacts to something, you let him look until he relaxes again."

"Good thing Bonnie isn't along. She'd go after that cat." Eddie leaned forward and

347

patted his horse's shoulder. "Good boy." Breaking Free snorted, and Maggie walked forward again.

"The snort was his sign?" Eddie asked.

"One of them. What did his ears do?"

"Ah, I forgot to look. Sorry." Going back up toward the house, Eddie looked down at his father. "How much time?"

Gil checked his watch. "An hour. But you need to get cleaned up."

"Can Maggie come to lunch too?"

"I think it might be better, sport, with just us this time."

Maggie breathed a sigh of relief.

"Can we bring Mother down to see Breaking Free? Maybe she could watch me ride?"

"We'll suggest that."

"She could help me brush him."

Gil choked back a laugh. "We'll see."

When the doorbell rang at exactly noon, Gil motioned for Eddie to join him. With both Eddie and Bonnie at his side, Gil paused for a moment, gathered a breath, and reached for the doorknob. He plastered a smile on his face, winked at his son, and opened the door.

"Hello, Sandra. Come on in." His insides were screaming, *Go away, don't do this.* He stepped back and motioned her in. "Eddie, this is your mother." She was still beautiful, but in a used sort of way; her smile seemed forced. Most likely she was as uptight about this whole thing as he was.

"Hello, Eddie." Her voice was still musical, although he figured the deepness and slight rasp were probably the price she paid for smoking. He could smell cigarette smoke on her, overlaid with the musky perfume she'd always preferred.

"Hello, Mother." Eddie nodded with a slight smile.

"It's good to see you." She glanced at Gil, obviously a plea for help.

"Maria has lunch all ready. We'll be eating on the patio since it is such a nice day. The restroom is the first door on the left."

"Thank you." She handed him a shopping bag with wrapped packages. "I brought some things."

"This is Bonnie, she's my assistance dog." Eddie stroked Bonnie's head.

"Oh, well, I'm glad to meet you, Bonnie." Sandra smiled and reached to pat Bonnie's head, but the basset drew back.

"You should always let a dog sniff your hand before you try to pet them," her son explained.

"Oh, I see. Well, I'm not very conversant with proper dog procedures." She stepped to the side and around the dog and the wheelchair. "I'll be back in a moment."

Gil watched her walk down the hall. Matching cream silk slacks and long-sleeved shirt with an abundance of gold at her throat, ears, and wrists, and she was wearing high heels. Not the best thing for a trek out to the barn, but so be it. Hair cut so it swung just so and lightened to ash blonde, makeup that didn't quite disguise the wrinkles at the eyes and lips. Just what he'd expected.

"She's pretty."

He ruffled his son's hair. "Yes, she is. Let's go help Maria carry the trays out."

He heard her high heels first on the tile floors, then on the hardwood. She greeted Maria who managed to be barely polite and followed her out to the patio.

"You have a lovely house, Gil, but then I am not surprised. I've watched your career take off and soar. Congratulations."

"Thank you. Would you like some of Maria's marvelous lemonade? We don't drink much sangria around here any longer."

"That's a shame — Maria made such great sangria. But then I don't drink it or anything alcoholic any more either." She took the tall glass tinged a deep red by the syrup Maria added and held it while smiling at Eddie. "I brought you a couple of things for your birthday." She nodded to the bag Gil had set on a chair by the table.

"That's very nice of you. Thank you." Eddie glanced to the bag, took his glass of lemonade, and after a sip looked to his father.

"Go ahead and open them, Eddie."

The blue package was a Game Boy. He smiled. "Thank you." And didn't tell her he already had one. The last package was a digital camera, small enough to fit in the pouch were he kept dog treats. "Thank you very much. I'll send you a picture of me and Bonnie and Breaking Free."

"Why Eddie, that is so sweet." She glanced at Gil. "He is so polite."

He's also sitting right there. Don't talk around him. Gil had a hard time just nodding.

Eddie put the gifts back in the bag and asked, "Do you live on the beach at Santa Barbara?"

"Close to it. Frank and I usually walk on the beach every day. You could come . . . ah, well, I guess your wheelchair wouldn't make it through the soft sand."

"Probably not."

Gil glanced at his son who was very carefully not looking at his father. He'd seen

Eddie plow through sand, over rocks, and through mud puddles. Only solid barriers like concrete walls stopped him. And when he needed help, he asked.

"Lunch is served." Maria set the basket of fresh baked rolls on the table.

Eddie rolled his chair to the empty space, and Gil motioned for Sandra to sit between him and Eddie.

"This looks wonderful," Sandra gushed as she sat down. "You always were a marvelous cook, Maria. Do you still make those wonderful enchiladas?"

"Sí." Instead of sitting down, Maria turned toward the house. She'd not set a place for herself; a definite sign she wanted no part of this *family* meal.

Gil took his place and spread his napkin in his lap. Sandra was trying far too hard. He thought of warning her, but then dismissed the idea. His ex-wife was an adult, and she was the one who wanted to come here. A shame she wouldn't see his home and family at their usual hospitable best. He dished up the chicken salad and fruit platter and handed the plates to his guest and son before passing the basket of rolls.

"I've always remembered Maria's fresh, homemade rolls. That was nice of her to make them for today."

Gil let that go by. Reminding him of earlier years together was not a good move on her part.

"So, Eddie, how is school going? You're in what, the fourth grade?"

"No, fifth."

"Oh. What do you like best?"

"About everything. I read a lot, and I write on the computer."

"Eddie is a very good student, pulls straight A's, and is a member of the debating club." Pride made Gil smile at his son's accomplishments.

"What school do you go to?"

"Pine Hills Christian Academy." Eddie slipped Bonnie a bite of chicken and let her lick his fingers.

She frowned, but turned to Gil. "I read that you are thinking of writing a book."

"Just thinking about it. I have a publisher who has been encouraging me." He caught Eddie's look of surprise. He should have already mentioned it to his son.

"Would you like to come see me ride this afternoon?" Eddie asked.

"Oh, you have a pony?"

"Not exactly." Eddie rolled his eyes toward his father. "Breaking Free is a retired racing Thoroughbred. Dad and I adopted him from the Thoroughbred Retirement Foundation."

Gil kept his smile inside but wanted to high-five his son.

Eddie looked politely at his mother. "Do you like to ride?"

"I don't think so. Horses are so . . . so big, you know." She looked to Gil. "Are you sure a horse like that is safe for-for someone in-ah, like Eddie?"

Gil's mouth smiled, but his eyes didn't. "You can be sure I am most careful with my son." Emphasis on *my.*

"Oh, I didn't mean to imply you weren't, but an ex-racehorse?"

"He's retired." Eddie's answer lay flat on the table.

Sandra looked down to see Bonnie looking up at her, a blob of drool dropped from her chops and onto the cream colored pants. "Oh, look what you have done!" Sandra dabbed at the spot with her napkin, making a face as she did so.

"Come on, Bonnie." Eddie pushed his chair back. "Please excuse us." Without waiting for permission, Eddie wheeled up the ramp and into the house, the dog trotting beside him.

"I've hurt his feelings, I'm so sorry."

"You owe him the apology, not me." Gil let her dip her napkin in her water glass and dab at the spot on her trousers. Wait until her heels sank into the lawn and the gravel.

"I'll do that later." She laid her napkin on the table. "Gil, sometime I'd love to take Eddie to El Capitan Theatre for the release of one of the children's movies."

"I think not." Gil leaned back in his chair, his salad half eaten. "Let's talk straight, Sandra. You said you no longer drink or do drugs?"

"That's right. I still attend weekly AA meetings, and I've been clean and sober for two years. I got my driver's license back . . ."

His eyebrows went up.

"Well, I had a slight accident. But that turned my life around and helped me realize that I made some pretty big mistakes, all thanks to-to my illness."

"Illness?"

"Well, you know substance abuse is an illness. And I'm glad to say that day by day, I've stayed in recovery."

Lady, you say all the right words, but . . . "I see. Well, I have a policy of not letting Eddie ride with strangers."

She leaned forward and extended one manicured hand. "I don't want to be a stranger any longer, Gil. I want to be his mother, at least as much as you will allow me to be."

Was she really this sincere or had her acting skills improved through the years?

"I-I think I'd better be going. It's a long drive home, and Frank doesn't like me on the freeways late in the day." She pushed back her chair. "Thank you for letting me come. I'll be in contact." She motioned to the gifts. "I hope he likes them."

"I'll get Eddie." Gil stood before she did. Nothing like here's your hat, what's your hurry. He met her at the front door, Eddie beside him.

"Thank you for the presents. I'm sorry you can't stay to see me ride."

"I'll come another day."

"We'll set something up. Perhaps Frank would like to come too."

She extended her hand to her son. "I'm sorry I was upset with Molly. I-I'm just not used to dogs."

"It's Bonnie." Eddie's jaw tightened, and he shook her hand. "Thank you for coming." Father and son watched her walk down the ramp and to her car where she turned and waved. They waved back and waited until she was backing out before closing the door.

"She should have worn khakis like Maggie does." Eddie heaved a sigh. "I'm glad that is over."

"You did well, son."

"She really doesn't like Bonnie."

"Her loss. Let's go swimming."

"Can we invite Maggie?"

"I think she's riding."

"Oh. Just think, if we had two more horses, we could all ride together."

"Two more now?" Gil rolled his eyes and made Eddie grin. "You think Maggie would be a good enough teacher to teach me to ride?"

"She could try." Eddie ducked away from his father's fake punch and sped down the hall to change.

Wouldn't it be nice if Sandra had her fill and never came back? *Dream on, Winters.*

TWENTY-SEVEN

Riding while Gil, Eddie, and their guest ate lunch seemed a good way to keep herself from stewing. She'd taken Breaking Free out on the trails before to make sure the horse would behave in different circumstances than the round pen. He ignored barking dogs, but shied at shadows until she gave him time to see there was nothing to be afraid of, and finally he enjoyed the rides as much as she did. Like today. She stood straight in her stirrups, stretching her legs, and inhaling fall, the scents of dried grass and pine pitch and freedom.

While paying attention to her horse, she also let her mind roam. If Gil adopted another Thoroughbred or any horse, she could ride with Eddie. She looked up and ahead to see the ravens that scolded her from the tops of the pine trees, while around her scrub jays and sparrows flitted through the brush. A family of California quail ignored both horse and rider, fluffing their feathers in the dust baths beside the trail, chattering like the giggle of little girls.

On the way home she saw a roadrunner running head forward, tail straight back and then turning into a stick when it stopped, totally melded with the grass and weeds. *How Eddie would love to see all this,* she thought as she patted her horse's shoulder. Never would she have dreamed that the horse that had once tried to slam her into a wall and raked her shoulder would become such a steady friend and companion.

Hard to believe it was mid October, the weather had remained so nice. While she'd not left Breaking Free outside overnight, she'd thought about it. Maybe she should mention it to Gil.

She took the drive to the barn, noticing that the guest's car was no longer in the driveway. That hadn't been a very long visit, especially when the woman had come so far. As soon as he saw her, Eddie and Bonnie blew through the yard gate and along the path to the barn.

"Did you have a good ride?" he called before he stopped far enough away to avoid startling Breaking Free. Bonnie felt no such restrictions, sitting up for her mutual greeting. She gave her equine friend a quick nose lick, and when he snorted she dropped to all fours and shook her head.

Eddie giggled and drove up to hand his peppermint candy to the horse. "Did you have fun?"

"We did. We even saw a roadrunner, until he camouflaged himself. They are amazing creatures."

"Did Breaking Free spook?"

"Not once. He likes looking around though. One of these days I'll lead you along that path so you can see the same things we did."

"Dad and I've walked up that direction sometimes. Up until the trail gets too steep. But we never saw a roadrunner. Beep-beep."

Maggie paused. "I'm sorry, Eddie, but you better go ask your dad or Maria to come down here with you."

"Oh yeah. Come on, Bonnie." He turned with a grimace and headed back to the house.

"What a stupid rule," she muttered to the horse.

Eddie and his father wandered down to the barn a few minutes later and helped her finish brushing Breaking Free. When they let him loose in the pasture, he ran the perimeter of the fence, dropped to roll, and then began grazing.

"He does the same thing every time," Eddie said, peering through the rails.

"Horses are like that."

"So are people pretty much, unless they make a concentrated effort to change." Gil turned his head to glance at Maggie.

She could feel his look, but stared straight ahead. What was happening that she could feel his look and sense when he was near? Her thoughts roamed around what he'd said and added, *Or some tragedy happens and they have no choice.*

"Maggie, Eddie and I've been talking and I think he's right. Now that he can ride alone in the round pen, you don't really need me down here, or Maria."

Maggie stared at him. "Thank you." So she'd finally gained his trust. She knew she should be more pleased but acceptance was enough for now.

A week later Gil was out of town giving a presentation when Bonnie announced a visitor. Eddie and Maggie were working in the riding corral when a cheery voice caught their attention.

"Hello, I've come to see you ride." Sandra waved from the side of the newly finished riding corral, which was much larger than the round pen.

"Hello, Mother." Eddie smiled politely.

361

"Mother sounds so formal, Eddie. I'd love it if you called me Mom like other kids do."

Eddie nodded.

Maggie could tell by the look on his face that he had no intentions of calling her by the more common nickname. The boy who made friends with everyone was not showing the affable side of himself in this situation. She wanted to tell the woman "don't push" but decided to keep her mouth shut too. After all, she was only the horse trainer, not the mediator in a family brouhaha. But it made her wonder what had gone on. Eddie had described the first visit with his mother in very uncomplimentary terms.

"And you must be Maggie. I'm Sandra, Eddie's mother."

Maggie nodded. "I'm pleased to meet you." Sandra was pretty as Eddie had said, but she looked worn about the edges other than her jeans that looked like she'd removed the price tag just before putting them on. Gil hadn't said she was coming. Did he know she was here?

Everyone was on alert, even Breaking Free and Bonnie. Of course animals were usually far more perceptive than humans anyway. She remembered Mr. James saying "horses never lie." In this case, both of these animals were protecting Eddie.

But protecting him from what? Should she ask Maria? *Don't get involved. Just get through.* The words echoed in her mind. That was advice for a woman in prison. When would she be free of needing that advice? *Mrs. Worth, I need your wisdom right about now.*

"Okay, Eddie, once around the arena, walk, reverse, and repeat it going the opposite direction. Pay attention to your posture, your hands. Make sure Breaking Free keeps an even stride and a nice distance away from the rail. Any questions?"

He grinned at her and touched the rim of his helmet with one finger. "Walk, Freebee."

The horse stepped out, the very picture of relaxation. Eddie, with his legs in the casings and his booted feet in the stirrups looked as comfortable as the horse. Obviously, he was no longer concerned about the unexpected visitor.

Maggie stayed in the center of the ring, mainly so she didn't have to talk with Sandra and wouldn't be as easily distracted. "Don't let him go to sleep on you."

The only place Freebee eased away from the rail was when he walked past Sandra.

Bonnie whined at Maggie's feet. From the first day of training in the bigger arena, Bonnie had decided this was her proper place.

Part of the time she watched Eddie on his horse, part of the time she did her basset thing — slept. "What is it, girl?" Maggie leaned down and patted her russet head. "You are one beautiful dog, you know that?" She stroked down the black back. As a tricolor, Bonnie had beautiful markings, including her white feet which changed color when she insisted on coming into the sandy arena. No wonder she'd been a champion show dog in her younger life.

"All right, Eddie, pick up a trot and do the same thing again — once around, turn and reverse." Since the boy had no leg power, he sat the trot rather than posting. Good thing his horse was easy on the gaits, unless he got excited. Maggie remembered him trotting hard and high, not comfortable but sure flashy.

When would she be able to put them in a ring with other riders, like in a preshow so they would know what to do? She glanced over to find Sandra was no longer standing at the rail. Where had she gone? "All right, Eddie, when you get back to your starting point, ride diagonals at a walk, straight across, turn and take the next one going back, just like we did the other day. You remember?"

"Yes."

"Are you all right?"

He nodded. But something was bothering him — he kept looking around the arena and back at her. Breaking Free had raised his head and swished his tail.

Maggie signaled them in to the center. "Okay, what's wrong?"

"Where did she go?"

"I don't know. You want me to go check?"

"Please."

"You stay right here in the middle then. I'll be right back." She debated leaving them. Eddie always rode supervised. But getting him on and off was rather a major operation, especially for just this brief moment. "You call if you need anything."

"Maggie, I'm not three years old."

She nodded, giving him a raised eyebrows salute. "Be right back."

She trotted to the barn, seeing Sandra's car where she'd parked it. "Sandra?" She looked in the tack room, checked the stall. "Sandra?"

"In here." The answer came from the bathroom on the far side of the tack room. Gil had one installed with deep sinks for washing gear, a commode, and cabinets for storing supplies.

"Oh, sorry. Eddie was concerned about you." Was that a cabinet door she heard closing? What was the woman looking for anyway? "Do you need anything?"

"No thank you." The toilet flushed.

I must be paranoid. Not surprising. She still watched her back and made sure nothing was left out that could be stolen. "If you're all right, I'll be back out in the ring with Eddie." She strode out of the barn and waved an all right to the boy on the horse, then signaled them around again. Bonnie met her at the fence, watching the barn. Maggie turned to see Sandra strolling out into the sunshine.

Maggie had Eddie back up his horse, walk three paces forward, and back again. Then they came to stand in front of her. "You two might have been riding together for years rather than weeks."

"He's a supremo horse. Maggie, did you ever think he would be like this?"

Maggie shook her head. "No, 'cause I saw them unload him when he first came to Los Lomas. And my shoulder is still a bit tender where he ripped into me."

"And you never told anyone?"

"Just you." Eddie had grilled her about every detail of Breaking Free's care and actions so she finally told him. She made him promise never to tell anyone. Although she knew if Gil ever asked her, she'd tell him.

"I trust him."

"And he trusts you. That's what makes the two of you so good together."

"I'm getting stronger."

"I think so too. Probably because you're riding every day." Maggie glanced at her watch. "Maria will have lunch ready in half an hour. Let's put him away."

"Will you swim with me this afternoon?"

"You don't want to ask your mother?"

Stiffness dropped across his face. "I could, but maybe she doesn't swim. You do, and you know my dad won't let me go in alone."

"Ask her. That would be the polite thing to do."

"All right," came out on a long drawn out sigh.

"Are you finished riding?" Sandra asked as Maggie opened the gate.

"Yes."

"Mother, would you like to stay for lunch?"

"Oh, I'd love to. Thank you, Eddie, for asking."

"And you'll come too, Maggie?" Maggie nodded, then gave a speaking glance to Eddie.

He sighed again, but this time only a little one. "I'm going swimming this afternoon if you'd like to come, Mother."

"Oh, well, I — I didn't come prepared to swim."

"Gee, that's too bad."

Maggie rolled her lips together, but kept quiet. Eddie knew there were various sizes of swimsuits for guests in the cabana, but if he didn't want to tell his mother, she for shooting sure wasn't going to.

Instead of staying for a longer visit, Sandra left shortly after lunch. It was a rather strange meal. If Eddie or Maggie asked a question, Sandra went on and on without ever giving the others a chance to join in. Maria spent her time sending their guest daggered looks. Both Eddie and Maggie breathed sighs of relief when the woman finally went out the door.

"She not to be here." Maria propped hands on her hips and glared at Maggie.

"Maggie didn't ask her to stay, I did." Eddie wheeled his chair to the window, as if making sure the car and driver had left.

"But why?"

"Because Dad always says to be polite. It was lunchtime and she was here."

"You did well, Eddie." Maggie joined him at the window. Should she tell him or Gil the woman was a snoop? She'd been snooping in the tack room, and she'd heard her investigating the cupboards in the bathroom.

"She be back, you watch." Maria turned back to the kitchen. "I don't trust her. Not farther than I can throw that horse."

Eddie chuckled. "That horse could throw you."

"I know he could, and you too, chico. You be careful."

"Breaking Free won't throw me." Eddie's smile lit his face. "He's my friend."

"He's a horse."

"Not intentionally he won't, but accidents do happen." Maggie supported the housekeeper's admonition. *Do I ever know that accidents can happen.* The thought of Eddie being injured made her want to shield him from all harm, especially his mother. Why did she have the feeling Eddie needed protection from Sandra? She knew there was more story to this whole thing, but Gil and Eddie were entitled to their secrets like she was entitled to hers. "Aren't you going swimming?"

"Later."

"Then I think I'll go get some things done at my house. Call me when you want to swim, and I'll come watch."

"Don't you like to swim?"

"Yes, but . . ." But what? *You know you*

could use one of those suits from the cabana. One of these days you are going to have to go shopping. Two pairs of jeans, one pair shorts, khakis, and a couple of T-shirts were not an adequate wardrobe. It was past time to go see her attorney and find out the state of her finances and, the most horrendous of all, go see the grave. "I'll see you later. Page me when you need me."

Maggie left the house and strode down the path like she was stamping snakes. Why did the miserable thoughts have to intrude and spoil what might have been a perfect day — had Sandra not arrived? She said she wanted to visit with Eddie, but spent half the time in the barn. Or had she gone to the car? And if so, for what?

A little nip, do you suppose?

The thought made her stop. Why would she even think that? Because of all the stories she'd heard at AA meetings. Perhaps the nonstop talking at lunch was the product of a few pulls on the bottle or a pill or two. She'd not smelled liquor on the woman's breath, but she'd come back chewing gum.

Had Gil said anything about his ex-wife having an alcohol problem? Maggie racked her brain, sorting through any conversations or wisps of dialogue. Not that she knew much of what had gone on. Perhaps it was time to start asking questions. Perhaps it was better to continue playing ostrich with her head in the sand.

The next morning Gil joined her at the barn before Eddie would be up. "I hear you had a visitor yesterday."

"We were pretty surprised." Maggie put Breaking Free's hoof back down and stuck the pick in her rear pocket. "She acted like you'd invited her to drop in any time."

"Suffice to say I didn't, but it sounds like you all handled it very well."

"You should be really proud of Eddie. He invited her to stay for lunch and even invited her to go swimming, but he didn't push when she brushed that off." *Do I mention my thoughts about Sandra or . . . ?* Keeping a low profile won out.

"I hear she disappeared into the barn for quite awhile."

Maggie nodded. "Has she had a drinking problem?" The words slipped out before she could catch them.

"Yes, why do you ask?"

"I'm not sure. Just a hunch, I guess."

"Well, trust your hunches. I don't want her around here when I'm not here. I'll make that clear to her next time I speak with her on the phone. There will be no more drop in visits." He started to leave, then turned back. "I forgot to tell you, the contractor turned the keys to the office over to me. You want to go look at your new quarters?"

Maggie shrugged. "The trailer is really comfortable. And near the barn."

"I hope you'll like this better. We need to get some furnishings so the move won't be right away. If you don't have anything planned, we could all go shopping tomorrow. Maria is planning on spending the day with Enrico so we'll eat out."

"All right." *Come on, Roberts, all he asked was for you to go shopping with them. Surely you can manage that. After all, you work at Rescue Ranch all the time — there are lots of people there. This will be a good test for you.* Like she wanted a test. The argument continued as she finished picking hooves and let Breaking Free loose in the pasture. Right now she wished someone would let her loose.

To her surprise, everyone had a good time shopping. Eddie made her lie back on the beds to make sure she got one she liked. Both he and Gil helped her choose a chest of drawers, a small drop-leaf table and two chairs, lamps, and linens.

"I think a recliner would be a good idea," Gil advised. So they tried out recliners. One tilted back so fast it nearly threw her overboard, which made Eddie tease her about how she could ride a horse and fall out of a chair.

"You need a television with Xbox so you can get good."

"Like I need a hole in the head."

"A bookshelf would make a good room divider."

"For what, my three books?"

"No pictures? Collectibles?" Gil motioned toward a display.

"Actually, I have pictures and some personal things stored at my attorney's office. I need to go talk with her one of these days."

"Where is she located?" Gil stopped at a variety of end tables. "How about one of these by the chair?"

Maggie shrugged. "I guess so. That's one of the things I like about the trailer, all the furniture is right there." She nodded when he pointed at an oak table with a lower shelf and a drawer. "She's . . . my attorney's office is down in Long Beach. Please, haven't we bought enough?"

"You don't want any art for the walls?"

No, I just want to go home. She shook her head.

"If you like, I'll take you down to see your attorney. We just have to figure out a time."

"You would? I mean, you could take me to Bakersfield and I could take a bus."

"No, this would be easier."

"I'm hungry, Dad."

Saved by a boy who looked at her as if he knew exactly how she felt. Thank God for Eddie.

After they were seated at a table in the restaurant and had ordered, Gil looked from Eddie to Maggie, his fingers templed under his chin. "I have something to tell you, but you'll have to keep it a secret for now. Can you do that?"

Eddie leaned forward. "You know I can keep secrets." He turned to Maggie. "I used to not be able to. One time I told Maria what we had gotten her for her birthday. Dad was a little upset with me."

"More than once you blabbed." The two shared matching grins.

Maggie watched them; she'd not realized how much alike their grins were before. Of course they usually weren't sitting so close together, perhaps that was why.

"So what's the secret?" Eddie laid his napkin in his lap with a sigh. "Do you have to take so long?"

"It's about Maria."

"Oh yeah." Eddie rolled his eyes. "She has the hots for Enrico."

"Eddie!"

"Well, she talks about him all the time and even sings his name. She really likes him, I know."

"The hots is not exactly a nice thing to say."

"I could have said she thinks he's a hottie."

Now Gil rolled his eyes and shaking his head looked at Maggie. "What do I do?"

"Give up?" Eddie giggled behind his glass of soda.

"Never. So I guess that was no secret."

Maggie shook her head along with Eddie. "Nope."

Gil leaned forward. "Well, you don't know that Enrico came to talk with me. He said he wants to marry her, but he hasn't asked her yet."

Eddie's eyes and mouth formed three Os. "But she can't leave us. What would we do without her?"

"That's what I said, but then I invited him to move in with her after they are married and he said he'd think about it. He could rent his house out. So, we'll have to see, but remember, you promised. This is a big secret."

"When is he going to ask her?"

"Maybe tonight."

The dinner would linger in Maggie's memory, not only for the secret shared. How pleased she was for Maria. If anyone deserved happiness, she did. But besides that, Maggie had forgotten how good a real, flame broiled, medium rare steak tasted. And would again tomorrow as she picked up the plastic bag holding the box with the remainder of her dinner. "Thank you."

"Anytime." His hand touched the middle of her back as he motioned her to go before him. The spot stayed warm clear out to the van, which was now loaded with boxes and bags. The larger pieces would be delivered in the next few days. Had Gil really meant it when he said he'd take her to Long Beach?

TWENTY-EIGHT

Two days of cold, rainy weather kept Eddie off the horse and made him grumpy.

"I wish we had a covered arena like over at Rescue Ranch." Eddie propped his chin in his hands and looked toward his dad.

"I thought having an arena in general was pretty good."

"But there's lots of time in the winter when I won't be able to ride."

"Well, it's not even November so winter won't be here for a while yet." *A covered arena. Pretty soon we'll have all twenty acres covered with buildings and then I'll have to buy more land.* Gil had already been thinking about buying the parcel that butted up against the west end of their field. And here he'd been the one who thought forty acres far more than they needed.

That evening he went back out to his newly relocated office and settled in to work on the outline for the book he'd promised a publisher he would write. He could hear Maggie moving around in her new apartment next door, cupboards closing, a chair scraping. Surely the urge he felt to knock on her door had more to do with procrastination on the book than on a desire to talk with her — without Eddie around. "Get real, Winters, you're the one who teaches people to be honest."

He leaned his chair back and put his feet up on his desk, a pad of paper resting on his thighs. Maggie might have been on the property little less than two months but she was taking up more and more of his thinking time. Maggie riding Breaking Free. Maggie working with Eddie in the round pen, her voice firm but always encouraging. What he couldn't picture was Maggie laughing because he'd never heard her do so. What was her laugh like? Surely she had a nice laugh along with her contralto voice.

Sandra's high giggly laugh got on his nerves. It was worse when she was nervous, which she'd been the day she came for lunch. He'd warned her not to just drop in like she had when he was gone. As if she'd just been passing by. Santa Barbara was too far away to be "just dropping by."

He smelled the coffee before the knock came on his door. "Come in."

Maggie pushed the door open and entered carrying two coffee mugs. "I made decaf."

"Thanks, but you didn't need to do that."

"Meaning you'd rather have high-octane?" She handed him a cup. "I don't want Maria on my case. Or don't you want any coffee?"

"I always prefer leaded but then I wouldn't sleep."

"Me either."

"Thanks for this." He raised the mug. "Have a seat." Setting his mug on the desk and his feet on the floor, he pulled a chair closer to the desk and motioned for her to sit.

"How do you like your quarters?" He watched her over the lip of his mug, now held in both hands.

"I thought the trailer was big, so this seems huge in comparison." She sipped her coffee. "But I'm adapting."

"When do you want to go to Long Beach?"

"I don't want to go. I just know I need to."

"Your attorney could ship the boxes."

"I know, I've thought of that. But, there's . . . more."

He nodded and waited for her to continue. The scene felt so comfortable, like they needed to do this more often. No matter how much he cared for Maria, this was different.

"You don't have to tell me if you don't want to."

"I think I want to." She chewed on the side of her lower lip.

He watched her, such a different woman than the one he met what seemed so long ago at the prison. Even then there'd been something about her that stayed in his mind. She'd been so out of place there, a mouse in a room of hungry cats. Now her hair glowed in the lamplight. Her eyes held secrets, but the fear that seemed such a part of her had vanished along with the mouse-like demeanor. She wore confidence well. Had Breaking Free done for her what he'd done for his son?

"I-I . . ." She studied her cup, then looked up at him. "I need to go see the grave, my son's grave."

"You've never been there?"

"No, I was in the hospital recovering, and they wouldn't allow me to go to the funeral or anything."

"Ah, Maggie. So much for you to bear."

She slowly moved her head, as if battered, too heavy, and held up a hand. "Don't."

"Don't what?"

She blew out a breath. "Don't be —

ah . . ." She swallowed and stared at the upper wall, then inhaled a breath and pushed it out again. "It's far easier for me if you don't be too nice." Her whisper hesitated between words as though they were pulled hand over hand from a deep well.

"Too nice?" He could feel his forehead wrinkle, his jaw drop, like he was standing outside his skin, watching this scene from the room's corner.

"I-I don't want to cry." She surged to her feet and bolted for the door. "Night."

He watched her go, wishing she'd stay, grateful she had come. "Tomorrow night, I make the coffee," he promised himself.

But the next night Maria invited them all to a special dinner.

"You made Chili Rellenos." Eddie grinned up at Maria. "So what's so special? And who else is coming?" Eddie pointed to all the place settings on the table.

"You wait and see." She set a warmer of homemade tortillas next to a platter of tamales.

"She's gone all out, Dad. This is major." Eddie looked toward Maggie. "This is celebration food, only for holidays or big-time events." He grinned at his dad and raised his eyebrows, mouthing "the secret?"

Gil shrugged and started to sit down but rose when the doorbell rang. "I'll get it."

"No, me." Maria waved them away to go open the door herself.

Gil and Eddie swapped high fives.

When Maria ushered Enrico and his two sons and one daughter into the room, Maggie glanced at Gil and raised her eyebrows. He nodded.

"Sit down, sit down, you are almost late." She pointed them to their places, not their usual calm Maria but more a high-strung filly. She blushed when Enrico winked at her.

Conversation was lively during the delicious meal with Eddie teasing Maria. She tried to hush him but then Gil picked it up and one of Enrico's sons joined in, while the daughter giggled at their antics.

"Oh." Maria threw up her hands and gushed a stream of Spanish that made everyone laugh but Maggie.

Eddie leaned closer. "She just said we were all impossible, and she wasn't going to serve us dessert if we didn't calm down." He grinned and waggled his eyebrow. "As if . . ."

Maggie helped clear the table in spite of Maria's objections and stacked the plates on the counter while Maria freed her masterpiece from the coolness of the refrigerator.

"Tres Leches?"

Maria nodded and carried the tray to the table. Maggie followed holding the coffee carafe in one hand and a pitcher of pink lemonade in the other.

Enrico stood and the others quieted. Maria set the tray on the table and went to stand beside him. "Today Maria and I want to announce that we will be married the day after Thanksgiving. We will not have a big wedding, only our families with us," swinging his arm he included all of those present, "before the priest. We will have dinner at Los Palominos in Bakersfield and then we will go on a honeymoon until Monday."

The clapping and cheering nearly drowned out the last of his speech. He raised his voice. "God willing."

Gil stood. "My turn." More clapping. "We wish you both every blessing, and I have only one suggestion? Complaint?" Maria's smile faded. "You aren't giving us much time to get ready."

"Nothing to get ready. Very simple." Enrico slid his arm around Maria. "I love her, she love me." His accent deepened as he spoke.

"Be that as it may, every bride needs flowers and a cake, and I will provide those."

Maria rolled her eyes. "We have dessert now before it melt away." As she brought each one a piece of her special three-cream cake, she kissed them on the top of the head.

Maggie fought back the tears. "Thank you for including me," she whispered. Her family, she'd been called a member of Maria's family. She who had no family was now part of one.

The weather was fine that Saturday, so Maggie picked up a book she'd ordered and took it out to the chaise lounge on the patio on the back side of her house. But instead of reading she laid it open on the low table beside the chaise and let her eyes drift closed. Pictures of Charlie floated through her mind. Charlie smiling up at her from his crib, his baby fists beating the air in anticipation; Charlie learning to crawl, determined to reach the red ball; Charlie staggering from one step to another, always on the move, always seeking something more. Such a happy guy until thwarted. Then his temper showed. Like when she told him no, he couldn't have the basket of flowers from the coffee table, and he slapped his palm on the glass and said "no" along with a stream of indignant baby talk right back at her. It was all she could do not to laugh. So instead she'd swung him up in her arms and kissed his neck and belly until he giggled.

Tears followed the others in trickles down her cheeks. "Charlie, I'm so sorry." But sorry never did anything to bring her son back to her.

"Maggie?"

"Out here on the patio." She brushed the tears away and picked up the book again. If only she had some tissue, but her shirt hem would have to do. She mopped her eyes and watched the concrete walk that circled the building. Bonnie came into view first, running over and putting her front feet up on the chaise, tongue lolling, eyes bright. Maggie patted the dog and nodded when Eddie appeared.

"I thought you were going to call me." Maggie patted the cell phone on her waistband.

"I was, but I'd rather ride than swim."

"Up to you, it's your Saturday."

"I wish we had another horse, then we could ride up the horse trail. That would be more fun than the arena."

"You bored with the riding corral already? Your Dad just got it in."

"I know. Do you think I'm ready for the

show? Carly does."

"She knows more than I do."

"It's three weeks from now."

"I know." Maggie thought of riding the trails that had been laid out through Horse Country. They could even go up into the BLM land and ride for miles. A picture of her, Eddie, and Gil riding up there dove through her mind like a hawk on prey. How silly, they didn't have three horses and Gil didn't like to ride. Or at least he thought he didn't. Back to the moment at hand. "You'll do fine in the show, Eddie."

"I hope so. I wish you could drive me and Freebee over to the arena at Rescue Ranch so I could ride him there."

"Sorry, Eddie, but you know I don't have a driver's license."

"But you could go get one."

How do you tell an eleven-year-old boy you are scared to death to get behind the wheel of an automobile again, that you have promised yourself you never ever have to drive again? "Let's go saddle up if you want to go riding."

"Can you teach me how to braid Freebee's mane and tail?"

"You don't need it braided for the classes you ride in." *Besides, how can we get you up high enough for that?* Her mind flitted around looking for the answers. Anything she could help him do on his own added to his independence, not only physically but also mentally.

"But it looks so cool."

"I can show you how and you can practice, then we ask Carly if it is appropriate." Maggie heaved herself up from the lounge and started for the barn. Thanks to the way Gil had designed all the paths, she could walk beside Eddie's wheelchair and they could keep talking.

"Okay. I thought maybe I could reach his mane from the mounting block."

"We'll try. The tail is easier. Have you ever braided anything before?"

He shrugged. "Don't remember."

"That is some sight," Gil said to Maggie later that afternoon. Out in the pasture the setting sun caught the fire in Breaking Free's coat. Eddie threw something, and ears flapping, Bonnie shot out to retrieve it. Breaking Free tossed his head and started forward like he would like to follow the dog too. They heard Eddie laugh and call him back, handing him a treat. Bonnie bounded back, dropped the bone in Eddie's lap, took her treat, and waited to do it all over again. This time Breaking Free went after her.

Maggie watched as Gil joined in Eddie's laughter. "Those three have such a good time together." She turned from resting her arms on the fence rail. "Eddie was wishing we could ride up on the trails. Have you thought any more of getting another horse?"

"No. Yes. Well, thoughts only, but no inclination to do anything about it."

"Eddie could go trail riding now. It would be really good for him — and you."

"I suppose I should adopt another Thoroughbred." He grinned at her, letting her know he was teasing.

"Why not? You have an experienced trainer on site already."

"You'd do that?"

"Do what — take care of another horse or two?" There, she'd snuck that in for him to think about. "Piece of cake."

When they finally found a day to drive to Long Beach, Maggie fought off an attack of not only butterflies but also dragonflies that felt big enough to carry her away. Gil insisted they should take his truck in case they found some other things to bring back — he'd mentioned he'd like to stop at a housewares store and perhaps she might think of somewhere she might want to visit too.

The sun hadn't made it up yet when they drove on to the freeway. Wisps of fog hung in the cuts between the foothills, green peeking through golden grasses thanks to the recent rains.

"We're greening up a bit early this year." Gil broke the silence.

"Oh." Maggie stared unseeing out the window. Why had she ever mentioned that she needed to do this? Shipping the boxes would have been so much easier. The butterflies and dragonflies were dive-bombing each other inside her. She rubbed her middle in the hopes of settling them down.

Even the Grapevine and the Angeles National Forest where they used to go camping couldn't break through the thick glass that separated her from her surroundings. The first mention of Long Beach on the highway signs made her shrink back, trying to melt into the seat. Her breathing ratcheted up a notch.

"Maggie, we don't have to do this if you don't want to." Gil touched her hand, making her flinch.

"N-no. I need to get this done."

"Then you have to give me directions."

"Take 710." As they neared Long Beach, she told him where to turn and finally said stop in front of a four-story stucco building in the older part of town, but not the seedy area.

As she started to get out, he took her hand. "Maggie, I'm coming with you. If nothing else, I can tote the boxes." Her relief caught him by the throat. "Did you think I was going to let . . . make you do this alone?" Shaking his head, he got out and came around to open her door and give her a hand down.

"Th-thank you."

"You look nice." He wanted to tuck a strand of hair behind her ear but refrained. That might send her flying right over the truck, let alone back into it. They took the elevator to the third floor and walked a carpeted hall to a sign that said Law Offices and a list of several attorneys. He opened the door and ushered her ahead of him.

"I'm here to see Lawana Carlson."

The receptionist punched a button and said who was there. "She's in the second office on the left."

Maggie nodded. She inhaled a breath, walked to the door, and let him open it.

"Hello, Maggie." A woman whose hair was probably gray under the blonde tints came around the desk, her hands outstretched. Maggie walked into the hug without saying a word.

After a moment of silence, the woman said softly, "You're looking well, Maggie. You made it through and now your life can begin again."

Maggie took in a deep breath and pulled back. "It already has. I want you to meet Gil Winters, my employer."

"The man who adopted Breaking Free?" She reached around Maggie to shake his hand. "Sit down, please."

"You know about it?" Maggie asked.

"There was a write-up in the paper about the program up at Los Lomas, and your picture on the horse was included. I wouldn't have known it was you if it hadn't said so."

"I looked pretty ghastly."

"No, the helmet shaded your face." She guided Maggie toward the nearer chair. "Sit down and fill me in on what's been happening."

Maggie gave her a brief rundown, and Gil filled in a bit too. Lawana leaned back in her chair. "Well, that is certainly good news. And you've been reporting to your probation officer and attending AA meetings?"

"Of course. I'm not going back there."

"Good. That was just the lawyer talking, we like to cover all the bases." She nodded again. "I have your boxes." She pointed to four cartons in the corner on a dolly. "And I have your financial records here, including your savings passbook. I invested your part of the divorce settlement in diversified mutual funds, which in spite of the crash managed to keep making you money — not much there for a while, but they've made up for that in the last couple of years. I kept a thousand in your passbook in case you needed anything, like I told you I would."

"I guess. I don't remember much of those days."

"Not surprising. There's also a letter here from Dennis, telling you where Charlie is buried. I wasn't sure if he sent you that information or not."

"His attorney did. Dennis never contacted me again."

"That . . ." Lawana paused and gathered herself together. "Well, at least we didn't have to go after him for your share of the house and assets." She tapped the folders in front of her. "It's all here. Is there anything else I can help you with?"

"No, but I do thank you. You took your fees out as you went?"

"Yes, you don't owe me a dime." Lawana gathered the folders and put them into a manila envelope. She stood and brought the envelope around the desk to hand to Maggie. "I take it Gil is here to wheel the boxes down?"

"Yes, ma'am." Gil stood when she did. *And take care of this woman whom I'm lucky enough to have in my life.*

Maggie took the envelope and gave Lawana another hug. "Thank you."

"The best thanks would have been to have gotten you off." She sighed and hugged Maggie again. "Don't let this ruin the rest of your life."

"It won't." Gil tipped back the dolly. "Let's go."

Maggie looked at him as if to ask, How could you know how my life will go? She opened the door for him and waved to Lawana.

Gil loaded the boxes in the backseat of the dual cab and, whistling, trucked the dolly back upstairs.

Maggie watched him go. She knew she should look in the envelope, but it might as well have been locked with three padlocks, none of which had a key. She laid it on the seat and buckled her seat belt. Her eyes burned so she closed them and leaned her head back against the headrest. One more chapter of her life was over.

Gil got back in the truck, and she could

feel him looking at her but opening her eyes took more effort than she could dredge up.

"Would you like to get some lunch now?"

She shook her head.

"Coffee?"

She nodded. "If you want to eat, go ahead."

"Later." He started the engine. "Do you have a map to the cemetery?"

She dug in her shirt pocket and handed him a folded paper, faded by time.

He unfolded it, read the directions, and pulled out onto the street.

Every turn of the wheels tightened the ropes binding Maggie's chest. When he turned the truck into the granite gates of the cemetery, she let out a whimper. "No, I can't do this. No."

Gil wheeled the truck around and drove back out onto the street. "You don't have to do this if you don't want to. We're going home." He glanced over at Maggie to see tears meandering down her cheeks. "Home, Maggie. You'll be safe there." He wiped away the tears with his thumbs.

Maggie crumpled into a heap, held up only by the seat belt.

Twenty-Nine

Every day as soon as he'd changed out of his school uniform, Eddie spun his way down to the barn. One afternoon, a few days after her and Gil's big venture to Long Beach, Maggie had left Breaking Free loose in the pasture. Eddie whistled and Freebee raised his head, his dark mane floating with the movement. When the boy whistled again, the horse started for the barn. "He learned fast, didn't he?"

"That he did."

Breaking Free leaned over the fence railing to get his candy treat and pats from Eddie and his nose licked by Bonnie. When he tossed his head, looking at her, Maggie stroked his shoulder while Eddie rubbed between the wide-set eyes and smoothed his forelock. Opening the gate, they led Breaking Free down to the barn where Eddie fetched the grooming bucket, and they started brushing.

"I've been thinking."

Maggie glanced down at the boy who looked up at her, eyes serious for a change. "And?"

"Can I ask you a question?"

She turned to face him. "Like you haven't been asking me questions?" One eyebrow cocked.

"This is kinda personal."

Fear hissed a warning. "You can ask, but I might not answer."

"Okay." He turned his wheelchair so he could watch her face. "Why are you afraid to drive?"

Maggie closed her eyes. Here it comes, ready or not. To tell, or not to tell, that is the question. When she opened them, Eddie was staring at her. Bonnie sat at his side, watching her also. Tell. Don't tell. Run. Stay here.

"It's not that I'm afraid so much as I swore I'd never drive again."

"Why?"

"I had a little boy."

"Charlie?"

"How do you know?"

"You said his name one time and then you scrunched your eyes and got all quiet. I could tell it hurt a lot."

"It did — and does. One night my husband didn't get home from work on time. I had prepared a really nice dinner because it was our wedding anniversary. A phone call came and said he'd been in an accident. I put Charlie in his car seat and drove to the hospital. It was late and dark, and I missed a stop sign. A car plowed into us. Charlie and the driver of the other car, an old man, both were killed in the wreck. I swore I'd never drive again." Tell him the whole thing, that you'd had two glasses of wine, that you were angry and . . .

"How old was Charlie?"

"Three."

"And you went to prison for that?"

"Yes."

"Seven years?" Eddie's mouth rounded. She nodded. "So Charlie would be almost the same age as me?"

"Yes."

He stared at her, his eyes glistening with tears. "I'm so sorry, Maggie."

"Me too." She glanced up to see Gil standing a few feet away. How long had he been there? Her feet itched to run, to hide. But she didn't need to do that any longer. While, as the social worker had said, she'd paid her debt to society, there was no way she could ever bring Charlie back. Or Dennis. The divorce took care of that. She tried to block the scenes with willpower she'd built over time, but the bars were down and the memories she'd kept locked away came pouring out. Dennis saying she killed his son and he could not stay married to her. The divorce papers. The family of the old man accusing her of murder. The headlines in the papers. Drunk Driver Kills Son. Drunk Driver Charged with Vehicular Manslaughter. Roberts Sentenced to Maximum Time. The media frenzy, as if she'd chosen the whole thing, as if she deliberately set out to kill her own son and send herself to the hospital so she couldn't even attend the funeral.

Breaking Free turned his head and nudged her arm. Eddie kept brushing the horse's side, as far as he could reach. He laid the brush in his lap, turned his chair, and rolled closer to her. Reaching out he took her hand, the one that had been brushing the horse, and held it. Silence, other than the sounds of breathing and sniffing, filled the stall and wrapped comfort around Maggie's shoulders. With every inhale, she breathed in healing. With every exhale, she leaked out pain. When she looked, Gil was no longer there.

Breaking Free swished his tail at a fly, then stamped a foot at another offender.

I need to spray him, Maggie thought. *I need to . . .*

She knelt by Eddie's chair. "Thank you." With tentative fingers, she reached over and brushed back a lock of hair from his forehead. His loving smile made her mouth twitch. Slowly, ever so slowly, the muscles in her cheeks strained against seven years of inactivity. A tear escaped. Eddie brushed it away and patted her face.

"You'll be okay."

"I know. Thank you." Her facial muscles struggled further, and one side of her mouth inched toward a smile. The other side followed suit and her lips stretched. Her eyes shimmered with more tears, but lightened with the efforts of her face.

Eddie traced the curve of her cheek with one finger. "You're smiling. I've never seen you smile before."

"I guess I haven't smiled for a long time."

Breaking Free nudged her back, and she grabbed the arm of the wheelchair to keep from tumbling over.

"Hey, horse." She glanced over her shoulder to see him nodding his muzzle.

"He wants attention."

"I know." Maggie stood up carefully, feeling like she might hit the roof she was so light. She ruffled Eddie's hair and patted the horse's neck. She could see every chip in the shavings, every black hair in Breaking Free's thick mane. A swirl of dust rose from the light force of her hand on his shoulder. He needed a bath.

Eddie grinned at her and picking his brush up again moved around to the other side of the horse to continue his job. "We need to give him a bath. He must have rolled out in the pasture."

"Maybe tomorrow." Saturday would be a good day to wash a horse. Saturday would be a good day to be alive.

Confession must indeed be good for the soul.

Maggie lay on her bed, staring at the ceiling. She'd fallen asleep after returning to her apartment and now sunset burnished the room through the western windows. She should get up, but something was missing. And it felt so good to have it gone. How to describe it? The rat that had been gnawing at her gut for all these years had gone. Or rather, had slunk away.

"Thank you, Eddie, for asking." She remembered reading somewhere, "when the time is right, the teacher will come." Who'd have expected an eleven-year-old boy to be a teacher?

She and Gil had never discussed this, but she knew he knew. He'd said he'd gone over all her records. But he'd hired her anyway. That said something for the man. A man who made his living teaching others how to live more successfully. Were there things he could teach her? Or would teach her — if she asked?

That was the hardest part of all, asking for help.

Just get through. No, that axiom no longer applied. *I don't want to just get through anymore. I want to live.* Marion Worth had once told her, "Jesus said, 'I came so you could live life and live it abundantly'." Had she ever lived life abundantly?

Not really. If she were really honest, and what sense was there in not being honest always, she'd begun to question her marriage even before the accident. Dennis had been working late an awful lot those last months. But Charlie had been nothing but her delight. Sometimes she'd wondered if Dennis was a bit jealous of her love for their son. Sure, he loved his little boy, but he wasn't around him 24/7 like she was. And Charlie never got to be of an age where Dennis could play football with him, take him to games, all the things that Dennis liked best.

Her carelessness had stolen all that from him. He'd said so more than once.

But drunk driver? Two glasses of wine. She who never had more than one. Classified as a drunk driver. Convicted as a drunk driver. Did she need AA? Not hardly. Would she continue to go? Probably. Although she'd never told her story, it was a good place to make friends, friends who understood that life changes in an instant and you don't have any control over those things. The accident might have happened even if she'd not had two glasses of wine. Maybe she'd tell her story there too.

A knock came at the door the same time as the phone rang. She picked up the phone and punched the green button while she made her way to the door. "Hello?"

"This is Gil."

"Just a minute." She opened the door to see Eddie and Bonnie. She beckoned them in and responded to the phone. "Yes?"

"Number one: are you all right? Number two: are you coming up for dinner?"

She glanced at the clock. "Yes to both. Sorry, time got away from me. Eddie is here. We'll be right up." She clicked off and nodded to the boy. "That was your dad."

"He was worried about you. Me too." He ducked his head, then looked up at her again. "I'm sorry I asked you that question."

Maggie squatted down so they were eye level. "You did a good thing asking me that. A very good thing. Remember, I had the choice to answer or not. It was time that I answered."

Eddie leaned forward, arms wide. The hug they shared made Maggie's eyes leak again. "I don't ever want to make you sad," he murmured into her ear.

"I think you helped some of the sadness go away. You and Breaking Free."

"And my dad?"

"Yes, and Maria."

Bonnie nosed her way in between them and licked Maggie's wet cheek. "And Bonnie too."

Eddie chuckled and laid his cheek on Bonnie's head. "She doesn't like people to be sad."

Maggie wiped her eyes with the heel of her hands. "Let's go eat." For the first time in a long time, like years, Maggie was hungry — and looking forward to a meal. The three of them ambled back up to the house, Bonnie, nose to the ground, stopping to sniff something with great determination, then charging ahead of them, long ears flapping, tail twirling in a circle behind her.

Gil was grilling and Maria carrying a tray with the side dishes on it when the trio walked onto the patio. "Perfect timing. The swordfish is just about done." He glanced at Maggie. "You ever had swordfish before?" He studied her face, as if searching for answers. He must have found something for he nodded and smiled.

"Not that I can remember."

"Then you are in for a treat. Maria made mango salsa, and I've been using lemon butter. This will be supreme."

After the delicious dinner — she did like swordfish with mango salsa — Eddie asked, "Dad, when my mother was here the other day, she invited me to come visit her. I don't have to, do I?"

"No, you don't have to."

"I don't think she really likes Freebee. Or Bonnie either. She called Bonnie 'Molly'."

"She never was much of an animal lover."

Maggie watched Gil for any signs of fear or worry. For some reason, she felt really sure that he didn't want Sandra around any more than Eddie did. But Maria's flashing eyes said there was far more to this story than was being discussed at the moment. Should she ask her or wait for Gil to tell her? Most likely, it was no business of hers at all.

That night Maggie slept without nightmares or restless legs and feet for the first time in so many nights she couldn't remember. She woke to birds singing and tucking her hands under her head, just lay in bed. The blinds couldn't keep out the sun, sending narrow lines across the comforter. Glancing at the clock she saw the 7:30. She'd not slept so late since the day she'd been bound over to the jailers. She inhaled the rich scent of vanilla from the air freshener Maria had given her for her new quarters. She'd not noticed it before. Did tears no longer clog her nose?

Throwing back the covers, she headed for the bathroom and took a fast shower. One of these days she'd stand under this shower until she drained the hot water tank. But not today — today she and Eddie would give Breaking Free a bath. Perhaps Gil would like to help again. Her mind leaped back to her days at the stable and the water fights when she and the other teens who worked there washed the horses. Old white Silver once took the hose and soaked them all. If horses could laugh, he'd been roaring that day. She stared in the mirror and really looked at her face for the first time in — in forever, winked and after promising to buy some more makeup one of these days, dressed, and headed out to the barn.

Breaking Free didn't bother to nicker. He whinnied and banged the stall door with an impatient front hoof.

"I know, you're hungry and I'm late." She patted his nose and rubbed between his eyes, then made for the feed room. Carrots from the fridge in her pocket, a can of feed and a thick flake of hay in her hands, she hurried back. His nickering made morning music. What would it be like to have another horse here? *One day,* she promised herself, *one day I will adopt a horse from Los Lomas.* A thought shocked her. *Maybe I should go visit Kool Kat. Would they let me go visit the barn and look for a horse there? What if Gil does get another horse? Will he go there or look in the ads? What kind of horse would be good for him?* The thoughts flashed through her head, as if they too had been confined for too long. Dreaming was a new adventure.

That evening, after what she might have called a perfect day had she taken time to make an observation, she could hear Gil working in his office right next to her ear since his computer desk took up the same wall as her recliner. She liked the sound of his keyboard, but when he dropped something heavy, she jumped. So much for reading. She filled the coffeepot and leaned against the counter in her kitchen while she waited. When the machine beeped, she poured two mugs and took them out the door using her little finger to ring his doorbell.

"Come in."

Clutching both handles in one hand, she opened the door and entered. Papers everywhere.

"Looks like it snowed in here."

"And you brought leaded, I hope."

"Sorry, no. I prize my head too much."

"Maria wouldn't notice — she's so befuddled with this *simple* wedding, she started the day with mismatched shoes." He reached for the coffee and shoved some papers out of the way to find a coaster.

"So, you've ordered the cake and flowers?"

"She ordered them, and I paid the bill. That way she got what she wanted."

Maggie took the chair he pointed at after removing a couple of books to join a stack on the floor. "Is this preparation for a speech or . . . ?"

"I'm working on this book proposal. I thought I could just use the information from my presentations, but somehow it all got more complicated." He leaned back in his chair and inhaled the coffee aroma, watching her over the rim of the cup. "Have I told you how much I enjoy your smile?"

Maggie paused in mid sip. While her face was still getting used to the new exercise, she flashed him a small smile. "It feels good. Thank you. Really it is thanks to Eddie."

"He felt terrible for making you cry."

"I know, but it was a good thing. And I told him so." She looked around at the mess. "Could you use some help?"

"I wish. I've never done something like this before. See that stack of books?"

She nodded. Far as she could tell, the stack would fall over with the slightest breath.

"Those are about writing a book or a book proposal."

"I see." She glanced at the titles. "Solid reading."

"Good for holding the carpet in place or as an end table for your coffee cup."

"Too precarious."

"I have to be out of town again before the horse show."

"But you'll be back when?"

"On Friday. I've already talked it over with Eddie." He stacked some papers together. "Do you think he's ready?"

Maggie was more concerned about Breaking Free than Eddie. "I'd hoped this week we could work them with another horse or two in the arena."

"What about Monday?" He pushed some papers off the desk calendar. "Nope, I can't do that then. I'll be in LA for the day."

The look he gave her zeroed into her middle. *Come on, Roberts, he's just trying to figure out a schedule.* How easy it was to be in the same room with him now, especially this one. "You made this room comfortable so easily."

"Thank you. I need good working surroundings." He motioned to the wall behind her. "Eddie and company make for good decorations."

"I'd get the pictures taken and developed and then never framed." She found several in that stage when she unpacked her boxes. The framed pictures she had of Charlie were her meager decorations. She had more to go. She could feel his gaze upon her, as if he'd touched her. She pushed herself to her feet. "I better go and let you get your writing done." She reached for his coffee mug, and her fingers touched his as he handed it to her. She felt a jolt of electricity. Most likely she was just imagining things. "Night." Was she running away? Definitely.

■ ■ ■ ■

Her phone rang as she set the cups in the sink. Who could be calling at this time of night? "Hello?"

"Maria is making something special for breakfast so how about joining us?"

His voice sent a charge up her spine. "I guess so."

"Eight thirty, and I've promised Eddie I'd go to church with them. We'd like you to come too."

"I, ah, I guess."

"Night."

Maybe she wasn't imagining things.

THIRTY

"You going to church with us?" Maria asked.

"Uh, well, I don't have any church clothes." Maggie glanced down at her T-shirt and jeans.

"They wear anything these days." Gil glanced up from his waffle.

"They might, but I don't." Maggie caught the disappointment in Eddie's eyes. "Sorry. Maybe next Sunday."

"You going, Dad?"

"Of course." He caught Maggie's gaze and grinned at her. "And then I have a surprise for you all, so be ready, we'll swing back here and pick you up."

"A surprise?" Eddie leaned forward. "Tell me."

"If I tell you, then it won't be a surprise."

Clothes shopping was a must. Maggie spent the time with Breaking Free, then changed into clean clothes when she figured they would be home again. Gil sure had been insistent that she go along for the surprise.

Maria sat in the back of the van, and she and Eddie spoke Spanish to each other as they drove toward town. When Gil swung into a trailer lot, Maggie had a pretty good idea what the surprise was. Sure enough, he parked next to a horse trailer that had a changing room in the front.

"Wow, Dad, did you buy this one?"

"One like it. Four horse, instead of two."

"Four horse?"

"Just thought we might as well be prepared. Easier to buy the extra size now than turn one in later." He stepped from the van and waited for the others to join him. "You think this will be all right? I'll pick ours up on Tuesday before I leave so we'll have it for the show or use it to haul Breaking Free over to Rescue Ranch." He turned to Maggie. "Have you ever driven a trailer before?"

She shook her head. "No. And I don't have a driver's license, remember?" *Besides which, you said if I ever drove one of your vehicles, you'd send me down the road.*

"Right. But that might change."

Don't count on it. She turned to the trailer. While she'd seen fancier, this one was more than adequate for what they wanted. Per-

412

haps he was thinking of getting a horse for himself after all. "Have you ever driven with a horse trailer before?"

He shook his head. "But I've driven with other trailers. Backing it up will take some practice."

Maria came out of the living quarters. "Very nice." She smiled at Eddie. "Will make it easy for you."

On the way home they stopped for Eddie's favorite treat, milk shakes at the B & R with a dish of vanilla for Bonnie. Watching her chase the dish around made Eddie laugh. Maggie looked from dog to boy and then at Gil. She'd read about hearts turning over and thought it a bit over the top. But the look in his eyes did something to her midsection. A slow smile made the edges of his eyes crinkle. She felt the muscles tugging at the corners of her lips. Her face felt soft and pliable, like it might melt — just like her insides.

Her fingers itched to reach out and take his hand. What would it feel like? It had been so long since she'd deliberately touched a man's hand. Last night's finger brushing didn't count. She'd not counted the time one of the OCs grabbed her arm to hustle her away from a fight. A fight she'd not started and he'd finished. But Gil had touched her back several times and helped her out of the truck in Long Beach. He'd leaned across her to help her buckle her seat belt when her fingers refused to comply. Were those only the polite touches of a considerate man? If so, someone forgot to tell her nerves. They remembered each touch, each near brush of his arm against hers in passing.

She sipped her drink and watched the scenery go by. Prison life seemed like another world, far away and never to be revisited again.

"Now, I'll be back on Friday," Gil promised as he loaded his bag in his car on Wednesday. "Call me if there is anything, you have my speaking schedule."

"I know," Maggie said with a nod.

"I hate to be going away right now, but it's been booked for so long."

"We'll be fine."

He started to get in the car but instead turned back, strode up to her, hugged her close, and left for the car again. No words, just a look that set her heart to hammering. She waved good-bye and watched him drive away. Was he possibly thinking and feeling some of the same things she was?

On Thursday after school, she and Eddie were just finishing up his riding time when Sandra drove up to the barn, parking with a spurt of gravel. Bonnie woofed her warning bark and stayed by Eddie, rather than going to greet the newcomer.

Sandra got out of her car and waved, then dug something out of her purse and came on over. "Hi, Eddie, I hear you have a big show on Saturday."

With Maggie's help, Eddie swung into his wheelchair and rode down the ramp from the mounting block. "Hello."

"So, what time is your class?"

"I — I'm not sure." He glanced to Maggie for support.

She could tell by the look on his face that he did not want his mother to come to the show and was only trying to be polite. "We haven't seen the program for the day yet. This is Eddie's first show."

"Oh, I am so excited. I can't wait to see this."

Maggie tried to figure out what to say. Did Gil know his ex-wife was planning on being at the show? "Does Gil know you were coming out to visit today?"

"No, where is he?" She looked around like Gil might be hiding behind the wheelbarrow or something.

Maggie's radar kicked into full gear. Something was definitely wrong here. If only there were some way to see behind the dark glasses. Was she on something? Had she been drinking? Or was this who she really was?

Sandra reached out to pet Breaking Free and he backed up. "He's not a very friendly horse, is he?"

"Usually he is. He just doesn't like strangers much." Eddie sounded stiff, like he was afraid to say very much.

"Well, he better get to liking me because I don't plan on being a stranger." Her laugh set Maggie's teeth on edge. "In fact, Eddie, I think it is time you came to visit me."

Eddie shrank back in his chair. "I — I have too much to do to get ready for the show."

"We need to get Breaking Free taken care of," Maggie announced, motioning Eddie to the barn.

"Oh good, I'll go with you." Sandra laid a hand on Eddie's shoulder.

As Maggie led the horse out of the arena and to the barn, she thought about ways to get them out of this situation without offending the woman and possibly causing more family problems. She met Eddie in the aisle of the barn. "Where's your mother?"

"She went to her car for something."

"Hold Freebee." Maggie handed him the reins and ran into the stall that had a window looking out on the parking area. Sandra took one more drink out of her flask and tucked it back into her bag. *I knew it! She had to be on something. Now what do I do?*

Keep her away from Eddie. The order came through loud and clear. Surely she wouldn't hurt the boy she said she so wanted to get to know. But rationale didn't count with alcoholics — how well she'd learned that fact after all the stories she'd listened to. How much had Sandra had to drink already? She was willing to bet the woman was drinking hard stuff not wine, and if two glasses of wine could impair her own reflexes. . . . But the biggest question of all, why was she drinking when she said she wanted to get to know her son better? Nothing made sense.

Back in the aisle, she cross-tied the horse and set about removing the tack. Breaking Free shifted his weight and twitched his tail. Bonnie glued herself to Eddie's chair. "Easy, big boy, it's all right." But it wasn't all right and even the animals sensed the tension.

Maggie hung the saddle and bridle where they belonged and returned to the aisle to see Sandra coming in the wide front door. Taking a brush out of the bucket, she began brushing Breaking Free's shoulder, her senses tuned to the approaching woman.

"He sure a big horse. Hey, big horse, you want a apple?" She aimed a smile in Eddie's direction. "I brought apples for him." She held one in each hand. "And you." The hand that held an apple out to Eddie wobbled slightly.

"Thank you." He took it politely and laid it in his lap. "I'll give that one to Breaking Free if you like."

"No!" She staggered just slightly. "I'll give it to him."

She came toward the horse in a rush, as if losing her balance, and held out the apple. Breaking Free threw his head in the air and backed up as far as the ties allowed.

"Easy, fella. Hey, come on, Sandra, you're scaring him."

"Aw, he a big horse. Here ya go." She held out the apple, but the horse refused to take it. Eyes wild he swung his rear and snorted.

"Back off!" Maggie's command rang through the barn.

Bonnie stood between Sandra and the wheelchair, her lip lifting in a growl.

"Eddie, get out of the way." Maggie's voice remained firm as she took hold of the tie ropes.

"I'ma give that horse an apple."

"He doesn't want it." Maggie knocked the apple to the ground. "Now back up before you get hurt."

"You . . ." Sandra swung in a circle, arm outstretched and caught Maggie on the shoulder.

Breaking Free surged backward and one of the lead ropes snapped. He swung around, bumping Sandra with his hip and knocking her on her rear.

"That horse tried to kill me!" A stream of foul language blackened the air.

Maggie hung onto the remaining lead shank, jerked the knot free, and hustled the horse into his stall where Eddie and Bonnie had already taken refuge. While the woman screamed her rage and hauled herself upright, Maggie calmed the horse and boy. "You'll be okay in here. I'm going to get her out of the barn." Breaking Free nuzzled Eddie's hand and crunched the apple he held out.

"Breaking Free didn't mean to hurt her." The boy's face was white with shock.

"He didn't hurt her, other than her pride. It'll be okay." Maggie soothed her charges and shut the stall door behind her as she returned to the aisle.

Sandra leaned against the wall, regaining her breath. "I'll sue you for this and make sure Gil fires you. You just watch me."

"Why don't you come and sit in your car?" Maggie tried to take her arm. "Can I get you a glass of water or something?"

"I got enough out there — I don't need no water." She jerked her arm away and while dusting off her rear almost fell on it again.

Maggie caught her. "Here, let me help you." Now she could smell the fumes that had been hidden before. "How much have you had to drink?"

"Not enough." The names Sandra called her sounded more like words she'd grown accustomed to in prison than here in the peaceful barn.

Using as little force as possible, she helped the woman out of the barn and opened the car door for her.

"You're gonna pay for this."

"I'm sorry to hear that. You rest here a minute, and I'll have Maria call you a taxi." Maggie wasn't sure if taxis came out this far, but offered enough money, they probably would.

Sandra dug in her bag and brought out the flask. "You oughta try some of this, loosen you up some, you self-righteous witch." She took a swig and held the silver flask in the air. She stared at it for a moment, her face crumbling.

Maggie glanced down at her belt to realize she didn't have her cell phone. It must have gotten knocked off in the fracas. "You wait here, I'll be right back." As she turned, she remembered — Maria was gone to town. She'd have to call the cab herself. She strode back in the barn to pick up the phone lying in the aisle. At the same time, she heard the car motor roar to life. "Oh, dear God, I didn't take away her keys. I never . . ."

The engine thundered, obviously not in gear. The woman floored it and the engine screamed. She threw it into gear, and the machine rammed into the corner of the barn, the stall where her three charges were supposed to be safe. It sounded like the whole barn was coming down — metal screeching on metal, wood splintering as the side caved in. The horse screamed, the boy screamed, Bonnie barked in a frenzy. Sandra shifted into reverse and, peppering the fractured wall with gravel, tore away from the barn and out the drive.

Maggie hit the stall door to see the wheelchair on its side and Eddie laying on the shavings and straw, pieces of shattered wood scattered around and on him. Bonnie licked the blood seeping from a wound on the side of his head. Breaking Free nuzzled the boy's chest, a huge splinter of wood protruding from the horse's shoulder.

Maggie knelt by Eddie, checked his pulse, fast but steady. What to do? Was he in danger of dying? Concussion? What? She looked at the wound again. Steady bleeding but not gushing. That wasn't so bad, but he was still unconscious. If only Maria were here. Flicking her phone open, Maggie dialed 911.

A woman answered on the second ring.

"I have an eleven-year-old boy with a head wound, bleeding and unconscious." She kept her voice even as much for her own sanity as for the dispatcher. She answered the questions as to address and location. "How long until someone will be here?"

"I'm not sure. I have a call in now. Our local ambulances are already out on calls. Stay with me."

Maggie's heart was pounding so hard, she could barely hear the woman. *Hurry up. This is a little boy.*

"Do you have someone there with you?"

"No."

"Do you have a vehicle to transport him?"

"Yes. Call the hospital and let them know we are on our way. I'll be driving a white pickup."

Dear God help us. Carefully she lifted Eddie in her arms and carried him out to the truck, laying him on the seat. Bonnie jumped up in the cab, daring her to order her out. Maggie climbed up in the driver's seat, dug the keys out of the side pocket where she'd seen Gil leave them, and started the engine. As she pulled onto the street, she hit speed dial for Maria's cell.

When Maria answered, Maggie fought to keep from crying. "There's been an accident. I called 911 and there is no ambulance available. I'm taking Eddie to the hospital. Please call the vet. Breaking Free is hurt. Bonnie is with me."

"Madre Dios, what happened?"

"Call Gil too, please." She drove out the driveway, being extra cautious on the speed bumps. Once on the freeway, she floored it.

Never had she prayed so hard and long in her life. Not the long nights in the cells, not when other women were attacking her. She prayed for Eddie, she pleaded for a police escort. She drove with such intense concentration, she almost missed seeing the police cars parked by the road. But when she tore by them honking her horn, one pulled out behind her. "Thank you, God."

When she didn't stop at the flashing lights, he pulled up beside her with his bullhorn.

"Pull over!"

She rolled down her window. "I have a severely injured boy here. We have to get him to emergency as fast as possible!"

"Follow me."

With a car in front of her and one behind, they reached the hospital through flashing lights and sirens. The ER crew had the gurney ready and the door to the pickup open almost before it stopped.

Bonnie met them with teeth bared.

"Call off the dog, lady."

"Bonnie, here." Maggie grabbed the dog's collar and hauled her back enough for the men to lift Eddie to the gurney and rush him through the emergency room doors.

"Come on, ma'am. Shut the door so the dog is confined, and we'll get you inside too." The policeman spoke gently.

Maggie patted Bonnie and slid out the driver's side. She slammed the door just in time as Bonnie hit it, her howls heartbreaking in their agony.

"She's his care dog. She hardly lets him

out of her sight." Maggie fought to keep from dissolving in tears. She had to be strong for Eddie. Surely Maria had gotten through to Gil. How soon would he be able to get home? She strode to the door, the policeman at her side.

"Are you all right?"

At his gentle question, she nodded. "I just need to see Eddie."

"They won't let you, you'll just get in the way. Come over here and answer their questions so they can help him better."

Maggie stopped at the counter, gripping it till her fingers turned white. "No, I'm not his mother — his mother is what caused all this. He has spina bifida and gets around in a wheelchair." She gave name and age, the address and phone number. "His father is out of town on a business trip. I'm the horse trainer and his riding instructor. And no, I don't know what kind of insurance they have. Call Maria, she's the housekeeper/nanny, she'll know." She handed over her cell phone. "It's three on the speed dial." While they talked, she tapped her foot — anything to let the adrenaline out. "Please, can I see him?"

"I'm sorry, dear, but you'll just be in the way." The woman behind the desk patted her hand.

"But he'll be so frightened in there, all . . ."

"You have a seat, and I'll find out what I can."

"Thank you." Maggie turned and nearly bumped into the policeman standing behind her.

"Ma'am, I'm sorry but I need to see your driver's license."

Maggie started to say she'd left her purse at home, but sucked in a breath. "I don't have one."

"You mean it's expired?"

"No, I've not had one for the last seven years. Somehow a driver's license didn't seem important when I saw the blood coming from Eddie's head, the piece of wood sticking out of his horse's shoulder, and the dog going crazy. His mother was drunk, she backed her car into the barn and the stall where I had sent them to be safe." Maggie staggered so the man caught her. "I sent them there to be safe and look what happened. It's all my fault."

"Easy, ma'am. You sit down here, and I'll get one of the nurses." She collapsed in the chair. *Gil left them in my care and I failed. Just like I failed before. God, please don't let Eddie die, please let him live.*

"Can I get you anything?" The woman who sat down beside her took her hand.

Maggie slapped her pockets. "My phone is gone. I need a phone to call his father."

"Right this way."

"No, wait a minute, I gave my phone to the woman in ER."

"I'll get it for you."

Maggie braced her head in her hands, her only possible plea, *Help us, please help us.* When the woman handed her the phone, she nodded. "Thank you."

"You're welcome. Is there anything else I can get you?"

"Information about Eddie." Like now, she felt like screaming the words, but hung on to her control by sheer will.

"I'll see what I can find out."

Maggie punched number three. "Did you get ahold of Gil?"

"Sí, he will catch the next flight."

"And the vet?"

"He fix the horse."

"Good. Can you come here?"

"Sí. Almost there. How's Eddie?"

Maggie gulped a sob. "I don't know. He's in the emergency and they won't let me go see him."

"I be right there."

Even in the hospital, she could hear the dog howling. She looked up to catch the police officer's eye. "Look, I need to go out and take care of Bonnie, she's probably torn the truck apart by now. Will they let me back in here?"

"I'll take care of that."

Maggie stared around. "I don't know how to get out of here."

"I'll show you."

The policeman walked her out to the truck where Bonnie went crazy to see her, yipping and barking. Maggie patted her and held her in the truck since she had no leash to restrain her with.

"I'll get something. Wait here." The officer returned in a few minutes with a length of nylon rope. "Here, tie that onto her collar, and we can let her out for a few minutes."

"Thank you." Maggie did as he said, feeling as if he were talking from a far distance. She walked Bonnie over to a grassy strip so she could pee and then back to the truck. "Do you think you could get a bottle of water for her? She's been barking so hard, she . . ."

"I will." He brought one back from his car. "Here, but I don't have a dish."

Maggie opened the bottle and tipped it so Bonnie could drink. "Eddie taught her to do that." Maggie removed the rope and gently closed the door.

"Easy, girl. Stay." Bonnie whined but

settled back. "She's pretty protective of Eddie."

"I can tell. She wasn't going to let those medics touch him."

When they returned to the ER waiting room, the woman who had promised her information met her. "Okay, here's what we know. The X-rays showed a skull fracture, but not a severe one. They stitched up the laceration, and he is resting now."

"Is he conscious?"

She shook her head. "No, but that's not surprising."

"Did they sedate him?"

"No."

Maggie sat down in one of the waiting room chairs and leaned back, closing her eyes. She opened them when Maria sat down beside her. "He's not regained consciousness."

"You mean what?"

"He's sleeping."

"That good."

"No, he's . . ." How could she explain unconscious? She went on to repeat what the woman had told her.

"Madre Dios." Maria crossed herself and bowed her head, her lips moving in prayer.

The hours passed. They moved Eddie to intensive care, and Maria and Maggie moved to a waiting room close by.

When Gil walked through the door, Maggie stood and walked into his arms. "You go pick up the phone by that button to the right of the door, and they'll let you in."

"How is he?" Gil kept her hand as they walked to the closed door and he followed the instructions.

"They won't tell us anything, other than he is resting comfortably."

He identified himself, and they buzzed open the door. Maggie watched the door close behind him and returned to sit next to Maria. Surely Eddie would be all right. They'd said the fracture wasn't severe. But what did she really know about head injuries?

THIRTY-ONE

Time never passes more slowly than in a hospital waiting room.

In order to keep her sanity while Gil went to see Eddie, Maggie called the vet. "Breaking Free will be fine, pretty stiff in that shoulder for a while but I believe I got all the slivers out. He'll have a scar, but he should be fine." He gave the instructions for caring for the horse and asked about Eddie.

"He's still unconscious." Every time she said the words, she had to fight back the tears.

"We'll all be praying for him. He's one tough young man."

"Thank you. I'll tell him you said that."

Gil came out of the ICU and sat down between Maggie and Maria. "Here's what they could tell me. Eddie has a skull fracture, probably from a flying two-by-four, but the bones are still together rather than crushed in, which is really good news. He is stable and comfortable."

"But is he starting to wake up?"

"No, and he is not sedated so we wait. The sooner he wakes up, the better."

Maggie clutched his hand. "Can he hear you?"

"We don't know." Gil squeezed her hand back. "We just pray." He swallowed hard, sighed, and turned to look directly at her. "Now tell me what all happened."

Maggie told him everything, wishing she could do something to wash away the sorrow in his eyes. He looked weary beyond measure. When she'd answered all his questions, she asked, "Can I get you a cup of coffee or something?"

"No thanks. Why don't you and Maria go on home and get some rest. They said I could stay in there with Eddie."

"All right. I'll take Bonnie home and see to Breaking Free. Then I'm coming back."

"You don't drive."

"I do now and they're going to hang me for the first offense so I don't think another one much matters."

"Get some sleep, both of you. I'll call you if there is any change. And Maggie, don't drive."

Maggie let Bonnie out to do her business,

and she and the dog both climbed into Maria's car. *Jail, will I end up in jail again? What if — don't go there. Eddie is going to be fine. What do I need to do? Call Mark first thing. For you can bet the police will. Thank God Gil is back.* When Maria stopped the car in front of the house, Maggie said, "You take Bonnie into the house, and I'll go check on Breaking Free, all right?"

"You get some sleep."

"You too."

The horse nickered as soon as he heard her open the door. She ignored the desire to check out the barn damage and turned on the lights. The vet had put the horse in a different stall and even left a full water bucket and hay in the rack. "How you doing, big boy?" She stroked his neck and shoulder, staying away from the bandages. "Your boy is going to be all right, you hear? None of that was your fault, and you behaved wonderfully." Tears slipped down her cheeks, and she sobbed into his mane. Another accident. More damage. *All my fault.* She patted him some more and eased out of the stall. "You sleep now, and we'll all feel better in the morning." Shutting off the barn lights, she followed the moonlit pathway to her house. After taking a shower, she set the phone on the pillow next to her head and after praying for Eddie again fell into a restless sleep.

Gil called at seven a.m. "He's the same, but the doctor says it is only a matter of time."

"I need to feed the horse and call my parole officer and then we'll come. Can you see any change?" *Please, please, let there be change.*

"Not yet, but he doesn't seem to be in any pain either and that is good."

"Gil, I'm so sorry, I . . ."

"Listen to me, Maggie. This was not your fault. And by the way, Sandra was involved in an accident. She was in the ER earlier."

"Is she all right?"

"I think they carted her off to jail for driving under the influence."

What could she say?

Maria set a small suitcase in the backseat. "Eddie will have clean clothes to come home in."

Maggie nodded. "You keep thinking that."

"I keep praying."

When they entered the waiting room, Gil met them. "He's moving around more. They say that is a good sign. The nurses said you could come in." He beeped the button and the door opened. Maggie stopped at the foot of Eddie's bed. He looked so small in that bed of white. Even his sandy brown hair was covered by bandages. One eye had turned purple.

She stroked his feet. "Come on, Eddie, Breaking Free needs you. Bonnie needs you. She hasn't quit crying."

Maria held his hand, tears raining down on the slender arm. "Que bueno, chico. You come home."

Gil joined Maggie at the foot of the bed. "How are things at home?"

"Breaking Free will be fine. The barn will need to be repaired."

"What did your parole officer say?"

"Not to worry. Come see him at four this afternoon. He said I probably wouldn't be sent back to prison." She looked up at him. "But I'll need to go before a judge, most likely." She shuddered. "I-I can't go back to prison, I just can't."

"Maggie, if it takes every dollar I own, I'll keep you out of prison." He put an arm around her shoulders and gathered her into his side. "Thank you for saving my son." He breathed the words into her hair and her ear. "Thank you."

For saving my son. All she could think was she'd nearly killed him. *But I didn't do it.* She said the words three times. *I was lax. No, I wasn't. His mother is at fault. I should have marched her out of there, but I was trying to be polite. I should know better than trying to reason with a drunk.*

"Chico?" Maria moved to Eddie's head and touched his cheek. "Come now, it is time to wake up." She turned to Gil and Maggie. "See, his eyes, they blink." She smoothed the back of her fingers over his cheek. "Come, Eddie, wake up."

He blinked again and slowly his eyes opened. He sighed. "Hi, Dad."

Gil clung to Maggie's hand and pulled her along beside him. "Hey, sport. You had a bit of a nap."

"Maria?"

"I'm here." She squeezed his hand. "I get the nurse."

He turned his head and his smile widened. "Maggie, you're here too?"

"Bonnie would be if she had her way." She felt her face spread and smiled back.

"You smiled."

"She did." Gil turned her his way. "Well, I'll be — Maggie's smiling."

"You don't have to make a big deal out of it." But she could feel the warmth of her own smile clear to the soles of her feet.

"Am I hurt?"

Gil nodded. "But you'll be well soon."

"Good." Eddie's eyes drifted closed then

shot open. "Will I get to ride in the horse show?"

"I'm afraid not this time, but we'll be ready for the next one." Gil smoothed his son's cheek.

"I'm sleepy." Eddie's eyes stayed shut this time.

The doctor stopped at the end of the bed. "He should recover quickly now. He'll need to take it easy. The headaches could be fierce. We'll probably move him to the pediatric floor in the next few hours if all goes well."

Gil shook the man's hand. "Thank you."

Gil and Maggie left Maria with Eddie and wandered out to the waiting room, each with an arm around the other. They stood at the window and looked down to the green lawn below and the vibrant bed of ruby zinnias that surrounded a fountain.

"Turning into a beautiful day." He pulled her closer.

"Yes, it is. A breaking free day — for all of us."

"Well, at least I don't have to worry about getting dizzy and falling over." Eddie looked up at his dad as they waited in the vestibule of the church.

"Good point. But you will tell me if the

pain gets bad?"

"I will. But I am not missing walking Maria down the aisle." Eddie grinned at his dad. Wearing matching tuxedos, they looked more alike than ever. "Are brides always late?"

"No, not always." Gil glanced through the doors to see Enrico and his oldest son waiting at the front. The other family members lined the front pews. The group had grown more than the three children Enrico had brought to the dinner at Gil's house.

"She's ready." Maggie came through the door to the bride's room, wearing a long-sleeved, scoop-necked dress that fell loosely from gathers at the shoulder. The shimmery shades of blues made her eyes sparkle. The smile helped too.

Gil sucked in a breath. "You're beautiful."

"Dad, I told you that."

Maggie fingered one of the crystal dropped earrings in her newly pierced ears. "I feel so strange, dressed like this." She gestured to the entire ensemble.

Gil swallowed. She'd caught him by surprise. And yes, Eddie had said that, but then he'd seen her in this dress — and Gil hadn't. "Just remember, the first dance is for me."

"I thought Eddie was first." Maggie tipped

her head and smiled up into his eyes.

She was flirting, yes she was. His Maggie was flirting. When had he begun to think of her as his?

The door opened and Maria came through, fussing with her lace mantilla.

"Leave it," Maggie whispered. "You look beautiful in it. Enrico is getting impatient."

Maria took Gil's arm and motioned for Eddie to take his place on her other side. Maggie stepped in front of her and when the organ changed the tune walked through the door to lead them all to the altar. When she was halfway there, Gil kissed Maria's cheek, she bent down and accepted a kiss on the other cheek from Eddie, and the three of them proceeded down the aisle.

Gil watched Maggie's face as the minister led the service. The sun beams through a side window caught the glimmer in her gown, making her glow. She held the bouquet of lilies and chrysanthemums that Maria had chosen and arranged the mantilla after Enrico kissed his bride. After the bride and groom walked back down the aisle, she came over and took Gil's arm.

"I'd rather walk with the two of you." And so she did.

That evening back home after they had dinner and the animals were fed, Gil tucked his son in bed and sat down for prayers. "I have a question for you, Eddie."

"What?"

"What if I asked Maggie to marry me?"

"Do you love her?"

"I sure do, how about you?"

"Can I walk her down the aisle?"

"I'm sure you can."

"When?"

"I don't know. She'll have to decide that."

"Well, you better go ask her. I can say my own prayers for tonight."

Gil leaned over and kissed his son good night. "Right away, huh?"

"Before she gets away."

He found Maggie in her apartment. This didn't seem like a real romantic proposal but like Eddie said, he might want to hurry. While he knew she felt the same attraction he did, what if she didn't want to get married? After all, the first time had not been the best — well, not for either of them.

He returned to the kitchen for leftover cake and plates to serve it on. He had coffee in the office already. A few minutes later, he knocked on her door, balancing a tray on one shoulder. "Room service."

"Come in."

Maggie had changed into a long caftan of a slinky fabric that touched her in all the right places and fell to the floor in attractive folds.

Gil set his tray on her table. "Tonight was my turn to bring the coffee. And I must say, you look lovely. Two dresses in one day?" He arched an eyebrow at her and wiggled it like Eddie did.

"It's nice to feel feminine for a change. Thank you for the cake."

"Let me serve you, madame." He knew his English accent wasn't real well done, but it made her smile. He'd do anything to make her smile more often. "If you will be seated."

Maggie took the chair he suggested and sank back with a sigh of delight.

He handed her a plate, a napkin, and a cup of coffee. "Decaf, even."

"Good, then we won't have trouble sleeping tonight." She took a bite of cake and rolled her lips together, eyes half closed. "This is so delicious."

"Not quite as good as Maria's, but a close second." He sat down on the ottoman in front of her. "I have a confession to make."

"Oh, really?"

"Uh huh, I confess that I have fallen in love with you."

Maggie's eyes opened wide. "What did you say?"

Gil leaned closer. "That I love you." His voice deepened. "Please say that you love me back."

Maggie cut another bite of her cake and held it out to him. "Do I need to make a confession too?" Her voice took on a slow, rather sultry resonance.

"No, a profession would be fine." He held out a forkful of his cake.

She took it and licked a bit of frosting off her lower lip. "That I love you?"

He set his cake down and leaned forward to share their first kiss. When their lips touched, he tasted a sweetness of cake, and another that could only be Maggie. When he pulled back he smiled. "What do you say?"

"I say yes."

"Yes, to . . ." He nodded to encourage her.

"Yes to I love you. I wasn't sure until the wedding today."

"Me too. Eddie told me to hurry up and ask you before you got away."

"So he approves?"

"Oh my yes. The look he gave me said, 'What took you so long, Dad?' "

"Good." Maggie kissed him this time. "Will it be another breaking free kind of day?"

"But first a coming together kind of day."

He set their half eaten cake out of the way and stood, pulling her into his arms. "Guess we better go get two more Thoroughbreds. Good thing I bought a four-horse trailer."

"And maybe rescue another basset too?"

"We'll be known as Rescue Acres." He kissed her again.

And so they three became a family along with Breaking Free, Saturday's Song, Diamond in the Rough, Bonnie, and Sampson — better known as Sammy, or Down Boy.

READING GROUP GUIDE

1. What causes Maggie to agree to participate in the Thoroughbred Rehabilitation Program?
2. Mr. James says that "working with horses reveals who we are. No matter how hard we try to hide it." How does the program and working with Breaking Free help Maggie? In what ways do you see it helps the inmates?
3. Why is Maggie afraid of being vulnerable? How does this help or hurt her while she is in prison?
4. How has the lack of forgiveness for her own mistakes affected Maggie's life while in prison?
5. What parallels do you see in Maggie's and Breaking Free's struggles and recovery?
6. What lessons of forgiveness and second chances does Maggie learn by taking care of and rehabilitating Freebee?

7. How does DC's bullying help Maggie learn to fight for herself?
8. Compare Carly's, DC's, Kool Kat's, and Maggie's approaches to life. Who do you find yourself identifying with most?
9. What lessons does Maggie learn about God's grace in meeting Gil and starting over?
10. How is Maggie's presence in Gil's and Eddie's life good for each of them?
11. How does Maggie's life experience challenge Gil's role as a father to Eddie?
12. How does Maggie's and Breaking Free's brokenness help each of them to heal? Can brokenness be beautiful?

ABOUT THE AUTHOR

Award-winning and bestselling author **Lauraine Snelling** began living her dream to be a writer with her first published book for young adult readers, *Tragedy on the Toutle,* in 1982. She has since continued writing more horse books for young girls, adding historical and contemporary fiction and nonfiction for adults and young readers to her repertoire. All told, she has up to sixty books published.

Shown in her contemporary romances and women's fiction, a hallmark of Lauraine's style is writing about real issues of forgiveness, loss, domestic violence, and cancer within a compelling story. Her work has been translated into Norwegian, Danish, and German, and she has won the Silver Angel Award for *An Untamed Land* and a Romance Writers of America Golden Heart for *Song of Laughter.*

Lauraine helps others reach their writing

dreams by teaching at writer's conferences across the country. Her readers clamor for more books more often, and Lauraine would like to comply, if only her ever-growing flower gardens didn't call quite so loudly.

Lauraine and her husband, Wayne, have two grown sons, and live in the Tehachapi Mountains with a cockatiel named Bidley, and a watchdog Bassett named Chewy. They love to travel, most especially in their forty-foot motor coach, which they affectionately deem as a work in progress.

The employees of Thorndike Press hope you have enjoyed this Large Print book. All our Thorndike and Wheeler Large Print titles are designed for easy reading, and all our books are made to last. Other Thorndike Press Large Print books are available at your library, through selected bookstores, or directly from us.

For information about titles, please call:
  (800) 223-1244

or visit our Web site at:
  http://gale.cengage.com/thorndike

To share your comments, please write:
  Publisher
  Thorndike Press
  295 Kennedy Memorial Drive
  Waterville, ME 04901